101 JOKES

by

ALEX GALL

BALBOA.
PRESS
A DIVISION OF HAY HOUSE

Balboa Press books may be ordered through booksellers or by contacting:

Balboa Press
A Division of Hay House
1663 Liberty Drive
Bloomington, IN 47403
www.balboapress.com
1 (877) 407-4847

Because of the dynamic nature of the Internet, any web addresses or links contained in this book may have changed since publication and may no longer be valid. The views expressed in this work are solely those of the author and do not necessarily reflect the views of the publisher, and the author hereby disclaims any responsibility for them.

The author of this book does not dispense medical advice or prescribe the use of any technique as a form of treatment for physical, emotional, or medical problems without the advice of a physician, either directly or indirectly. The intent of the author is only to offer information of a general nature to help you in your quest for emotional and spiritual well-being. In the event you use any of the information in this book for yourself, which is your constitutional right, the author and the publisher assume no responsibility for your actions.

Any people depicted in stock imagery provided by Thinkstock are models, and such images are being used for illustrative purposes only.
Certain stock imagery © Thinkstock.

Print information available on the last page.

ISBN: 978-1-5043-3251-4 (sc)
ISBN: 978-1-5043-3252-1 (hc)
ISBN: 978-1-5043-3253-8 (e)

Library of Congress Control Number: 2015907271

Balboa Press rev. date: 02/22/2016

Dedication
To my wife Anna,
Words cannot do her justice

INTRODUCTION

Telling jokes was always second nature to me and I've always enjoyed it especially when I told the jokes of the many great comedians and writers, past and present. Happy and humorous movies always appealed to me and I tended to remember great lines not only from movies, but from all of the great comedians.

I love to tell people a joke when least expected, it's a habit I can't shake. Years ago I was at Delaware Park, one summer, and I wanted a hot dog. I went to the food counter where I saw a little old lady, too old to work, who had a deadpan look about her, somewhat similar to Buster Keaton. No doubt she had been working at the track for many years. She may have been a widow or someone's grandmother, but after I paid her, I said, "You know, I bet a horse at ten to one and it did not come in until two-thirty." She looked at me with an unchanged stoic expression when from deep within her a smile started appearing, something that in her job rarely, if ever, occurred. I told her a couple of horse racing jokes. After all I was at the race track, and she ended up smiling as I left her relishing my hot dog.

I frequently go into supermarket and on rare occasions my wife would say, "Bring home some parsley." At the express checkout counter, out of the blue, I said to a dead tired cashier, "Do you know what's green and dances?" She replied, "No, what?" I said, "Elvis Parsley". I know that joke is not all that funny, but it broke the ice, and I told a couple of really short jokes that I considered can't fail material. When I left the express lane the cashier was happier and laughing. This ritual happened over and over, without the parsley, and it came to a point that whenever I was leaving the store I was asked if I had any new jokes. Sometimes when that happened my mind went blank and it was hard to come up with jokes that are normally second nature to me. Most of my jokes are triggered in conversation and when a topic is mentioned I remember one or more jokes to fit the occasion.

Only last week, an elderly gentleman, selling produce along the highway, told me that some scoundrel, my word not his, had stolen

36 watermelons on Sunday night. I felt so bad because he's not rich and his prices are very reasonable and I'm sure that he is not making a lot of money there. I've told him frequently that his prices were too low, since my first part-time job, while attending high school, was as a produce clerk at the 'Good Deal' supermarket in Irvington, New Jersey. After commiserating with him for several minutes I told him three or four jokes and his whole demeanor changed from a sour down-in-the-dumps countenance to an increasingly larger smile which seemed to cheer him up. In the past, whenever I stopped there I'd tell him a few jokes, which he liked.

Intellectuals and professionals seem to laugh just as much, if not more, than less educated people. I told my wife's surgeon about one half of one dozen 'doctor' jokes, there are so many of them. Once in a while I forget that I told the same joke before, but even then if the joke is good enough you can tell it many times and it's still funny. Not quite as funny the second time, but it's still funny. I told a Henny Youngman joke to a hip and knee specialist and I got a faint smile from him. I followed it up with a couple of other physician jokes, but the doctor was very business-like and merely acknowledged the jokes somewhat reluctantly. What I can't get over was that on a follow-up visit I told him a joke and he told me the Henny Youngman joke that he had forgotten that he heard from me.

Most of the jokes in this book have been processed through my wife, the ultimate critic. If she laughs it stays, if she doesn't laugh, it's tossed into the joke graveyard. Her instincts are infallible. There are many excellent and creative authors. Many jokes omitted were 'inside' jokes that require some expertise or background in the job or sport involved to fully appreciate the joke. I must confess that I know nothing about English cricket jokes because I don't know a thing about cricket, notwithstanding the fact that the joke may be hilarious to certain parts of the world. Other jokes are no longer as funny as they once were in another era. Many acronyms of government bureaus from the World War II are no longer extant, while excellent in their day, they were not timeless. When I mention Greta Garbo, Clark Gable or Randolph Scott, I get a lot of blank stares from a lot of people, but by the same token I do not recognize current stars and when I see them on TV, I say, "Who is he or she?"

I did not include some very good jokes about how many people does it take to change a light bulb, yo' momma, and most knock-knock jokes, many of these are often funny, but in many cases really stretch the imagination to make a point. I know that there is a joke in there somewhere and occasionally the humor dawns on me.

The majority of limericks are degenerate and border on, or are outright bawdy or uncouth. While humorous, many would be troublesome to a large cross-section of the population who, no doubt could take offense at many of the limericks. Some people would groan or frown immediately and dislike not only the limerick, but perhaps condemn the book in its entirety.

I prefer short jokes. I can recall hearing 'shaggy dog' stories where I wanted to crawl under a table or head for an exit as the story dragged on and on, and the story was never that funny, and became increasingly distasteful as it progressed, particularly if I heard it before. Noel Coward said, "A gentleman never heard the story before," so I would not blurt out the punchline although I've been there when that happened and it was as if someone had taken a safety pin and popped a balloon. I can distinctly recall hearing 'shaggy dog' stories when I enjoyed every minute of them and hoped they would never end. I could see the narrator falling in love with himself as he told and meticulously embellished every minute of the story, particularly with his considerable talents at storytelling, the telling of the story was far superior to the anti-climactic deflating punch line.

Short jokes are immediately funny or they are not. When I read a lengthy, say one half or full page joke, there are many opportunities to figure out the punch line before it arrives and I wonder why it took so long to get there and when the last spasm of the joke is told I end up saying, "So?"

Many people are starved and anxious to hear a joke that will make them laugh and improve their spirits, this was epitomized by a senior gentleman that I met at a Barnes and Noble bookstore in Bel Air, Maryland. We met at the humor book section — what a coincidence?

We exchanged jokes for about twenty minutes, we both enjoyed the experience and I could see that he was ecstatic whenever he heard a new joke. We both hated to leave. There has to be a lot more people out there with similar interests.

Many entries in this book are not strictly jokes, but things that I found interesting. Since I'm interested in a lot of things, I had to bite my tongue limiting the interesting non-jokes. The jokes included, rise or fall on their own merits. I hope that you get a good laugh out of them, I did.

The final part of this book includes essays on topics that interested, appealed or concerned me and are my own thoughts and impressions, right or wrong, merely my opinions on the topics. Some ideas and thoughts needed to be said by someone, ideas long overdue, or am I just another voice crying in the wilderness.

CONTENTS

TOPICS OF INTEREST

PREFACE

Perhaps I didn't fully appreciate the power of the written word. I fantasized that in the worst case it would be reported that *Jokes 101* was so funny that three people proofreading had been stricken and convulsed with laughter but were currently improving. My sympathies would go out to them and I would wish them a speedy recovery, after the laughter subsided.

How would it be possible to predict the debilitating effects of the jokes? I have it on good authority that a part time psychic heard about *Jokes 101* and she hasn't stopped laughing since despite the fact that she never saw the draft much less read it. Perhaps as she perfects her craft she would be better able to cope and avoid any future trauma.

When I began to comprehend the unexpected turn of events and possible complications I was almost ready to throw in the towel and nearly quit writing and even telling jokes. This state of affairs lasted all of five minutes when I hit upon a bright idea on how to minimize negative repercussions and safety hazards on any future written comedic endeavor.

I decided that perhaps affixing a warning label in a conspicuous spot on a book, one that bears the blessing and approval of perhaps a federal government agency, who better than Environmental Protection Agency (EPA), might do the trick. I knew that the EPA likes to get its sticky fingers on everything and since the book is in the environment it is a part of it. The EPA prides itself at saving people from themselves so they would be comfortable with a task of this nature.

I would not have to worry about CO_2 emissions associated with the book and the related consideration of a carbon footprint, whatever one of those looked like. Contentious issues are a strong suit for the EPA since they can always issue a government grant to fund a comprehensive study of the 'effects of laughter on the human condition'. No doubt many professors, and their associates would be glad to sink their scholastic teeth into this pithy topic to approve a predetermined conclusion. No challenge is too great for the EPA and I am confident in their ability to create an acceptable warning label, merely a warning with no fine or penalty associated with it.

Then when the next fun-seeker reads the warning label, and is forewarned if he breaks out laughing uncontrollably the nearest person to him could take quick and appropriate action and forcibly slap the reader so that he may proceed calmly until the next outburst. A sure sign that the fun-seeker has come to his senses is that tell-tale affirmation, "Thanks, I needed that."

When will all of the merriment end? For now you have been summarily forewarned based on the preponderance of the questionable evidence, and you may proceed reading at your own in peril.

ACCOUNTANTS

What a strange story, an accountant died with a smile on his face. It seems that he was at a picnic and was having his picture taken when he was struck by a bolt of lightning.

He chose accounting as a profession because he didn't have enough personality to become a mortician.

Everyone wants to be a singer nowadays. A few people have beautiful voices, many have nice voices, some have terrible voices, but all that accountants have are invoices.

He was an accountant and an account executive and by all accounts could count and be counted on but his wife called him a no account and that really summed it up.

Accountants are quiet and reserved and when they threw a giant bash and they wanted someone to liven up the party so they hired a party pooper who was the hit of the party.

A dog asks a business man for a job. The business man said, "We are not hiring now, why don't you check with the zoo?" The dog said, "Are they looking for an accountant?"

An accountant's wife was tossing and turning one night. She did not have any sleeping pills and out of desperation she asked her husband what he did at work.

While most tax returns are filed, my neighbor does quite a bit of chiseling on his return.

The accountant wanted to liven up the party, so he left.

An accountant always wanted to join the circus he said, "I've been juggling the books for so long, I have lots of experience, it's taxing work."

ACTING

He was a character actor who played all of his characters uncharacteristically well.

He was a failure as an actor, he realized this after a performance when the audience gave him a five minute standing boo.

I remember that they referred to a movie star as the 'Blonde Bombshell'. I wondered if she had an explosive personality.

Victor was mature for his age, come to think of it he was mature at any age.

He said that as an actor he needed more exposure so he spent a lot of time sunbathing.

He was a consummate and accomplished actor, he had to be because he slept late, drank, smoked, chased women, loved himself, loved to brag and when he had a real job he never accomplished anything.

He was a magician and he frequently said, "Abra cadabra, hocus pocus, first you see it and now you don't", but things went horribly wrong when instead of pulling a rabbit out of his hat he pulled out a duck who wanted to sell everyone insurance.

He acted in western movies, he was a relative unknown but he made a good living and never argued with anyone, he was a 'yup' man.

A circus performer made a living walking on stilts dressed as Uncle Sam, he wasn't much of a conversationalist because even his conversation was always stilted.

She was a dancer in Las Vegas who lost the sequins from her costume so she just danced out of sequins and not in order.

He said that it was his second time at a rodeo but he felt at home, he was a dancer and he was used to cattle calls.

He used to work building streets but he had higher ambitions. He thought that acting might suit him because the actors told him that as a start he would get his first job in a road company to put on road shows and gain experience, unless he ran into some road block.

His jokes were so funny they were riotous and they called in the police to calm the crowd.

He practiced magic but when he threw a rock into a lake he couldn't get a ripple, he didn't know his own powers.

A hypnotist ran into some bad luck he tried to hypnotize an owl but got outstared.

He wanted to follow in his father's footsteps but his father was a circus clown so he had some big shoes to fill.

Minnie Pearl was a wanted woman she had a price on her head.

He was an actor that spent a lot of time in the pool hall when he acted he was never behind the eight ball because he always entered on cue.

In a play the actor was a cook and during rehearsal he had to make grits and as he kept stirring the plot thickened it was a gritty scene but before long he had to break for lunch.

He wanted to play the devil in an off Broadway play but he was burned out and didn't have that fire in his belly to be properly motivated.

The actor was to be in an underarm deodorant commercial. He was a method actor so he went out and purchased a pair of castanets and rented a Spanish flamenco outfit to prepare for the role.

I asked a French woman if she could dance, she answered, "Yes, I can can."

She went to a masquerade party dressed as a banana but at midnight she had to split.

He wore a giant yellow bandana to a costume ball, the host said, "I thought that you were coming as a banana."

At the Academy Awards they asked a starlet, who used to be an English teacher, who she was wearing? She replied I'm not wearing anyone, I have shoes, under garments, and a dress that was designed by Malcom of Bayonne, New Jersey.

After the play the audience cried "Author, Author!" Luckily the author was wise enough to be out of town during opening night.

I visited Hollywood, they call it Tinseltown it made sense, turned out I was visiting it at Christmas.

A character actor who was very ugly was desperate for an acting part so he tried out for a part as a vampire in a horror film. He was selected immediately and they told him to show up the next morning for filming and not to go to makeup, he was perfect just the way he was.

During a snowstorm, an actor got lost in the Swiss Alps, in desperation the Swiss rescue authorities sent out three Saint Bernards each with a small barrel of brandy and a hairbrush.

He wasn't a big star, his fan club met in a telephone booth.

He was so used to sleeping late, his career path inevitably led to a job on the night shift or the acting profession.

He was such a bad ventriloquist, his dummy not only walked out on him, but took the first bus out of town and the next plane out of the country.

The guy that's been heckling me for the last ten minutes is very bad, can you believe I thought that he was the president of my fan club.

ADVICE

If I'm not back in five minutes, just wait longer.

It's pointless to write with a broken pencil.

Never take a sleeping pill and a laxative on the same evening.

If at first you don't succeed, try management.

If at first you don't succeed, redefine success.

If you find yourself in hot water, be nonchalant and take a bath.

"The philosophy of the school in one generation will be the philosophy of government in the next generation". *(Abraham Lincoln)*

Have a nice day. Response: "I have other plans."

If you want to improve your lot, start a flower garden.

He who hesitates is lost and probably five miles from the next exit.

I couldn't think of a word to the wise, brevity was never my strong suit.

If you are up to your ears, keep your mouth shut.

Be proud to be humble.

"Don't drill for water under the outhouse." *(Cowboy Wisdom)*

"A good scare is worth more to a man than good advice." *(Anonymous)*

"Zeal should not outrun discretion." *(Aesop)*

AIRLINES

A man stole one million dollars from the business where he worked. He crammed the money into a suitcase and headed for the airport, where they managed to lose all of his luggage.

A new airline served two small meals, one on the plane and one while you waited for your luggage.

Airlines are going out of business very quickly nowadays, by the time I found my luggage the airline was bankrupt.

ALCOHOL

I know a guy who just couldn't hold his liquor; he was just jumping on a trampoline at the time.

When I met her she was so beautiful that a chill went down both legs, but then I noticed that the clumsy klutz had spilled her drink and ice cubes on my lap.

My buddy said that he was unlucky. He said that his beer was warm and his girlfriend was cold.

Bill had an alcohol drinking problem and he wanted to try a new and novel cure which he thought had possibilities, he spent two weeks 50 feet in the air in a treehouse. Now he's a tree-totaler.

He wasn't sure just how much that he had to drink at the party, but it must have been excessive because the next day he was told that he had kissed his wife.

I was intoxicated with power, maybe I shouldn't have grabbed that live wire, I was drunk.

I asked the bartender if he served a pale ale. He said he did and he gave me a beer in a bucket.

I was at a party and began to get thirsty when I noticed that there was a punch bowl in the far corner of the room as I worked my way towards it, a boxer beat me to the punch.

He was a loose cannon who was loose with money, his girlfriend was loose and he was fast and loose in his business, loosely speaking; but he got tight every weekend.

He was stout because he drank too much stout, he wanted to be a stout hearted man.

He was a mechanic, he liked to drink at a bar that catered to all types of people, it was called the 'Universal Joint'.

He was a crack shot whenever anyone made a crack he drank a shot.

He was double jointed as soon as he left one joint he headed for another.

When he drank with both hands he lifted his spirits.

He said he only drank to forget but unfortunately he had a lot of memories.

When he came home drunk his wife put her foot down and stepped on his hand because he was passed out on the floor.

He was so fat that whenever he bellied up to the bar he could not reach his mixed drink.

I used to drink heavily but I got a job in a plant that smoked hams and now I'm cured.

He dined and drank wine until he felt fine but he was a highbrow who tippled on toddy until tipsy, then he slept it off.

It was stormy outside and I was thirsty, I looked around but all I had was a bottle of port so I decided what the hey, any port in a storm, but I had to be careful because if I ate and drank too much I may become portly.

I drank port on the port side of the ship until there was nothing left, but I couldn't throw the empty bottle out of the port hole and ruin the environment.

Don't tipple until you're tipsy, don't drink until you're drunk, don't toot until you hoot, don't drink whiskey until you're frisky, don't chug until you lug, no rum until you're dumb, no Vermouth until you're uncouth – just a few sobering thoughts that have been distilled.

Most of the wine made by farmers in my area was made from concord grapes. French wines have good and better years and a great year can be expensive at a fancy restaurant, most of the wine that local farmers make doesn't last for years when they have a good wine they say that the bottle was from a good month, that's good enough for me.

When Don was poor he said he guzzled beer, when Don became wealthy he quaffed beer, either way it tasted the same, wet.

I was down south in a lovely section of woods and I decided to get a few still pictures, they turned out great both of the moonshiners were smiling.

The only time that drinks were on Angus, the Scotchman, was when he was run over by a liquor truck.

Is it any surprise that I am against liquor, it was the cause of my father's demise. Three cases of beer fell off of a beer truck and hit him, the demon alcohol killed him.

He has no respect for age unless it's bottled.

My water bill went through the roof in August. I didn't know that the lawn and trees on my property had a drinking problem.

I once lived on water for one week, but finally the luxury liner reached England.

I did not realize that he was drunk until one day I saw him sober.

Cicero was dining with a friend who offered him a glass of forty year old wine. After tasting the wine Cicero remarked, "Young for its age."

ALIENS

I went to the supermarket to get something to eat. I was intrigued by a can marked alien beans, it claimed to taste out of this world. What a gas?

ANIMALS

I suspected that my dog was slowing down, he brought me last week's newspaper.

Our dog is like a member of the family, he looks a lot like my uncle, but he really takes after the postman.

They have a new computer crime dog, he takes a byte out of crime.

I bought a parrot from a pirate. I hypnotized my new parrot so he only says nice things to visitors, and doesn't use salty language.

Did you get a free haircut at a dog grooming school?

My friend said that he was a bookkeeper, I lent him a book and he kept it.

Talking to you is like putting my car in neutral, the engine is running, but I'm getting nowhere.

Even cows make mistakes one cow went to a lawyer for a divorce she complained she got a bum steer for a husband.

I was amazed when I visited Rehobath Beach at the Maryland seashore. While sitting on a bench on the boardwalk, I could throw French fries in the air and the seagulls would catch them, unfortunately I forgot to wear a hat.

Do you think that everyone is afraid of black cats? Response: "That depends." Question: "Depends on what?" Response: "That depends if I'm a man or a mouse."

My dog doesn't dance very well, he has two left feet, but if he stands up on his hind feet he does a pretty good imitation of a cha-cha.

The fort was under attack by a bloodthirsty band of Indians. The men in the fort were out-numbered and didn't have a man to spare. Under the cover of darkness they wrote a message for help and attached it to the back of a snail. Help was very slow in arriving, and when it did all of participants were collecting social security.

To measure speed there is an expression that is appropriate, they say he was as fast as a duck on a June bug. I never spent much time on a farm and never on one with ducks, but I have seen June bugs. They are very pretty, but if a duck got it, it came to an un-colorful end, but evidently tasteful for the duck.

As a hobby, a friend raised pigeons that carried messages. One day he wrote an extremely long message because he was poor at editing and besides he didn't know when to stop. He placed the message on the pigeon's leg but when the pigeon flew it listed to one side. After five miles the pigeon threw in the towel exhausted from the weight. He managed the final distance by walking. It took two months before the pigeon flew home safely.

I used to watch TV when a doctor out west was paid in goods like a chicken, a rabbit or a duck. One enormously successful doctor out west made a lot of money when he opened a zoo containing all of the animals he accumulated. He was quoted as saying, "I can only eat so much."

I like your clothes they are different, did the tailor have a fit when he fitted you?

My father owned a small plot of land and we weren't sure if he owned the mineral rights beneath and the air space above it. If he owned the air space we could charge birds for flying through.

The horses pulling my horse carriage were talking to each other I suspected that they were plodding against me.

I used to think I was a dog, but since I hypnotized myself I'm cured. Friend: "How can you tell?" Reply: "Just touch my nose."

My dog was smart, whenever we had company or family over for a meal he would go around to each person for a food handout. Things got out of hand after six months, since he had gained 50 pounds from table scraps. So we put him on a diet and now he begs with a tin cup.

I noticed that when two dogs meet they tend to sniff around until their curiosity is satisfied. My Mexican Chihuahua was doing great until a neighbor moved in next door who owned a Great Dane. My dog showed him who was boss because he beat up the Great Dane and taught him some manners.

My dog used to chase a stick after I threw it, until one day he got mad for some reason and after he chased a stick he picked it up and never came back, what happened?

My cat comes over and lets me know that he wants to go out late at night. I said, "Isn't it a little late to go bumming around at all hours, just where do you go and who are you seeing?" He showed up the next morning, ate, slept all day and perked up when he wanted to go out catting around at night again, another of life's mysteries that remains unanswered.

My dog thinks that I am a great guy, in all modesty, who am I to argue with his judgment?

I asked my cat a question but go no reply. He indicated that he would sleep on it and get back to me when he awoke. No reply yet.

My dog didn't seem hungry often and I wondered if he had a circuit around the neighborhood where he bummed meals from neighbors with dogs that were his pals. He frequently came home with a group of friends who were looking for a free meal and hung around until they got one. When they finished they pursued their dog gone business for perhaps an even more sumptuous meal.

For snacks Noah had two cases of animal crackers.

My dog was extremely proud and fetched the newspaper off the lawn each morning. My dog was out of a job when I cancelled the paper delivery but even unemployed he couldn't get an unemployment check.

To keep his paw in, I tossed him a newspaper every morning. Real work didn't interest my dog, he was a boxer, I think he's interested in sports.

Chickens have a hard time getting into heaven, during their lifetime they used nothing but fowl language.

My dog took me out for a walk. He just never seems to tire. He likes fire hydrants, posts, car tires and sniffing around people or other dogs he meets. Home, he eats, curls up and looks at me almost as if to say, "Just another rough day at the office."

Domesticated elephants have learned to stuff mud into the cowbells around their necks before they go out to steal bananas.

If a person that delegates is a delegator what do you call a person who allegates?

They crossed an owl with a goat and got a hootenanny.

Everyone knows that a bumble bee is too heavy and its wings are too short to fly but no one told the bumble bee. Don't get close enough to whisper in its ear.

They told me to take the bull by the horns and run with it. I couldn't find a bull so I'll just have to go to Pamplona Spain to run with the bulls.

Bees can't spell, just ask them. If you're lucky you may get a bumbling bee but eventually they buzz off, just like a bee.

When calm, Humpty Dumpty was a good egg, but he just cracked up when he got mad.

I wanted to soar like an eagle but I was told my efforts were for the birds.

My dog and I are very compatible. I'm happy and he's pat-able.

I had a contented cow she was always in a good mooood.

My neighbor worked like a dog so I asked him to retrieve ducks during hunting season.

My neighbor walked my dog and upon their return I said. "Here Rufus!" My neighbor came over and I said, "I said Rufus, not doofus."

My Great Dane was so frightened of noises at night I called him the 'not so Great Dane'.

A midget took a Great Dane out for a run, he returned home dog tired.

I went to the ocean and did birdwatching on the beach, I was sea gullible.

He lost his dog and went out at night with his flashlight looking for Fido when he heard Fido barking he beamed with satisfaction.

A horse will go to any lengths to win.

His wife called him an animal, he acted like a pig, had a horse laugh, was hungry as a wolf, liked to monkey around, pussy-footed everywhere, drank like a fish, was a pool shark, sang like a canary and ran like a deer, but for some strange reason he enjoyed his job at the zoo.

He was a purebred dog, his name was Whole Wheat.

He was as busy as a beaver, this idea came to me because I noticed that he had buck teeth.

My dog was either a chemist or a scientist, all of her puppies were labs.

My dog wanted to wrestle but how could he, he was a boxer?

I asked an elephant if he wanted to hear a secret he said that he was all ears.

I wanted to teach my cat to dance but all he did was pussy-foot around.

Two pigs were eating lunch, one remarked, "I ate too much, did I make a pig of myself?'

I wanted a pearl of wisdom from an oyster but he soon clammed up.

I worked at a zoo and my girlfriend called me an animal, I said, "Can you be more specific?"

He developed muscle pain while visiting Australia and he applied a thick coat of muscle rub containing eucalyptus oil he began feeling better but he was attacked by a hungry koala bear.

In Australia they have a court at the zoo, it is a kangaroo court.

He had a dog that used to chase rabbits through a corn field, he was one of the corn dogs.

A wild horse could be considered an unbridled success.

He was an excellent cowboy who proudly straddled his saddle but he was a poor businessman because he was saddled with debts and he no longer felt at home on the range.

The giraffes were getting sore throats in the winter so the zookeeper asked his grandmother to knit woolen neck covers to keep the giraffes necks warm. His grandmother said, "That's a tall order."

He was a professional rustler but every once in a while he reflected before he took stock.

He said he was similar to an orangutan because his arms were very long. I actually believed him because I saw him hanging around a lot.

A giraffe had a sore throat the veterinarian had to buy and use a case of throat lozenges.

In the zoo a wolf had a tickle in his throat the veterinarian managed to remove the feather.

He was a bird watcher and while out one day with a friend he saw a large bird that he didn't recognize, his friend said that the thought that it was a religious bird, one of those birds of prey.

He wasn't sure of the breed of his dog but he suspected its parents may have been French, the dog only ate gourmet food.

The hunter had a dog that was a retriever that never brought back a duck, but he was good at retrieving a can of beer from the refrigerator.

He thought that he owned a thoroughbred dog but it did not possess any papers. However, he suspected that the dog had good blood lines because it never liked getting its paws dirty.

He tossed a stick but his dog just sat there and refused to fetch it, the dog told him that he came from a strong union and that it was his day off.

He always wanted a roof over his over his head but there were so many to choose from but any roof satisfied him, he even taught his dog to say 'roof'.

I taught my cat to use the Xerox machine she was so good they called her a copycat.

He was an exterminator but he began to notice the people started to bug him.

My cat loved to sit and stare out the window I think she's looking at birds but doggone if I know.

He was a cat burglar and the police dogged him day and night.

I asked a large mouth bass why he didn't speak up his brother said, "He can't, he's got a frog in his throat."

Two catfish hadn't seen each other in a long time when they said goodbye one said, "Don't call me drop me a line."

The Chinese take very good care of their panda bears, all of them are pandered.

My neighbor asked if my dog had done a job on his lawn but I pooh-poohed that idea.

I adopted a German Shepherd police dog who had a been used by the police to sniff out dope, but when I got him home he spent a lot of time sniffing at my friends.

He had a lazy dog it was supposed to be a pointer but he was too lazy to point, instead it just wrote a note saying, "Two in the bush."

He was a true friend of wildlife he even bought a wig for a bald eagle.

The cow was very messy, a visitor to the farm asked the cow, "You are sloppy, do you live in a barn?"

I had a computer canary, he was not very good at chirping but he loved to tweet. Tweet, tweet.

A pair of enterprising monkeys were capitalists at heart and opened up a fruit stand specializing in selling bananas. A man from the state sales tax division came by and asked one of the monkeys, "How long has this monkey business been going on?"

A beaver was lamenting "Woe is me, so little to do and so much time." His brother, Weaver, said "What's the problem?" Reply, "Well I'll tell you, my beaver dam is completed and I'm ready for the winter but I munched up all of the neighboring trees and I can't find anything that I can sink my teeth into." Weaver's reply, "Why don't you try whittling, it will expand your horizons and allow you to hold two jobs instead of one, it's cross-training." Reply, "Why didn't I think of that, thanks?"

My friend had a dog that begged a lot we called him a moochin' pooch.

A priest caught a large insect in the church yard, he thought it was a mantis, but it didn't look as if it was praying.

A calf walked into a barn looking for his fodder, he said, "My mom sent me."

An Arab offered me twenty camels for my wife, I told him that I didn't smoke but thanks for the offer.

I finally taught my dog to bring me slippers, but now my wife started barking at me.

My wife said that the dog had eaten her meatloaf. I said "Don't worry, I'll get you two new puppies."

Dead owls don't give a hoot.

A pig had a skin problem. The doctor wrote a prescription for oinkment.

A disgruntled pig is an unhappy pig that lost its voice.

Someone stole my watchdog. Did I get what I paid for?

Two ducks were saving their strength, instead of flying south for the winter they took a bus.

Ugly? - They gave him a doggie bag before he ate, without his asking.

My friend thought that I should buy a seeing-eye dog, he said, "After all you've been on a lot of blind dates."

A night mare is a horse who wins at night but can't win any races during the day, when the sun is out.

My dog was barking near the front door. I thought that he wanted to go out, as it turned out he wanted me to leave.

An ant is busy all day long, but it's not all work, they go to cookouts and picnics frequently and dine out.

I once had a job at a zoo in Florida, my job was to feed the pelicans. It wasn't the best job but at the time it filled the bill and allowed me to pay my bills.

I told my wife I wanted to hear the pitter patter of little feet, she put little shoes on our dog.

Pigs have a tendency to squeal, that's why you can't expect them to keep a secret.

A number of horses is a herd, a group of sheep is a flock, and twenty camels are a pack.

A cat burglar broke into an apartment and stole a canary, a goldfish and a pint of milk. He got away undetected.

Give me a home where the buffalo roam and I'll show you a dirty house.

Never try to kill a fly on a window pane, monitor or TV screen with anything other than a fly swatter, and under no circumstances use a hammer.

My cat is pretty smart. I asked her what two minus two is. She looked at me and said nothing.

Pet store owner: "Do you own a talking parrot?" Customer: "No but there's a woodpecker outside of my house that could be familiar with Morse code. I get a message every morning."

Laughing stock are cattle with a sense of humor.

We could use smaller fire hydrants to accommodate small dogs such as the Pekinese and Chihuahuas.

When is a seagull not a seagull? When it flies over the bay – then it's a bay gull.

An elephant wanted to look up its family tree, but it was a Monmouth task.

A horse wanted to be a big star in westerns, but his career went nowhere, he was always saddled with bit parts.

A monkey said, "I'll be a monkey's uncle," after his sister had a baby.

Camelot is a place where you park a lot of camels.

APPEARANCE

He was always cool, calm, and collected, I suppose that he was too stupid to fully understand the gravity of a situation.

Occasionally you're the statue and not the pigeon but some days you're the statue covered by a flock of pigeons.

You look familiar didn't I see your picture at the Post Office lately?

Your looks leave a lot to be desired if you were three feet taller you would remind me of big foot's twin brother.

Her lovely brown eyes looked wistfully sad but not quite as sad as a Bassett Hound that just had his hamburger snack stolen by a low life mongrel.

He had carrot colored hair, cauliflower ears, a nose as red as a beet, and lips like cherries; altogether a nearsighted female vegetarian's dream.

I went to an auction and the auctioneer came over and welcomed me. I said, "Do you know me?" He replied, "No but your face looks, as if it's forbidding."

He wore a mask during a bank holdup. He needed one because he was so ugly his face was unforgettable.

His outward appearance was satisfactory but I never got a look at his inward appearance, maybe an X-ray would help.

She looked like an unoccupied unmade bed which was unsettling and quite unsightly.

My wife got a permanent that didn't last it was a temporary permanent. Can she buy a temporary permanent that's lasts permanently?

I used to sell women's bras but sales fell off and business started to sag.

They say that she had a lot of oomph, she was called to oomph girl. I didn't see any oomph and if I did I didn't know how to recognize it, maybe they meant ooh or oops.

Her face was an open book but I think a lot of chapters were missing.

She appeared to be a vision of loveliness but he'd been having a lot of visions lately and he didn't know if she was real or imaginary, imagine that, she was a visionary.

He told his wife that he needed a new rug she bought him ten feet of carpet way too big to fit on his bald head.

"May I see you pretty soon?" "Don't you think I'm pretty now?"

She was a real knockout, she wasn't especially pretty but she was a fantastic boxer.

I have a fairly good nose, as noses run.

A lazy beautician had slightly dirty hands and could not wait for the next customer to come in who needed a shampoo.

My wife's beauty parlor has a recovery room.

When she left the beauty parlor they asked her to leave by the back door.

"If I were two faced would I be wearing this one?" *(Abraham Lincoln)*

ART

The artist bought paint that tasted like fruit which made it more palatable on his palette.

Was there anything common about Tutankhamen?

He was a sculptor but he was still a regular guy, actually he was a chip off the old block.

He was the picture of health but the artist was Salvador Dali.

He was a sculptor who married a lovely girl who was statuesque.

He painted a picture of a crowded shopping mall but a critic said that it was, "Too Busy."

She was very talented and interested in art but, Art was not interested in her.

An artist painted a still life of an orange cut in half. An elderly couple who knew nothing about art stopped and stared at the painting for several minutes. The husband said, "I don't get it." The wife said, "I think they need to be squeezed."

The artist fell on hard times and occasionally begged whenever he asked the same person for money twice he didn't feel bad as an artist he was just retouching a subject.

He was a rogue with roguish behavior who ended up in Rogue's Gallery but he didn't seem to care because he secretly longed to be an artist and he felt at home in any gallery.

They said that if I wanted to be good I had to sacrifice something for my art, it was a tough choice but I finally decided, I gave up poverty.

He was very conversant about sculpture, he was always very conversational and he liked to have conversations about his hobby. He even had a strange sculpture in his house just as a conversation piece which leaves his visitors speechless.

A visitor stopped at an art gallery exhibit and said to a guide, "Is this hideous monster called modern art?" The guide said, "No sir, that's the mirror."

I took an art class in finger painting in the evening at my local community college. I was gratified because after the class it only took me one year to paint my kitchen.

AUTOMOBILES

Speed bumps kept getting taller and a car's ground clearance keeps getting smaller. It may come to a point that an expensive sports car could get hung up on a speed bump with its wheels spinning going nowhere in a hurry. I hope that he has AAA coverage.

I am always a little edgy in a car when I'm a passenger, I feel better as the driver. I'm not as nervous as a hitchhiker in a car driven by the late Evil Knevil.

I found a dead car battery, it didn't cost anything, actually, it was free of charge.

I went to return a car at a rental car agency but the rental agent was a wise guy. I asked him what to do with the car he said, "Park it."

I noticed that on short trips my car got poor gas mileage and that when I took longer trips the cars gas mileage was a whole lot better, that's when I hit on a bright idea, I now do all of my daily shopping 100 miles from home.

I bought a car from a company that made cars and clothes dryers that way I could take either of them for a spin.

Have you read a copy of *"Consumer Reports"* buying guide and found out that the car that you own is rated as 'worse than average' with lots of solid black circles at trouble spots. Sometimes you choose a car based on beauty, status appeal, color, etc. which does not help when your car is stalled somewhere. Which reminds me of an old joke. Why do Yugo's have heated rear windows? Answer: So that you can keep your hands warm while you're pushing it.

When I bought my used car the smooth talking salesman said that it was easy on gas, but the price of gas went up, so I had to sell my car to pay for the gas. As soon as I did, prices went down. I saw the salesman again he told me that he was now on easy street.

I left my heart in San Francisco, and I left my wallet in Las Vegas and I left my rental car at Hertz.

I went to a high rise parking lot and managed to find a parking spot that was so high my ears popped and I worried about a nose bleed, if I was any higher I could parachute out and collect jump pay.

The court jester brought the King a wrench, which disturbed the King, who said, "I said a wench, you fool, I wasn't jesting."

A couple went to a night club and pulled up to the entrance. The owner handed the key to a parking lot valet while he would not trust his son with the same car, the parking lot attendant could be an intelligent car thief and you can kiss your Ferrari goodbye.

Why do gas station restrooms have a giant piece of wood attached to a tiny key? Why don't they just leave the door open, what's to protect? Each bathroom is messier than the next, maybe a Good Samaritan will take pity and clean the place.

The mechanic wrenched his shoulder patting himself on the back.

He carried a bottle of Geritol, but when he stepped off the curb he got that run down feeling.

When I needed new tires, the tire salesman had an unusual sales pitch based on his interpretation of the English language. He said that he car was not properly attired and that the front tires had no doubt been maligned in the past.

Years ago I was impressed when I heard that a robber left the scene at a mile a minute. On reflection that is 60 miles per hour which people do in their cars every day on I-95. How fast do you have to go to impress people today?

I would stop at nothing to be a cab driver.

When I bought the used van, the salesman said that I had four on the floor, he was right. It took me an hour to get those hippies out of the van.

My new sports car's glove compartment was so small the only thing that I can fit in it is a small pair of children's mittens.

My wife says that her car is her baby and I agree with her, she can't take her car anywhere without a rattle.

He was shopping with his wife and he thought that he heard a chirping noise coming from the back of the car when he remembered that his mother-in-law had come along for the ride.

He was a sloppy auto mechanic who was careless and wrenched his shoulder out of its socket.

I needed a ride home so I hitch-hiked. A driver stopped and said, "Jump in chump." So I jumped.

I took my car in for preventive maintenance and the mechanic told me that it was too late for preventive maintenance and too soon for necessary maintenance, he said that my brakes had about 5000 miles left on them and the tires had another 10,000 miles before being worn out, all I could do was to maintain my composure.

I was in a hurry to learn to drive a car so I took a crash course in driving from Evil Kneivel.

He had an all-terrain vehicle, he thought that he could go anywhere until he got swamped.

He hit the brakes so hard they had to scrape him off the front windshield.

He was an ex-serviceman who worked in the service industry as a service man at an automobile service center servicing cars his standard greeting was, "At your service."

He used to replace tires for a living but he had a habit of overblowing his own importance.

He had an unusual pickup line "Hey baby do you want to get in my pick up?"

My wife has a black belt in parking.

He sold car tires, he was always properly attired.

He was an old race car driver when he started going downhill this time his health began to decline.

A midget bought a mini car he used it primarily for short trips.

He owned a tire store every once in a while he had a blowout sale.

I was having a discussion with a friend in front of my house when he said, "I'd like to run something by you. Wait, I'll be right back." At that point he took off on a dead run around the corner and in no time rolled up in a lovely red sports car. He got out and said, "How do you like it?"

Believe it or not my neighbor ran over himself. He's getting old and no teenager wanted to go to the store to pick up his smokes so he ran over himself.

Traffic was so bad I got out of my car three times to make car payments.

Radiator Shop Sign: "Best Place To Take A Leak."

I was not an especially good driver but when it came to parking I did a bang up job.

The driving instructor told my wife that she was in the wrong gear, so she went home and changed her clothes to something brighter.

The quickest way to solve a parking problem is to buy a parked car.

Texas is a big state, even bigger than I imagined. While driving there I tried to open a map of Texas but ran out of room in my car. I had to get out on a level stretch of ground to open the map completely.

I got the bus driver mad, naturally he told me where to get off.

His new sub-compact car was so small that it only took one minute to go through a five minute car wash.

If they give a driver's license to a jackass, do any other animals need one?

I followed a truck for twenty miles and just could not pass it. I was in my car being towed to a repair shop.

Since I did all the driving I couldn't see why my dog needed a license.

While visiting Florida, years ago, I drove an older car with seat belts that buckled over my lap. On a very hot and sunny day I quickly jumped into my car and buckled my seat belt. The buckle was so hot I thought that I was branded and I began to feel sorry for branded cattle.

They say that the type of car a person owns reflects a person's personality. Some people have no personality, and many others don't own a car at all.

My wife wanted me to take her someplace expensive so we drove to the gas station.

So many pedestrians, so little time.

About ten years ago I was at a yard sale and bought a license plate holder with the inscription 'Happiness is living in Baltimore' but I never installed it because I was concerned that when I visited Baltimore the holder might walk off under its own power.

Bumper Sticker: Been Nowhere, Done Nothing.

BANKING

Rudolph the Red Nosed Reindeer was at liberty after Christmas because it was a slack period for him during the off season. He wanted to make some hay, but was at a loss because his glowing red nose suggested employment on a night shift. Willing to travel, an enterprising employment agency suggested Las Vegas where he would be readily recognized and a big hit. He landed a job at a big bank that had a special night shift where he convinced tourists of a Christmas Club Savings Account for visitors who still had money, and planned ahead. Because of the bank's generous profit sharing plan, Rudolph is now the richest reindeer at the North Pole, but that was easy because all of the other reindeer were broke.

Bankers around the Jordan River had lots of assets and were the most successful and the richest in the Bible, their banks were overflowing.

He was taking dance lessons and couldn't keep up with the dance class monthly bill payment so he robbed a bank and waltzed off with the loot.

My bank sent me a bill that stated my check had not cleared due to 'insufficient funds'. How do they expect me to pay it when I'm low on cash in my checking account, they are just digging the hole deeper.

It was a branch bank, all of the accounts were out on a limb.

He used to be a cowboy but now he's a loan arranger, in a bank and he makes loans pronto.

He wanted to make money the old fashioned way, he wanted to inherit it.

He had little or no interest in his savings account.

He wasn't too bright so the bank gave him simple interest.

He was a geometry teacher they kidded him they told him to sine on the dotted line.

She was forced to live under the most primitive conditions, she could not find her credit cards.

Someone said that his check bounced, just how high did it bounce, I never saw a check bounce? I got stuck with a couple of bad checks but my bank never said that they bounced, there was insufficient funds. I bounced when I was charged by the bank for a bad check given me.

I used to get 4% interest at a bank and now I only get 1%, I was concerned about the state of affairs but I soon lost interest.

Since the loan arranger was not in at my bank I told them I wanted to speak with his faithful companion.

My bank has one window open when it's busy, and two teller windows open when things are slow.

I can imagine that at a typical bank's corporate headquarters they establish a new vice president in charge of creative and imaginative billing techniques to ferret out additional revenue. Do we need more revenuers?

Big banks must have innovative and creative billing committees to dream up new commerce defying fees, charges, and penalties. After a solid week of all day meetings, and before they adjourned I can almost hear the bank CEO say, "Gentleman and ladies, have we possibly overlooked anything?"

After three years I found out that my bank account was dormant and it took me three months to get eighty dollars back from the state. I'm worried that the state politicians will want my account to take shorter naps in the future.

My one hundred dollar savings account showed a ten dollar service fee on the monthly bank statement. I hadn't been there in six months and received no service. I told them, "Within ten months my account will be zero." The bank was billed as a "Friendly and Caring" bank. I closed out the account and while we are still friends, we aren't close friends.

I received a new privacy statement brochure from my bank, evidently some federal regulations mandated it. I could only guess that the bank got a bulk mailing rate to deliver it. It was so heavy that to be on the safe side I added a couple of extra screws to secure the mailbox in case the regulations are improved.

After reading my latest list of fees, penalties and charges, I cautiously entered my local bank almost afraid to make a deposit. I looked around suspiciously and was careful not to do anything untoward. I managed to escape without any known fee, penalty or charge, but I won't know for sure until my next monthly statement.

A banker decided to sell left over promotional toasters that had cost the bank ten dollars each. He sold them for nine dollars each. He claimed that it was more profitable than banking.

Bankers have a new mixed drink. With several drinks they begin losing interest and eventually they start questioning their principles.

If we outlaw ball point pens, will bad check bank fraud be reduced?

My bank sent me last year's calendar, maybe I should have kept more money in my savings account.

If money is No.1, and power is No.2, what is 3 and 4? (Way too easy) Answer: 7.

BARBERS

I was told that I was developing a receding forehead. I went to a mirror and checked my forehead it had not receded but my hair was retreating from my forehead.

A barber decided to go on a vacation but before he left he had a few departing words that couldn't be combed over.

I received an expensive comb as a gift, I thanked my girlfriend and said, "I'll never part with it."

My friend's haircut was so bad that I asked him, "Did your barber have a seeing eye dog."

A bald man is a man whose hair is departed on both sides.

BARS

He was a pilot for a long time. He was used to going into a lot of dives.

When I asked for a double, the bartender went into the back room and brought out a guy who looked just like me.

BEAUTY

I asked her for a big lock of her hair so that I may keep it in my wallet, she said she'd like to give me a lock but that would make her wig looked unbalanced.

A giant woman from outer space landed on earth and she went to a beauty parlor. Her face was so large that they had to use a paint roller to apply her makeup and a trowel to put on her eye shadow, when done she looked out of this world.

Her hair looked as if she got her finger caught in a wall socket for too long.

She said that her face was her fortune. To be polite no one told her that she was dealing with a small fortune.

My neighbor's wife does not know how to apply makeup. The one day a year that she looks her best is on Halloween.

She had a natural look it looked as if she had just jumped out of bed in the morning.

I saw an amazingly beautiful girl and I never gave her a second thought, I was preoccupied with my first thought.

She was as pretty as she ever was, but now it took three times as long to achieve that.

She attended a beauty and charm school that gave a class on how to look beautiful by properly applying lipstick, eye shadow, face cream, eye liner and rouge. She could not take the test on this class and came in on the weekend for the makeup exam.

When he first met her he was mesmerized by her beauty, but after one year he was hypnotized by her monotonous voice.

I saw a young girl with painted toenails, which is a very common occurrence. How does this come in handy? It's okay if you want to hide your feet in a large pile of M&M's

Angel was not only cute she was too cute she had an acute case of cuteness they called her 'cutie', how cute?

BLONDES

A blonde blood donor was asked her type. She said, "I'm friendly and love animals."

BOOKS

I was reading a book and lost my place so I went place to place for the place I misplaced, but I finally found my place in the last place I looked.

I hesitated to order magazines because I only read them periodically.

"Once you put one of his books down, you simply can't pick it up." *(Mark Twain)*

BUSINESS

He had executive potential, if there was a major problem he blamed his subordinates and with all successes he took the full credit.

Management of a small company held two weeks of daily meetings to determine why productivity had tailed off during the last two weeks.

All employees at the brewery took an intelligence test, this included management. The company president was very happy that he was the owner.

"I could buy a box of nails at the store down the block for one dollar less than you are asking, but the other store is out of them." Reply: "Come back when I'm out of them, I'll be able to sell them even cheaper."

When things were slow my boss would come around and say, "Look busy, do something." My coworker was very talented he could look busy while accomplishing nothing. My coworkers 'talent' could lead to a managerial position.

In my business I was so busy that I was too busy to talk about how busy I was, I was just a busybody.

He had a strange talent, he was successful at failure.

I used to work for a big lumber company, but I got tired of the board meetings.

Andrew Mellon and Andrew Carnegie were called captains of industry, but a recent college student said that he outranked both of them because he was an accounting major.

My wife wanted me to buy some duck feathers for a pillow. I bought the feathers on time, they gave me a bagful after I made the down payment.

I did not know anything but I got lucky and made a fortune on the stock market. Just think what I could have made if I knew what I was doing.

Never go in business with an atheist, he does not believe in prophets.

It's none of my business but what business is it of yours? If it is no business of ours we're out of business. I plan on minding my own business and hope that you mind yours.

He took a business class in a business school near the business district. He became a business man with a business plan. He wore a business suit, handed out business cards, worked long hours at wholesale-retail with an ailing failing business that went bankrupt because times were tough now it's nobody's business. He's unemployed and gets a steady check every week, for now.

Inflation didn't worry me I went broke last year.

Two maintenance companies had sporting competitions with events in buffing, dusting, cleaning, polishing, and window washing, one side cleaned up and swept to victory.

He rented a storage locker for ten years but it wasn't very practical from a business point of view because the cost of the storage fee for ten years was ten times the value of what he was storing, he had bad news in store.

I wanted to climb the ladder of success but all I had was a six foot ladder.

It was so complex no one could uncomplicate it but the complexity seemed uncomplicatable so we spent 2000 dollars and hired a consultant to simplify the problem. After a thorough analysis he advised us to ignore the problem that simplified everything.

I visited a place with lots of signs, no smoking, no peddling, no walking, no running, no trespassing, no fighting, no profanity, no fraternizing, no kissing, no talking, no kidding, no fun, I stopped dead in my tracks not knowing which way to turn.

I wanted to compromise without compromising my principles, but my opponent was unprincipled so he compromised too quickly that I doubted his compromising attitude.

He was an advance man with an advanced degree but he wasn't advancing fast enough so he paid in advance for an advanced copy of a book on '*How to Advance*', now he has an advanced standing in his job. Thank goodness his first name was Vance on purpose and not by just happenstance.

Ralph was concerned about the toaster he bought which was guaranteed by the manufacturer, in a reply to a letter he wrote the manufacturer said, "Our concern is concerned about your concerns about our toaster. Concerning our toaster your concerned letter was the first that we have ever received with a complaint and that concerns us. What are you some kind of weirdo? Thanks for your letter we toasted it."

Charlie had a confab at work, he said that he was confabulating. I never heard of confabulating, I was used to small talk, chit-chit, rumors, gossip, chatter, bull sessions, sports talk, nonsense, etc., but Charlie was in top management and was paid the big bucks to confabulate all we could afford was small talk. It didn't help his business, fat chance.

I needed some furniture, saw an ad for used furniture, went over and bought it. The furniture did not look used, it may have been slightly used and never abused so in no time I got used to it. Visitors came over and I said, "How do you like my used furniture?" Company replied, "Used? It doesn't look used, if you didn't tell me I would have sworn that it was new because it looks barely used." My guest said, "Now that I know it's used somehow I feel more comfortable about it, and I could get used to furniture like this, it's so useful." I advertised it as reused furniture since I was the second owner and I had no further use for it.

The managers of the local gas and electric company had a meeting at lunch one day, they called it a power lunch.

He had a business that was barely making it, a consultant told him he needed to expand so he added 20 pounds to his weight. It didn't help his business, fat chance.

Sign in store window: "Why go elsewhere to be cheated when you can come here."

Being a telephone operator is neither a job nor a profession, but it could be considered a calling.

I went in to buy three suits for the price of one. I ended up buying four suits for two dollars, I bought a deck of cards.

Christmas is becoming too commercial. At a large retail store a sign in the window said, "Five Santa's, No Waiting."

The suggestion box was in the restroom. Our enlightened management was flush with new ideas.

The hotel business really fell on hard times, one doorman was nearly arrested for vagrancy.

"A person without a smiling face should not open a shop." *(Chinese Proverb)*

A farmer was big in the stock market, this year he sold five pigs and four cows.

CABS

I go to work in a taxi every day, I'm a cab driver.

CANNIBALS

Cannibals love to fight it seems as if they have a bone to pick.

An overweight cannibal went on a diet, he ate only midgets.

COOKING

Two cooks fell in love and were married, but he was unfaithful since his wife caught him basting a spring chicken she said to him, "I roux the day I met you."

"What you cannot enforce, do not command." *(Socrates)*

I watched dozens of cooking shows and all of the chefs 'popped' meals into the oven, they said, "Let's pop this into the oven." I tried for 15 minutes to put a meal into my oven and never heard a peep or a pop.

I was a chef and I got tired of people asking me, "What's cooking?" Maybe I should have been an accountant like my Uncle Bill, the only thing he ever cooked was the books but on one ever asked him, "What's cooking?"

During the war the enemy was as thick as lima beans so we decided to shell them.

My wife tried to bake a cake for my birthday but the heat of the oven melted the candles.

CROOKS

A man paid 5000 dollars to a man who said that he was a bloop maker. He paid the large sum out of curiosity, the bloop maker constructed a 50 foot high platform by the edge of a lake climbed up the platform and at the top he took out a large stone and dropped it into the water and it went "Bloop."

He wanted to be a member of a gang, any gang but he should have been more selective he ended up on a chain gang.

At the crime scene the detective found a deck of cards with all of the twos removed, he deduced they had been stolen.

She had no luck with men she picked her future husband out of a police lineup.

He was a police artist. He used to draw chalk marks around dead bodies at a crime scene.

He was the young son of a mafia boss, in grade school he would draw chalk figures on the blackboard and rub them out with an eraser. He said that he wanted to be a hit man in later life.

During a bank robbery all of the patrons were bound hand and foot. One of the ladies got a call on her cell phone, she removed it from her purse and said, "I can't talk now I'm tied up."

The rookie hit man was dressed to kill, but he had time to kill and he didn't want to kill himself so he waited in the bar until they killed the lights and because his feet were killing him he drove home and nearly got killed in a car accident. So he never made a killing.

He was a second story man he even lived on the second floor.

He wasn't too bright, he killed two people and he thought that the judge had given him a suspended sentence, but his lawyer explained that the judge said that he was scheduled to be hanged.

He answered a wanted ad they told him to forget it they were only hiring notorious criminals.

He was sentenced to a life term in jail but he was smart before he went to prison he purchased term life insurance.

The judge asked him why he stole the pearl necklace? The thief replied, "I don't know for sure judge but when I was thinking it over it just came to me."

He was handed a gift on a silver platter, he had never seen a silver platter so he threw away the gift and kept the platter.

A bank robber drove to the bank and held it up. His driver was his neighbor's son who didn't know how to drive a stick shift car, by the time he learned the cops had both of them in custody. How was the robber to know that the youth was shiftless?

A thief stole a dozen eggs from a farmer and he escaped scot free but with good detective work they nabbed him poaching again at breakfast.

The criminal wanted to be exonerated but the judge was being investigated for excessive leniency in his sentencing which complicated matters, the criminal had been on a losing streak which remained unchanged.

Ralph loved to play in the dirt as a child, he played dirty high school sports, he got a dirty job and was paid with filthy cash. He turned to a life of crime and robbed a bank, but in this case he said that he made a clean getaway.

A group of thieves planned an elaborate holdup and made off with one million dollars. They buried it in a waterproof container on the outskirts of town until everyone forgot about the robbery. When they met ten years later and went to the site of the cash, it was somewhere under a Wal-Mart parking lot.

It was one big happy underworld family with close family relations and for those relations that they couldn't relate to, they paid Guido to cement relations.

Paul was an unconvincing convict who couldn't convince the jury that convicted him, despite the fact that he said that he had been framed, after they took his picture at the crime scene. He had been framed several times before so he was used to it.

A pickpocket referred to victims that he hasn't pickpocketed yet as unenlightened.

He was a tough career crook and did not know the meaning of fear, this was quite understandable since he was thrown out of grammar school in the third grade for being a bully, and there were a lot of words he didn't know.

Two crooks were just starting out in New York City, they used rented blackjacks.

Last week I was held up by a thief with a knife, but he apologized, he said, "I'm only part-time and I'm saving up for a gun. Two more jobs should do it."

At a bar a young lady asked me, "Haven't I seen you someplace before?" To be different and impress her, I said, "Perhaps you've seen me on the FBI's ten most wanted list."

One evening two detectives were at the scene of a burglary in an upscale neighborhood. They were gathering evidence, dusting for fingerprints and making good progress when a rock came crashing through a window. The detective picked up the rock, removed a note from it, and read the note. His partner asked, "What does it say?" Reply: "We fix windows."

A convict was hoping for a pardon or a reprieve, but before that happened he learned that the governor had been indicted for bribery.

A mummy went to jail, he said he got a bum wrap.

Fooling some of the people some of the time is enough for most crooks.

A crook stole some strong coffee from a poor person. I hope that he's having trouble sleeping at night.

CROSSWORD PUZZLES

In forty years my wife and I never had a crossword, neither of us liked trying to complete puzzles, they are just too hard.

DATING

I dated a jogger, we ran around for two years before we married, now I'm getting the run around.

I dated a jogger who used to be a Playboy Bunny, and I always ran over to her house. When I married my honey bunny I really got a run for my money.

She was looking forward to his presence but was disappointed when he did not bring her any.

A girl scout dated a boy scout, but when he got fresh she told him to take a hike.

He told his girlfriend that he was as busy as a bee. She told him if he wanted to be all that he could be, could he please buzz off?

She wanted to be alone so she dated a guy who had no personality and who was a shadow of his former self.

She said, "Charles please leave me." Charles replied, "Marsha, I'm rich how much do you want me to leave you, or should I just take a cab?"

'There is a good reason why you're going home alone tonight'. When I read that sign I thought, hey, I don't like that sign above the night club mirror.

A pretty young lady, who had a dull personality, went out on a date. The next day her friend asked her "How was the date?" Reply: "I had to slap him twice, he wasn't fresh, but I thought that he had fallen asleep."

She was a gold digger who wanted to marry a wealthy man with x-ray vision, but he saw through her.

He wasn't much of a Romeo, but he was not worried because he had a calendar and lots of dates.

I wanted her to understand me so I vowed to stop mumbling.

A girl dated a guy that looked like a baboon. He told her, "I'm not like the other guys you've been seeing lately."

She didn't date perfect strangers so she ended up with the imperfect ones.

I dated a girl and the more we talked the more it seemed that we had a lot in common. We found out that we were both common.

He had a hard time getting dates and he wanted to get serious and settle down. He contacted an on-line dating service and he filled out an extensive questionnaire about his likes and dislikes. He was very successful they matched him with a lovely young lady with similar problems, so they were meant for each other.

He was overweight by 60 pounds and found it difficult to get a date, despite his intense efforts. Then he heard that the government had spent 450k of grant money on a study to determine why overweight people have a difficult time in getting a date. After an intensive two year investigation that employed several professors and assistants, the conclusion reached was: Women preferred dating skinnier men.

My friend was always dead broke, never had many dates, was overweight, lazy, and had no personality, we called him, Lucky.

He pointed to his ear when he couldn't hear, he pointed to his eye when he couldn't see and to his wrist when he wanted to know the time of day. When he pointed to his tail a lady slapped him.

Mom you misunderstood me, my boyfriend doesn't work in the space industry what I said was that he was spaced out often.

My girlfriend lived in a basement apartment she told me if I want to see her more often I'd have to take a step down socially and physically.

Gravity always worked against me I tried to pick up a girl and I couldn't and then when I did pick one up, with difficulty, she dropped me with ease.

I wanted to elope with my girlfriend, but we lived in New York City and I couldn't get a ladder long enough to reach her in her tenth floor apartment.

My girlfriend and I wanted to elope but she lived in a basement apartment so a ladder was out. I had to dig a tunnel to get her out.

My girlfriend said that she had been involved in one of the oldest professions in the world. She helped her father on a sheep ranch as a shepherdess in Australia.

She was a widow with an hourglass figure, but time was running out.

He was a real scientist whenever he went on a date with a beautiful girl in the clear moonlight all he thought about was naming a star after his girlfriend and related astronomy topics.

I sent her messages on my shoes, I called them footnotes.

I was watching an ad on TV for a dating service that will help you find your soul mate, are you looking for a pair of shoes?

He found the girl of his dreams unfortunately he'd been having nightmares at the time.

About to be married her hillbilly friends wanted to give her a shower but she kept eluding them.

His girlfriend asked him if he was ready for a commitment. He said that he just wanted to date and he hadn't planned on checking into a mental hospital.

She said that she wanted to take their relationship to the next level so we started meeting up on the roof of our apartment house during lunch.

She dated a fisherman and she fell for him hook, line and sinker.

He worshipped the ground she walked on especially when he found out that her father had a lot of oil wells on his Texas ranch.

I wanted to see my girlfriend in the worst way so I went to see her very early one morning.

I knew that my girlfriend sold lingerie because she had the bad habit of giving me the slip.

She was not just another blond, he thought that he was marrying a golden opportunity.

My girlfriend's father was a comedian. I asked for his daughter's hand in marriage and as expected he said, "You have to take all of her not just her hand." What a comedian?

I was in love and I wanted a lock of my girlfriend's hair to put in my wallet. She said, "Do you want hair from my red or the blond wig?"

His girlfriend said, "A lot of men will be miserable when I marry." I asked her, "How many men are you planning to marry?"

The diamond in the engagement ring was so small that it had no room for a flaw.

I made the mistake of proposing to my girlfriend in my car in my garage. I couldn't back out.

I told my girlfriend that I would call her but she insisted that I give her a ring.

My last date was memorable, I haven't seen her since.

He had a rendezvous with destiny, but his girlfriend Destiny said, "We've got to stop meeting like this."

I dated a girl who was once an elevator operator. She told me that she had a lot of ups and downs but never liked the jerks she encountered occasionally.

She thought that her boyfriend was on the US Olympic Diving Team, but he corrected her, he told her that he's been in a lot of dives lately.

She wasn't frightened of her boyfriend who was a wolf but she was afraid of a mouse.

Gold digger to date: "They tell me that you have a lot of money, is that true?" Her date: "Well not exactly, my name is Richard, and a lot of people call me Rich for short."

When my girlfriend graduated charm school she got a job in a circus, charming a snake in a basket.

My girlfriend went to two weeks of charm school, when she graduated she received a diploma and a box of mint flavored charms, she said that the entire experience was charming.

My friend wanted to smell really good so he bought cologne by the case but the entire neighborhood soon got wind of it.

When a Borgia in Italy wanted to show love in the middle ages she sipped the wine first before handing it to her date.

I used to kiss my date a lot but one time her father walked in and he told his daughter "I'm getting tired of your kisser."

My blind date was a little plump and I was surprised when she said that her name was Bovina.

My girlfriend was a real problem but a problem that I liked wrestling with.

I dated a female lifeguard at a pool but I soon found out that she was really shallow.

My girlfriend's name was Ivy and I was always itching to see her.

I dated a girl named Sherry for two months, but I couldn't get used to her whining.

He dated a girl from Washington DC. He was a geometry teacher who became a politician to be politically correct he kissed her on the ellipse.

I told my girlfriend Isabella to give me a ring whenever she was in town.

He was a rich baseball player when he was single he like to play the field.

He fell in love with a young lady that weighed 300 pounds at first he thought that he was infatuated but it was more serious.

I live in Florida and my girlfriend lived in Mexico, it seemed as if there was Gulf between us.

I told her that I would get her a fur for Christmas I can't understand why she was disappointed with the tree.

My girlfriend got mad at me and called me a louse and for some reason I began to feel lousy.

When there was a full moon in June I wanted to spoon and if someone crooned love's tune my date may swoon and I'll be married at noon, honeymoon and live happily ever after or not.

He was from Ireland and before he left the old sod to come to the United States he made it a point to visit Blarney Castle to kiss the Blarney Stone. The problem was that he was so charming that his dates didn't know when he was serious or it was just some of the same old blarney as they called it the Baloney Stone.

My girlfriend worked at a pizza parlor when she wasn't working she smelled like pizza, I was always hungry and strangely somehow I was attracted to her.

He was an electrician, he alternated between two girlfriends, and he met one of them in D.C.

She said that she had to scrape the bottom of the barrel to find a date. Where did she ever find a barrel nowadays? If she was a farmer's daughter she could have picked the cream of the crop.

I dated a dairy framer's daughter but it didn't pan out she said that she would marry me when the cows come home. I kept thinking that I live in the city and there are no cows.

He took his girlfriend for a ride on a Ferris Wheel they were used to going around together.

She used to be a campfire girl so she warmed up to him quickly.

My girlfriend said that she couldn't stand me, I suggested that she sit down for a few minutes.

I didn't want to go swimming but I had to when my girlfriend got mad at me she said, "Go jump in the lake."

He said that he would slap her silly but she beat him to it and he wants to be slap happy, is this possible?

She was kissed so often that she opened up her own tollbooth and charged what the traffic would bear.

He was very strong he didn't even know his own strength one evening he picked up two young ladies.

She would not hug him but she embraced his ideas.

I received a letter in the mail from my girlfriend, the letter was empty and then I remembered my girlfriend said that she wasn't talking to me.

My girlfriend was not too bright I asked her to bring me some polish she showed up with a guy from Poland.

Her name was Ivy she had a tendency of creeping up on me.

My girlfriend tended to poke me in my side at first I thought she was fast but later I learned that she was actually pokey.

My girlfriend said that she was complex. I couldn't understand her, she seemed normal enough. She didn't have a complex she was just simply complex. I told her that I liked complex there's an air about it. I told her a dumb joke and she laughed, there's hope for us.

Joe was stumped he wanted to buy flowers for his girlfriend Doris but did not know whether to buy a bunch, a cluster, a group, a handful, a bouquet of flowers, or a single rose. He agonized for hours suffering from indecision and was tormented no end. He finally decided and bought Doris a box of chocolates, she liked chocolates, case solved.

My girlfriend's name was Donna she was from Italy they called her Bella Donna, my other girlfriend was named Ivy, once in a while either one could be poison.

Sam kept showering his girlfriend with gifts that were more and more expensive until one day he took a bath.

My girlfriend said, "Don't you remember that on our last date I dropped a hint?" I asked her if she remembered where she dropped it? All of our friends are looking for it.

A young lady tripped and fell and was helped up by a bachelor who said, "I saw you fall, what's your name?" She said, "Autumn." He replied, "Perhaps I'll see you next fall, Autumn?"

His girlfriend wanted to break up, she complained that he was like an albatross around her neck or like an anchor at her feet. Her boyfriend disagreed and told her that he may be more properly called a ball and chain around her ankle. She liked his comparison better than hers and she felt somewhat unfettered and she didn't like being fettered.

She was the Belle of the Ball, perhaps I should give her a ring, since I was in the North she wasn't a Southern Belle and I was not in Philadelphia so she couldn't be a Liberty Bell. The harder I thought about it the more thinking began to take its toll. Was I getting a ringing in my ears? I don't know why I was attracted to her but I once worked as a bell boy in a hotel and perhaps it was a subconscious thing.

I wanted to kiss my girlfriend, Luna, but she declined. She said that she was, "Going through a phase." But that didn't phase me, I promised her the moon, the sun, and the stars. She said, "What am I going to do with them, I can't get my hands on them, they don't phase me." Unphased I couldn't figure out what made Luna tick, but I'm still crazy about her. She said that she wanted me to be committed, but I wasn't that crazy yet.

My friend Sam said that his girlfriend Darlene was fair. Did he mean beautiful, or unbiased and reasonable or both, or was it how she performed at work, or was her hair fair, or was she fair minded, believed in fair play or just a fair weather girlfriend? It wasn't fairly obvious or even fairly apparent. Sam told me that she had a fair amount of good qualities, what more could he ask for, fair enough?

My girlfriend's name is Wanda, she is more than just a girlfriend, I call her always Wanda-ful.

Sam was a salesman and he wanted to meet and date a young sales lady with parallel interests, but if he finally located a lady on-line with parallel interests she would be difficult to meet simply because people with the same distance between them or with parallel interests, would never ever meet.

Since she purchased a new wool sweater she's been itching to meet someone new.

One curious candle asked another, "Are you going out tonight?"

An elderly playboy was in the habit or putting a notch on his cane for each lady he dated. He was doing fine until he gained weight and leaned too hard on his cane.

My girlfriend said that the magic had gone out of our relationship shortly after that she disappeared – like magic.

An Eskimo wanted to get married, but his girlfriend got cold feet.

I dated a beautiful Eskimo girl in her igloo, but I got off to a slow start, I had a hard time breaking the ice.

An undertaker had a hard time digging up a date.

The couple went to an old fashioned dance -- couples were dancing together.

A man in a supermarket bought five frozen TV dinners. The woman at the check-out counter asked if he was single. He said he was and inquired why she asked? She replied untactfully, "Because you're ugly."

DEATH

I know something's funny when I burst out laughing, I really enjoy something that is so funny I can't stop laughing and it just continues, unabated, but that doesn't happen often enough. I don't want to die laughing but it may be better than other choices. If you die laughing your epitaph could be, "That last joke was a killer."

I was dying to live forever.

I thought about writing my memoirs but how would that compare to famous politicians, writers, military men, people who butchered their way into history and other luminaries. I was low profile and tried to mind my own business so I gave up the memoir idea and decided to say it all in my epitaph, "Just passing through."

Where there's a will, there's a relative.

Cremation burns me up.

Get enough sleep, eat properly, exercise and live healthy die anyway.

I was thinking about the expression "You can't take it with you." In my case it's even worse because I'm not certain where I'll be going, even if I could take it with me. Something that doesn't burn easily may come in handy.

He wanted to be buried at the crack of dawn, so that even forewarned all of his mourners will be mourning in the morning.

My lazy no good bum nephew Bolivar wanted me to mention him in my will. Guess what Bolivar, I'm mentioning that you get a job so that instead of putting on airs you could leave something to your heirs.

He heard that too many people were dying in bed, he had a clever idea to delay things. He started sleeping on an air mattress on the floor.

A comedian was so funny that he got a standing ovation at the morgue when he died, but the joke was on him.

If an optimist always saves the best for last does that mean that he is looking forward to dying?

A battery died, the coroner was brought in and said that the death was caused by a terminal illness.

He was so lucky, he died last week but it wasn't because of anything serious.

His last pill made him deathly ill, now let's read the will "Will, you read the will?" Will's response: "You bet I will, let's see what will it be" The money in the till and the cat on the sill goes to Phil. Since the deceased is over the hill and now under it, all this talk gives me a chill." "Thanks Bill."

He was the first computer mummy, he wasn't put on a sarcophagus he was encrypted.

Epitaph for a chef: May he rest in peas and hominy.

Pick up line at a funeral: "Were you familiar with the deceased?"

Pick up line at a funeral "Do you come here often?"

Pick up line at a funeral: "You know I think black is your color, and it matches your eyes."

He was a blue blooded Englishman even when he made out his will he was putting on heirs.

The cowboy said that I should die with my boots on but I didn't own any boots. I thought that I could live a long time unless someone gives me the boot.

They asked the murderer if he had any last words before they hung him, he said, "I guess I'm at the end of my rope."

He used to be a paratrooper when he passed away they buried him with a R.I.P. cord in his hand.

He was in charge of ringing the bells at his church for 60 years but since he passed away he's a dead ringer.

Question to Ms. Answer Lady in the local newspaper: I am relieved to report that my husband who went out for a newspaper one night ten years ago is dead, do I qualify for any of his social security benefits, I miss him terribly?

When he died he left all of his money to charity. Charity was his girlfriend whom he dated for his last ten years.

When he died of laughter they buried him happily.

Soupy had a pleasant personality and he was pleasant to look at. He liked pleasing people in fact he took a great deal of pleasure pleasing people it just pleased him, he was so easily pleased. Soupy was a natural salesman, in his conversations Soupy exchanged pleasantries. It was so pleasurable. Soupy became the top salesman in his field, became rich which pleased him to no end. In the end they buried him with a pleasant smile on his face, if you please?

A will is a dead giveaway.

My father had no last words, my mother was with him until the end.

I thought I heard him say, "I'll have a good time even it kills me."

Undertaker: The last guy to let you down.

A California widow wears a black tennis outfit, and a black garter. The garter was in memory of those who passed beyond.

Alexander the Great asked Diogenes what he was doing searching through a pile of bones. Diogenes replied, "I'm searching for the bones of your father but I can't distinguish them from those of his slaves."

Here is what you want to hear when everyone thinks that you are dead. "Look he's moving."

He was cryptic about how grave the situation was.

People are living longer today because they can't afford to die.

They had a rough time burying the man who invented the hokey-pokey. It all started with his coffin when they tried to put his left leg in.

It's better to be over the hill than to be under it.

Graffiti: To Kick The Bucket Is Beyond The Pail.

"Let us endeavor so to live, that when we die, even the undertaker will be sorry." *(Mark Twain)*

DENTISTS

"Doc I need a tooth pulled right now, I don't want novocain, a sedative, or gas, just yank it our quickly. The dentist said, "You're very brave."

The customer turned to his wife and said, "Mary, show the doctor exactly just which tooth is bothering you."

I had to pay a toll whenever I kissed my girlfriend, she had a lot of bridgework.

What do you give the Dentist of the Year? A little plaque.

What does a dentist give you for one dollar? Buck teeth.

A patient went to a dentist who was advertised as 'painless'. When he touched her tooth the patient let out a yell. She said, "Doctor, you may be painless, but I'm not."

DIVERSITY

Can a really lewd person be considered ludicrous?

A gay Australian left Victoria for Sidney.

Many hair dryers in California are actually owned by men.

DOCTORS

Even though I was told that my medicine was tasty I could not swallow that bitter pill.

Prostate problems are no joke. People in white coats or ex-football players on radio and television constantly remind me of its dangers and I know they are right. It is nothing to joke about and saw palmetto pills from Wal-Mart may help but in the end it depends on your inate ability.

Everyone is concerned with colon health so many people who look like doctors advertise large intestine medicine on television. I prefer a real doctor to look into the problem in the meantime bran and Metamucil will have to do. This may help colon problems come to an end.

"Never tell people how you are, they don't want to know." *(Johann vonGoethe)*

Based on your examination was the lady pregnant? Response: "She was pregnant before I examined her."

"Doctor was the deceased shot in the nether region, doctor, just how low on the body is the nether region?" Reply: "He was shot below the belt."

Besides a pharmacist no one can read my doctor's handwriting but I have no trouble understanding the bills he sends me.

"Doctor as an expert witness what was the cause of the broken leg?" Doctor, "Am I here for the prosecution or defense?"

I thought that I needed glasses and went to an optometrist who asked me to read the eye chart. He asked me to read the lowest line on the chart that was clear to me." I replied, "What chart?"

Actually Sigmund Freud had a brother, Sigmund lived in northern Germany while his brother lived in the south, he was known as southern Freud and he sold fried chicken for a living.

My doctor told me to drink water an hour before bed but within ten minutes I couldn't drink another drop.

Because I was itching, I went to see a skin doctor. He said that he didn't want to make any rash judgments but that he was certain that I was just scratching the surface and the problem may be much deeper than skin deep.

Do I look normal – so what if I don't have an official handicap placard?

Optometrists live a long time. If what I heard is true they have a tendency to dilate.

Moses must have been a doctor in the hospital, he had a staff.

The bum was qualified for hospital work because he was an expert at panhandling.

The nurse at the hospital took my pulse but after she left I checked and it was still there.

If you think that time heals all wounds, why bother going to a doctor?

"Doctor, do I have to take these pills forever?" Reply: "No just as long as you live."

Doctor, I think I'm a clock. Doctor's reply: "There's no cause for alarm."

I met a crazy cowboy in the city, he said that he was slightly deranged.

Doctor you've got to help me, last night I dreamt that I was a commode and today I'm feeling flushed.

I told the dentist that my false teeth didn't fit right, he told me when I took them out at night to put them into a larger container before I put in the Polident.

I opened my prescription bottle and there it was a small wad of cotton, what to do, throw it out or keep it? I was sick thinking about it because I couldn't make up my mind. I finally flipped a coin for the correct answer and I felt satisfied with my thought process. I began picking cotton.

She was disappointed, she said she went to the doctor to be treated, but so far she hasn't received any treats.

The dermatologist got a rash of complaints.

I was in Dodge City and a tenderfoot druggist walked into a bar and ordered a stiff drink. The bartender said, "Name your poison." Acting tough the druggist said, "Give me three fingers of rubbing alcohol and put it into a dirty beaker."

While I was fueling up my car, a pickup truck pulled up at the next pump. The truck bed had a couch in it. I recognized the driver who was a psychiatrist and I asked "What's up?" He replied, "I'm making a house call."

I noticed that my friend was coughing and I told him that I hoped that it was not terminal. I asked, "Are you coughin' often, because if you are it may lead to the coffin eventually. He was not amused.

If you are not patient you'll soon become one.

She was an excellent nurse, it was somewhat of a family tradition, her father was a panhandler.

My uncle was really cheap. He refused to get well before he ran out of medicine.

He was such a problem patient that his doctor and all of the nurses sent him get well cards just to get him to leave the hospital sooner.

I was a tenderfoot in the scouts, when I got a tenderfoot as a senior I went to a podiatrist who told me, "Scout around for more comfortable shoes."

Doctor did you say that this medicine can make a person impotent or important?

I called my doctor and the girl who answered the phone said, "We're busy now can I put you on hold?" Did I have a choice? So I told her no. Did she listen to me, out of habit she put me on hold. I looked around for something to help but nothing was handy, she must have forgot about me. After 10 minutes I hung up and tried again.

I called my doctor and the receptionist said, "We're busy now could you leave a message?" We'll call you back as soon as we get a moment to spare." That was six years ago, they must be really busy, without a spare moment.

Everyone dies of heart failure eventually.

I used to be dedicated but since I had a nervous breakdown, now I'm committed.

I was going to put my heart into the song but I needed it for circulation.

My doctor told me that I needed to improve my circulation so I partied five nights a week.

Before you see the doctor the nurse said that she just wanted some information about my health. She said, what type of insurance do you have?" I knew then that she really cared about my welfare. If I didn't have insurance would I have spent the next ten years in the waiting room?

I bought a crazy watch it developed a nervous tick.

He said that he was Doctor Jekyll when women heard that they wanted to Hyde.

I had a hearing test and I told the doctor that the noises sounded eerie.

He was eating black jelly beans in the doctor's office when the doctor put a wooden tongue depressor on his tongue, he said that things looked black.

I needed to get a vaccination but I got nervous when I saw the nurse using two large knitting needles to knit a scarf.

The word blood has a lot of uses but the idea of making someone's blood boil is a little creepy. The English use the word bloody a lot in their movies such as "That was a bloody good job." Think about the uses, blood bank, curdling, count, bath, feud, donor, line, letting, hound, lust, money, relation, shot, where does it end? I don't want to get too excited about it all it will just raise my blood pressure.

The doctor told her to put more fiber in her diet and eat bran, fruit, vegetables, grains and brown rice. She had so much fiber she took up knitting as a hobby.

I had trouble coping so my doctor recommended I purchase a coping saw.

Jim Duffy went to see the doctor and said that he was tired, the doctor examined him and said that he was too sedentary and recommended that he get off his duff.

They called him a retch but he didn't know what it was and didn't feel bad until one day he got a stomach ache and upchucked and his friend told him that he must have felt retched.

He was a quack doctor, he treated ducks.

He was a single bachelor surgeon but all of his girlfriends called him an operator.

A plumber went to a doctor and complained, the doctor said, "I'll have to check out your plumbing."

The pharmacist didn't want a long version of his weekend activities so he made a capsule version of it.

I have an eyeball, an eye brow, eye lids, eye lashes, eye sockets, eye drops, eye glasses to get an eye full, or an eye opener, or see a sight for sore eyes, or just make eye contact. It appears that the eyes have it, that is if we see eye to eye?

Occasionally I spend a lot of time waiting for a car repair or in the doctor's waiting room with nothing but tired, worn out, outdated magazines which are boring at best. What about 'People' magazine or 'Reader's Digest'? While I don't recognize most troubled stars and starlets in 'People' magazine it's always, interesting to learn who is dumping who. Lately if I find something interesting to read, no sooner than I am engrossed I hear, "Your car is ready or the doctor will see you now," couldn't they wait a little longer? I'm tired of not waiting.

I visited my doctor and told him that I was having a problem with my hand. I showed the doctor my hand, the fingers cooperated but the thumb seemed to be opposed.

A stockbroker went to a doctor with a weight problem. The doctor said, "If you weight goes up ten more points, sell."

The doctor told the zombie to get some rest, he was dead on his feet.

I asked the doctor for an extra intravenous bottle because I was expecting a visitor for lunch.

My doctor examined me and said I was as sound as the United States dollar. When I heard that I started to sweat.

A patient with a bad back did not believe in chiropractors, because of the pain he finally went and spent fifteen minutes on a table being manipulated. When done he said "I feel a lot better, I stand corrected."

My friend advised me to see his doctor, he said, "You won't live to regret it."

What a great doctor, my uncle was at death's door, luckily his doctor pulled him through.

A cookie started to feel crumby, so it decided to see a doctor.

A patient waited four hours to see his doctor, exasperated he told the nurse, "I'm going home to die of old age."

An outpatient is a patient who fainted, and a paradox is two physicians.

A patient complained he was having trouble breathing. The doctor replied, "Don't worry I'll give you something to stop that."

I noticed that the surgeon scheduled to operate on me was examining the 'Reader's Digest' large print edition and I needed microsurgery.

I was sick last year and when I paid the last doctor bill my doctor told me that he was feeling a lot better.

My doctor told me that the operation was not dangerous because it was only $1500.

I knew that she was an honest doctor, as the cause of death she signed her name.

Once in a blue moon a very successful doctor will tell a patient, "There's absolutely nothing wrong with you."

My doctor found out what I had and he took it.

Patient: "I think that I was bitten by a vampire." Doctor: "We have a test for that, you drink this glass of water and if your neck leaks in two spots we can stop it, temporarily."

A surgeon often told jokes, he liked keeping his patients in stitches.

She had fee-fi-phobia which is a fear of Walt Disney giants.

Doctor, I didn't feel sleepy when I went to bed, but I really felt sleepy when I awoke.

The elderly matron complained to the doctor, "I was in such pain I wanted to die." The doctor replied, "You did right in coming here to call on me, dear lady."

Many, many years ago, a noted London doctor and professor, was appointed Physician to the King. When he informed his students one of them said, "God save the King."

My optometrist was a part time psychic. He said that he could see the year 2020 clearly.

Optometrist to patient, "Can you read the bottom line?" Patient: "Made in China."

"The art of medicine consists of amusing the patient while nature cures the disease." *(Voltaire)*

DRACULA

Dracula could not make the baseball team because the coach said that during a night game he was afraid that Dracula would turn into a bat.

Dracula loved going to nightclubs, but he was somewhat reluctant because he always had to check his cape in at the cloak room.

Dracula started biting his victims in a humorous vein because he longed to be a stand-up comic.

Dracula was pretty bright he took night classes at the local junior college.

Dracula must have been a closet vegetarian because he was deathly afraid of stakes.

Dracula went to a blood clinic where they expected him to donate a pint, but he turned the tables on them when he said, "I vant your blood!"

I saw a hobo that looked like Dracula I was afraid that he'd put the bite on me.

Dracula's wife was in a foul mood and took it out on Count Dracula she said, "All you do is sleep in that coffin all day, why don't you get a job like other guys and then you are out all night, who knows where you fly off to. You never think of me, once in a while you bite me on the neck but I'm tired of your necking why can't we be like other couples? I think we may need marriage counseling but the counselor may not have a stake in this matter and may actually cross you up." Dracula: "What's your problem, I'm a blood sucker and you knew that when you married me?"

ECONOMICS

I keep trying all different types of paper towels, cheap versus expensive, plain or printed, strong or weak when wet, good or poor water absorption, and fall apart or resilient when wet. So many choices for paper towels. I finally solved the paper towel problem, my wife picks the one she likes – problem solved.

Whenever I had a large supply there was no demand whenever there was a large demand I had a small supply, no wonder I got a 'D' in economics.

He lived in a land of plenty and everything was plentiful so he had plenty of everything instead of plenty of nothing.

An ounce of prevention doesn't seem as if it is a lot of prevention, a pound of prevention is 16 times better avoirdupois and 14 times better troy.

I bought some paint and the salesman said that I would get five dollars from the manufacturer. I said, "Why don't I keep the five dollars and save the manufacturer the trouble of mailing me a check, besides I pay an extra 30 cents tax on that five dollars as a sales tax plus the stamp needed to mail in the rebate coupon for about 80 cents extra, well that logic didn't fly, it doesn't work that way. Months later, after I received the five dollar check, yippee, I got my money back as if I had found five dollars, thank me.

I bought a couple of the best heavy duty Rubbermaid trash cans hoping that they would not just blow away in the wind as the cheaper ones did. Within two weeks I was missing one container top and since there was no wind it didn't just blow away. I found out that it is almost impossible to buy the top, I had to buy both top and bottom. Is this some vast conspiracy? I needed a five dollar top and had to buy a 40 dollar top and bottom. I spent weeks driving 100 miles to locate a top, no luck. I became burned out and tired of all the trash talk and I nearly blew my top.

Harry Truman wanted a one-armed economist because whenever he got economic advice the economist would say, "But on the other hand."

I'll tell you the economy is really rough today. Things got so bad that even Disney Studios is feeling the pinch I heard that Snow White had to lay off two dwarves, Sleepy and Dopey.

EDUCATION

In a preschool class the teacher said that we are lucky to live in the United States because we are free. One young lad said, "I was free last year now I'm four."

"Wisdom begins in wonder." *(Socrates)*

"The wise man learns from the misfortune of others." *(Aesop)*

"I know that I am intelligent because, I know that I know nothing." *(Socrates)*

He received a Phi Beta Kappa key and he's still looking for a door that it will open.

I was in unchartered waters and sketched in the missing land mass and there it was right on my revised map of those islands. I thought about calling the new island lost and found island.

When they said that you had nothing upstairs I defended you, I told them that you had a flat on the second floor.

I used to do odd jobs in high school when I graduated college I kept doing odd jobs but now I have a college education.

"Teacher I don't like arithmetic, I can't seem to add properly." Teacher, "Don't worry Johnny if you keep it up long enough eventually you'll have sum fun."

His parents promised to give him ten dollars for every 'A' he got in high school. After four years he managed to accumulate six dollars on his own.

Teacher: "Class does anyone know Lincoln's Gettysburg address, how about you Johnny?" Johnny: "Teacher I did not know that Lincoln lived in Gettysburg."

I took an easy elective in basket weaving at the University of Miami. I was doing great until ten Seminole Indians joined the class. After two weeks they skewed the curve and I flunked out.

If you have such a bright idea, why not invent a better light bulb?

School administrators are tough today, one student said that he looked into the dictionary and found explosives which resulted in a school lock down for a day.

I wanted to swap ideas with you but you say that you have nothing to swap.

I was lucky someone gave me a thesaurus for my birthday, because it changed my life for the better, since then I was never at a loss for words.

He met a pregnant woman whom he recognized from high school days. Being observant he noticed that she was about six months pregnant. Indelicately he asked, "What have you been doing lately, it appears that you've been quite busy." She replied, "Oh how nice of you for asking, let me fill you in on the details."

A computer whiz enjoyed breaking into computers and computer systems but as fate would have it he got his just desserts, eventually when he developed a serious cold and died of a hacking cough.

English is a tough language with people mispronouncing many words but there is one word everyone pronounces wrong. "Ok what is it?" The word is wrong.

I liked him but someone said that he was a little slow based on the rumor that he had taken an IQ test and flunked it.

I wanted to discover the fountain of knowledge all I got was a glass of tap water.

I wanted to visit the hallowed halls of an old college in England when I get there I noticed that the halls needed a fresh coat of paint.

Teacher: "Johnny just because you're taking up space in the classroom does not mean that you are going to be an astronaut."

I had to take an elective in college for the credits, I took up bird watching for a lark.

When he signed his name he made a large 'X' he left his mark for posterity to see, he was going to use a 'Y' but he didn't know why.

I went to a grammar school party and was having a whale of a good time but I lost track of time and got home two hours after curfew and my mother whaled me for good measure.

While he was a lightweight intellectually he was an excellent heavy weight boxer.

I want to learn all that I can learn if I succeed I'll become learned.

He was a trigonometry teacher so he knew all the angles.

He was too smart to be a moron and too stupid to be an intellectual, he was just one of the boys.

When he took an aptitude test he found that he didn't have any, he was eminently qualified for menial work.

I'm old fashioned when I grew up bong was the noise made by a bell that idea is now up in smoke.

He was a true chemist he drank his coffee out of a beaker.

She sent her daughter to finishing school in Baltimore, MD when she graduated she was finished.

The chemistry teacher successfully interacted with his college students.

I couldn't carry on a conversation with my geometry teacher, he kept going off on a tangent.

He was a dim bulb people had a hard time insulting his intelligence.

The college had a faculty for learning.

My name was Junior, I was in junior high school my father was called Senior, I was a junior but my sister was five years my junior, when I graduated high school I'm going to junior college.

He was an English teacher and he was singular but his girlfriend wanted them to be plural.

In high school they said that I didn't appear to be too bright and that I was plebian yet at the naval academy I was a plebe, but I could be common or coarse but not vulgar. I looked up plebian in the dictionary out of boredom.

Two copulas are a couple of cupolas.

He went to Harvard but he owned an Oxford dictionary.

I did not know that I did not know and they told me that I was ignorant or clueless. I realized that I was clueless and that I didn't know but I was ignorant of that fact but even though I was ignorant I could learn if you are stupid you may never know.

He said that he didn't have his wits about him so he was dim witted but not half witted but no doubt he was easily outwitted.

The instructor said that he was going to grade based on a normal curve but no one in my class was normal, abnormal was normal and the last time I saw anything bell shaped was the Liberty Bell in Philadelphia.

They said it was obvious but I didn't get it. Then it was more than obvious, how could that be I couldn't understand it when it was obvious. Obviously I missed something.

He never graduated college cum laude he just left quietly with his diploma.

He flunked all of his courses so as not to embarrass him they called him an underachiever to be politically correct, years ago they called him a loser, today he is intellectually challenged.

In high school we were all supposed to take turns, when it was my turn I took my turn, but I told the teacher that one good turn deserves another but she turned the tables on me and said I turned out to be greedy so I missed my turn as it turned out.

I took a correspondence course from a correspondence school. I corresponded for five months studying all of the corresponding literature I wanted to become a correspondent. I flunked the mail in test, even when I had forever to complete it and it was an open book. Maybe they couldn't read my handwriting on the essay test.

Rufus was called a country bumpkin, how did he qualify for this position, is there a test? Anyone scoring higher than 50 is automatically too smart to qualify. I never heard of a city bumpkin but there must be a few in a big city that qualify. If they qualify do they have to move to the country and would they get a travel allowance or just hitchhike there?

Jim took a competency test which proved once and for all that he was borderline incompetent. After years of night school and applying himself Bob became less incompetent. But Bob was practical he got a job and eventually surrounded himself with total incompetents which by comparison made him appear to be a genius.

Maurice, the French mathematics teacher, was not an expert in English he was more of an exponent of numbers.

Todd wasn't focusing on his college studies, he told his counselor that he excelled in extra-curricular activities.

When Joe received advice it fell on deaf ears, so he had his hearing tested and Joe only had a partial hearing loss, with a new hearing aid he heard a lot better and when he was given advice again it was loud and clear and he knew exactly what he wanted to ignore.

Otto lacked motivation so he took a night class at the local junior college, searching for a motive to be motivated. The professor, motivated by money, taught a motivational program to motivate unmotivated students. He graduated at the top of his class but it did him no good, when he realized he lacked ambition.

Extreme is an extremely interesting word. There is extreme pressure, an extreme reaction, extreme measures, extreme north, driven to extreme, or between extremes. All this is extremely confusing, I prefer being driven to an extreme rather than walking to it. Under extreme pressure I get an extreme reaction and I take extreme measures, this may not interest you or you may even be extremely interested.

At the post office I told the post lady that I needed a stamp for a letter that I was sending to my old grammar school, the post lady said, "Do you want send it first class or second class?" I replied, "No, I want to send it to the principal.

"Students welcome to the first session of Barber College 101. We will be working in pairs to start and we will be practicing on how to properly part a wig on a Styrofoam dummy head. John and Max will be working in pairs. John, you will be the party of the first part, followed by Max known as the party of the second part. Stick together and don't part ways remember you are a team but I expect you both to do your part. When you graduate we'll have a party before a parting of the ways and you can go on to a part time job leading to full time employment eventually, possibly owners of a partnership, but before we depart it all starts with the proper part on your part, from the very start.

I used to be redundant but now I'm succinct. I used to be verbose but now I'm terse. I used to be loquacious but now I'm tight lipped. I wasn't used to being at a loss for words so to keep my hand in I bought a dictionary and now I'm singularly lingual.

You say that it depends on what is is. Well so so, what's what is a no no, so run run, chop chop, hurry hurry and quick quick dum-dum if you know what I mean, what does anything mean Izzy? Yeah yeah.

He went to a book suppository he thought that it was a place where they stored books, that's what happens when you don't pay attention in English class and too lazy to look up a word in the dictionary.

Sam copied a copy of a reproduction of an original, Sam said it was just a part of the reproduction process. It turned out that Sam was prolific because he had copied a lot of copies so many that he could be called copius.

I didn't have any trouble with any of the questions on the test. When it came to the answers that was a different story.

My brother was held back in school so often that when he graduated he got a dinner and a gold watch.

Gross ignorance sounds quantifiably worse than ordinary ignorance.

I didn't know I was late, class must have started before I arrived.

I don't know how the people in the supermarket express lane graduated high school. Very few of them seem to know how to count to ten.

I know a classy school teacher who was unemployed and technically had no class.

A teacher retired with a nest-egg of one half of one million dollars after thirty years in the profession. She had accumulated three thousand dollars from her teaching job and the rest she inherited from a recently deceased uncle.

The teacher said that my class was dim so she put all of the lights on to enlighten us.

My teacher used to ask me so many questions I began to wonder exactly just what does she know?

Fat chance and slim chance mean the same thing.

I thought that I was the teacher's pet until I found out that she owned a dog and a cat.

Our school assembly took a long time, I don't know why, Ikea was one of the school sponsors.

EPITAPHS

Epitaph: A victim of fast women and slow horses *(Kirkland Lake, Ontario)*

Boxer's epitaph: I'm not getting up, stop counting.

I told you I was sick. *(Unknown)*

"If you take epitaphs seriously, we ought to bury the living and resurrect the dead." *(Mark Twain)*

Here lies an honest lawyer, and that is strange. *(Epitaph of John Strange - England)*

Here Lies
Lester Moore
Four Slugs from a 44
No Les
No More   *(Tombstone, Arizona)*

EXERCISE

I was at a health spa and I was told that I needed to reduce. I walked, I rode, I exercised, took a whirlpool bath, and spent some time in a sauna and a steam bath. I think it worked when I was done I was an inch shorter.

FAMILY

Mom, please give me an unbiased positive answer: "Yes or no?"

I knew that I could be a comedian because whenever I told my family that I wanted to be a comedian they broke out laughing.

I wanted to be a comedian but my mother told me that to be a successful comedy was no laughing matter.

When I said I was making a will everyone thought that I was stuck-up they said I was putting on heirs.

My grandmother doubled her knitting speed so that she would not run out of the ball of wool before she finished knitting the sweater.

She had no children and was hard pressed to know what to do for aggravation.

I was watching my daughter praying when she turned to me and asked. "Dad is there anything that you need, as long as I'm praying I'll ask for it and kill two birds with one stone."

My kids put lipstick prints on the bathroom mirror but they stopped when my wife told them that she used toilet water to wash the mirror.

A nosey neighbor said to my wife, "I can't help it but I noticed that you are expecting a bundle of joy." Reply: "Oh but you are mistaken I'm just carrying it for a friend as a favor."

My sister married one of my buddies, could that be the reason that he dislikes me as a brother?

Do you have an Indian heritage? I heard that you're a ticket scalper on Broadway.

No one liked Jim and what was worse he had no sense of direction. He was lost in his backyard for two days before anyone realized that he was missing.

Two light bulbs who had been dating for one year tied the knot in an elaborate marriage ceremony and had a glowing reception, honeymooned at Disneyland for the next forty years whenever they went to sleep they were delighted, they were very long life bulbs.

Conversation on telephone: "My brother is a twin." "Oh really?" "How can you tell each other apart?" Answer: "That's easy I'm his sister and I have long hair and a dress."

My lazy bum son used to sit around the house and do nothing for hours now its respectable it's called meditation.

A family was expecting guest for a supper. The mother wanted her daughter to serve the meal and cautioned her not to spill anything. The daughter replied, "Don't worry Mom, I know how to keep family secrets."

The baby started walking when she was one year old and she was lost in the house for an hour before they found her.

I heard that there was a kidnapping in our town, but it was a false alarm. He woke up when his mother picked him up.

My brother had a talent for getting into hot water, that's what happens when you take a bath twice a day.

I was shocked when I met someone who told me that when he was born he cried like a baby. I would never had thought of that.

I knew many families who lived in their furnished basements, this was comfortable and convenient because they had no problem being upwardly mobile.

I knew a lady who had an all-white living room, the rug, drapes, sofa, chairs and couch were Snow White, her children and husband were allowed in there rarely but guests were always welcomed.

Ugly? I can't say that the baby was ugly but when the doctor delivered her he took one look and shot the stork.

I had been bad and my father said I needed to be taught a lesson, he said, "This is going to hurt me more than it is going to hurt you." Then to my surprise I saw him strongly slap himself on the face ten times.

My mom told me that I had to do my chores before playing baseball. What is a chore, it was a chore thinking about it? To save time I asked mom to give me a list of what each chore was because I didn't want to waste my time doing something unnecessary.

My mother said, "How many times do I have to tell you?" Reply: "I don't know I have not been keeping count, is this a test?"

He was Don Juan's brother he was called Juan Two.

The potholder Tommy made at camp and gave to my wife cost 500 dollars.

His family tree has no roots.

He admired his father who was a midget he said, "I wish I could be half the man that he is."

I told an Englishman that 'mum's' the word. He said, "Are you talking about my mother or a yellow flower?

Remember the Maine? Remember the Alamo? Remember Pearl Harbor? Remember Sam Wazalewski? Nobody does.

His name was Lot he was big in real estate where he sold lots of lots and made lots of money but the rest of his family were a bad lot.

When he was young he received an allowance, actually his parents had to make allowances for him.

When I was seven I wanted to be eight when I was eight, I wanted to be nine. In England when you're ninish you say tennish anyone? Sorry about that.

His father sold fishing goods and his mother told him that he came from a long line her husband sold her.

I inherited a grandfather clock from my grandmother.

He was like a father to me and you know that my father and I never got along.

He was like one of the family he didn't get along with anyone either.

We have/had American royalty there's: B.B King, Count Basie, Martin Luther King, Queen Latifah and Gladys Knight without the Pips.

My sister was a nurse when it rained she was a wet nurse. She used to be practical then unregistered but now she's registered. You have to be a little patient to look up to her I caught her nursing a drink after a rough day, she complained about the heavy workload and she said if things got any worse she could always work in a nursery.

My second father liked to climb stairs for exercise of course he was my stepfather which made sense to me.

He was a carpenter and they called him a stud but he was a married man and as a carpenter he knew what a stud was and he wasn't a stud.

He was six years old and he wanted a water pistol for his birthday but when he got one he pestered everyone with it and they began calling him a little squirt.

The kids made a rumpus in the rumpus room so everything was OK.

He was born into a Japanese family and he used to get up early he was considered the early rising son.

He evaluated his family members based on their relative merits.

Our family grew up in the gutter my sister liked birds so we called her a gutter snipe until she got married.

She was young and beautiful she wore a pony tail but her mother was built like a horse.

Question to Ms. Answer Lady in the local newspaper: Is it good form for me to go on a honeymoon after my fifth child?

His wife was gone for two weeks during that period he received the bad housekeeping seal of disapproval.

My name is John but everyone wants me to be Frank.

He was so compassionate he received compassionate leave. He lost a lot of relatives, relatively speaking.

Nicholas Copernicus said that the earth orbited about the sun, I have a son who circulates all over the earth.

The carpenter didn't know what to name his newborn son, after some thought he named him 'Brad', I think he nailed it.

Just because he was born in a basement didn't mean that he was low born.

He wanted to be assimilated but instead he was regurgitated, the group leader said that he was hard to swallow.

He wanted to be an aristocrat but left a lot to be desired he had no social skills, lacked class, was dull, with no old money and his family tree was shady. The only thing left was to marry the daughter of an aristocrat, but Patricia said that he was too plebian a word that he couldn't understand, understandably.

My uncle used to sell bedroom furniture, sheets, pillows, pillow cases, blankets and bed covers. Whenever we argued he would end up saying, "Oh, you're just making a blanket statement and you are not specific enough." How could I win, I guess he was in the bedroom business too long.

I had a lot of distant relatives, one lives in Africa, another in Russia, one lives in Australia and another one is on the run so I can't say where he is but he writes occasionally from parts unknown.

My aunt said that someone had left her fence gate open and now she's looking for closure, she was feeling defenseless.

My brother was afraid to go to sleep because he dreamed he was working.

"Who is that terribly homely man over there?" "It's my brother." "Oh, there's not the slightest resemblance."

How many brothers do you have? Response: "I have three brothers but my sister has four."

By the time I realized that my parents were right all along, my children would not believe me.

My father left the day before I was born. He probably had a premonition of what was coming.

I looked up my family tree and found that most of my relatives were still living in it.

He boasted about his family tree, but he came from the shady side of the tree.

They were twins, he was 52 and she was 39.

Nice girls take after their mothers because some mothers take first.

Here's a statement that breaks a woman's heart: "Mommy, I missed the school bus!"

I went to a kids amateur show. One contestant said that he wanted to do a little number that he had learned recently. He said "Three."

My uncle really deserves a lot of credit because he's always had a hard time earning cash.

I was single and I wanted to see a new movie without interruption so I went to see it with my family.

He was the relative who fell out of the family tree.

My name is John, I believe I have a room named after me somewhere in this building.

Where there's a will, there's a relative.

My parents never struck me when I was young unless you count the time when my father hit me with the Buick.

My mother said, "Don't forget to write." I said "No problem, I've been writing since I was five years old and I'm a lot better now.

I wanted to buy a Christmas gift, but by the time I found a parking spot it was the New Year.

His family tree needed trimming.

FARMERS

A farmer went to a doctor who told him that he had a case of shingles. The farmer decided to use the shingles to put a new roof on the outhouse.

His father was a farmer so he wanted his son to go to agricultural college. At college the son partied and did not apply himself. At his graduation the son was voted most likely to go to seed by his classmates.

I threw an apple out my window and an apple tree began to grow. When I threw a cigar butt out the window nothing happened. When I started smoking cigars they grew on me.

I was down south and confused, they said that I was in redneck country. How was that possible, I saw a pickup truck with regular tires, items secured by ropes not duct tape, no dog in the back of the pickup, breakfast without grits and no Beverly Hills Hillbillies on television, was I dreaming?

He worked at a farm cutting and bailing hay but he was so frustrated with his job he quit and said, "That was the last straw."

He signed up for the fencing team at the agricultural college when he showed up for class he received a roll of barbed wire, a pair of pliers, a hammer, a box of large staples and wooden posts for his class farm project.

I went to an art auction and a painting fetched a price of ten thousand dollars since I was from the country the main item we fetched was a pail of water.

I was a farmer who studied agriculture, I always wanted to put down roots. I loved roots I used to root around for my clothes, my wife is one of my best rooters, but now I'm searching for my roots which appear to be shallow.

She said that she was a country girl but she never said what country.

He was content, his wife was content he was a farmer with contented cows he avoided contentious arguments which allowed him to sleep contentedly, uncowed.

He owned a plum orchard he thought that the work was easy and said that he had a plum job but his wife often acted like a prune, during the picking season he worked 16 hours a day and at the end of the day he was plum tired.

He was a gentleman farmer he was very cultivated and had a cultivated personality.

Someone stole a barrel of wheat from a farmer, his hired hands' alibi was so absurd and preposterous that no one could make up something that far-fetched so on second thought the farmer felt that there may be more than a grain of truth to it.

He was a farmer who grew wheat, a worker made him very mad one day and he threatened to thrash the worker within an inch of his life.

He wanted to plant an idea in his friend's mind but the soil was barren.

In the north he went quite a distance on the Beverly Hillbillies he went a fur piece

The farmer grew peas all of his life but one day he just snapped.

My uncle said that he was rolling in clover, he wasn't rich but he had a farm and grew clover and that he planned to harvest it as food for his animals.

Jim the farmer had close cropped hair, a furrowed brow, cultivated manners, a fertile mind, a rooster that crowed, impeccable chickens and a rye sense of humor just a typical hard working dawn to dusk farmer with a sunny disposition.

When driving in farm country use caution if you pass a farmer driving a tractor and he's chewing tobacco.

You never know about farming. In a bad year with severe drought very little corn is grown. One farmer ate five acres of corn for supper.

FASHION

I bought a made-to-order suit. I got a good buy because the man that ordered it originally never picked it up. He passed away. I almost died when I heard how cheap it was.

Bathing suits are so small today that their designers are working themselves out of a job.

He wanted to be haberdasher, but he wasn't sure that he was suited for his work.

She looked as if she was bursting at the seams because she wore a size 8 dress when she was really a size 10.

I knew that you had something on your mind because that was the first time I've seen you wearing a hat.

He said he wanted his wife to buy the most expensive suit for his funeral he may have to wear it for eternity.

She wore a fancy outfit to a fancy restaurant where she fancied a fancy meal and champagne that came at a fancy price, fancy that, and they called her Plain Jane.

When I was young as a gift I got a beanie with a large propeller on it and strings to tie under my chin to keep it from falling off, the problem was that in a gust of wind I began to feel light headed.

He was a material witness in a law suit between two ladies clothing manufacturers in the garment district.

She was poor even her gown had no visible means of support.

She wanted to be in fashion so she went to a fashionable dress store where after a fashion they fashioned an outfit for her and now she's a fashion plate or a good looking dish.

He couldn't afford a formal outfit so he bought a cummerbund and wore it around his waist with a business suit, he considered himself properly encumbered.

It was a watershed moment he bought a waterproof coat that was fine for two months when it began to leak he read the clothing label and it said water repellent he felt soaked in more ways than one.

She was very thin and her hair was in the shape of a bubble when she dressed entirely in a white she looked like a Q-tip.

Her name was Olive and she wore olive green clothes or was it olive drab? She had many types of oil for cooking but she considered them all Olive oil.

He couldn't afford orthopedic shoes so he bought a pair of orthopedic flip flops and orthopedic sneakers.

Her hair was a bright grey, from a distance her hair looked like a giant Brillo Pad.

I wanted to quit smoking my fingers were brown and my teeth were getting brown but on the bright side the color did not clash with my brown suit.

W.C. Fields frequently described lovely ladies as wearing a diaphanous gown which turns out to be 'delicate or gauzy'. Lovely ladies wear delicate clothes but I've never seen one wearing gauze perhaps he was referring to a nurse?

Maurice visited Greenwich Village in New York City and he wanted to stand out and be different so he dressed as a normal person.

She got her clothes out of a dumpster and naturally she looked dumpy.

That's a nice suit. When did the clown die?

Dry cleaner in New Mexico: 35 Years On The Same Spot.

When I saw his new sports coat it became clear that somewhere in Baltimore there was a classic 1955 Chevrolet with the front seat covers missing.

The clothing store had a giant sale. A sign in their window said "Come In and Have a Fit."

The skimpy bikini had a name from the Pacific, it was called almost nothing atoll.

In order to be different many teenagers dress alike.

Her living bra committed suicide, it claimed it was leading an empty existence.

Sign in a dry cleaners window: "Drop Your Pants Here."

One hat said to another hat, "You wait here while I go on ahead."

Dubious compliment: "I wish I could look that good in cheap clothes."

"Clothes may disguise a fool, but his words give him away." *(Aesop)*

FLOWERS

He was a florist but his job was no bed of roses and coincidentally his wife from Maryland was nicknamed black-eyed Susan and when they kissed they put their tulips together.

I saw a rose in bloom, it was an Israeli rose. How sweet it smelled.

She wore a hat covered with real flowers after all it was the Kentucky Derby, unfortunately she had a bee follow her around all afternoon.

He was a gifted florist even his speech was flowery.

I went to a florist who told me a secret, he asked me to keep it quiet he said, "Mum's the word."

I bought a bunch of daisies for my girlfriend Daisy, on the way over I pulled the petals out of the flower one at a time, "She loves me, she loved me not." Great, she loves me, that night she dumped me, you just can't put your trust in one flower; a blooming idiot.

Her name was Rose she was aptly named, whenever she experienced any difficulty she always rose to the occasion as she got older she needed a new hip, they called it a Rosehip.

He met a young lady from California her name was Lily, he loved her and they were married she said that she was, "Lily of the Valley."

Her name was Orchid so I brought her an orchid for the prom, she was quick witted when she said, "Oh how lovely, you're so unpredictable." Maybe I should have got her a rose but Rose had made other arrangements.

What do you send a sick florist?

FOOD

I can't tell you how many times that I saw an item on sale at the supermarket and at the register I was charged the full price, it's a good thing that I'm observant. The cashier said that I have to buy two and I needed to buy a total of ten dollars in merchandise or I need to have the store's club card for the discount. All restrictions are listed in tiny print barely visible at first glance. Is this misleading advertising? Do I have to go into a food store with binoculars to read the fine print? My glasses are bifocals I'm too far away to use my reading prescription glasses and too close to see both the large and small print. Superman help me.

When my wife changed religions she wanted me to be a vegetarian for health reasons. I started eating more fruits and vegetables religiously complemented with soy products such as tofu and veggie burgers. When I read the veggie burger package I was impressed by the multitude of mystery ingredients needed to make the veggie burger taste good. I said, "Wow if the soy doesn't kill me the byproducts I buy will."

The supermarket had a two for one sale, if you buy one at full price, the second one is free. I can't eat more than one what would I do with a second one, probably throw or give it away eventually? When an item is ten for ten dollars I can buy one for one dollar at two for one I'm flummoxed. You have to be on your toes even in a supermarket, which makes it very good for ballet dancers I'm caught flat footed.

I looked at the wine list at a fancy restaurant, what to choose a red wine or a white wine? I let my wife decide, I was color blind.

I had beautiful ingredients and the tossed salad looked appetizing but no matter how much salad dressing I used the salad tasted funny, maybe I should have rinsed them before I tossed them.

I ate at an organic food restaurant they claimed the taste was earthy but there may have been a tad too much earth.

I entered a hot dog eating contest and came in dead last. I was accused of 'dogging it'.

I worked in Baltimore for the McCormack Spice Company, they called it seasonal work.

I was an unemployed baker and now I do not feel kneaded.

Frank please be frank, how does your frankfurter taste? Reply: "Frankly, not too hot."

My girlfriend was liberated she wanted to go 'Dutch treat' it took me an hour to find a Dutchman that agreed to the idea after I gave him 20 dollars, it was cheaper than flying to Holland.

When they call for take-out food in China, do they call for a Philadelphia cheese steak, a New York pizza or Maryland crabs? What do they charge for delivery and how much do you tip the delivery boy? You can't pay in cash anymore.

A pizza place bragged about their fast delivery, they claimed that they delivered before you hung up the telephone.

I loved working at Starbucks, I didn't get rich but when I made coffee there were lot of perks.

For an emergency I stored up a lot of water, I may have bought too much while I have liquid assets, I'm broke.

I had a couple of hours to kill so I ate an artichoke and I ended up with a pile of leaves bigger than its original artichoke, luckily I managed to lose weight in the process.

I heard that all strange or wild meat tastes like chicken, I ordered chicken at a fancy restaurant and it tasted like beef.

On a tour I ate a pizza in Italy and the shop owner was very proud. He said that the tomato sauce was imported all the way from the USA, and he called the pizza 'New York style'.

At the Mexican restaurant they had ten different types of hot sauces on the table. I chose the Habanero blend, the one that had a skull and crossbones on the bottle. When I put it on my Mexican beans and ate it, the sprinkler system went off.

I ordered breakfast of scrambled eggs, home fries, bacon and coffee. and I told them that I was in a hurry, so step on it. When the breakfast arrived I said, "Who put this footprint on my breakfast?"

I bought some condensed milk in a can at the grocery store but when I got home before I knew it, it was evaporated.

The cook was a little slow it took him 15 minutes to cook a three minute egg.

A polite cannibal asked his wife, "Whom are we having for dinner tonight, Dear?"

I love chocolate, one hot summer day I put two chocolate bars into my pants pocket and forgot about them. When I checked they melted in my pants and not on my hands. I put them into the freezer to solidify and out of desperation I went on a Snicker kick.

I wanted to eat a balanced meal so I carried a plateful of food in each hand.

I wanted a square meal so I started out with a round pizza.

A cowboy ate alphabet soup for quite a spell.

Waiting for supper, I asked my wife how far are we from eating? She told me the distance between the kitchen and the dinner table was 12 feet and six inches, she's always so precise.

I forgot my lunch and had no time to go out to pick up fast food, so I went down to the room with the vending machines to choose my poison. One can was worse than the next, I was desperate so for emergency rations I bought two packs of Lance peanut butter crackers and a bag of Utz potato chips, a balanced meal. Down south it's called 'eating high on the hog'.

I was a great chef, but as I got older I knew that I was running out of thyme.

Fast food means food prepared and served fairly quickly while you wait. It also means that the food doesn't last long, so you're done eating before you know it.

I bought some buns at the bakery one of them looked exactly like Elvis Presley's profile. Too bad no one else could recognize the resemblance, it could have been worth a fortune.

The craze today is energy drinks lasting three to six hours. When the time is up do you run out of gas and slow down, what's next a ten minute energy drink allowing you to jump over cars? The addition of prune juice could cut the wait time to five or six minutes.

He kept gaining weight because at supper conversation he couldn't get a word in edgewise so all he could do was eat continuously.

The favorite meal of acclaimed actress Marlene Dietrich was hot dogs and champagne.

I ordered a Whopper at Burger King but the cashier was a comedian and told me one unbelievable giant lie after another. I told him I just wanted one whopper, not three or four.

I went to a pancake house. Pancakes were selling like hotcakes.

A cannibal became a vegetarian because he was fed up with people.

I looked into my refrigerator for something to eat, while it was jammed with food there was nothing to eat. I bought yogurt this morning and my wife put it in a safe place, now it's lost forever. How is it possible for yogurt to hide in the back of the refrigerator, by the time that I found the yogurt which was ten minutes later, I lost my appetite and now I'm looking for that.

I'm old fashioned and I like writing and mailing letters. A friend of mine was worried that the glue on stamps wasn't kosher, a thought which never crossed my mind. I think that the glue on Israeli stamps is now kosher, which eased my mind because when I start licking I want to keep ticking.

My wife was a vegetarian at supper we didn't eat, we grazed.

The whole place was a mess, actually it was a mess hall, where no one messed around.

Is it possible to eat a pomegranate without a bib? I tried it and it looked as if I had been hit with buckshot. I wonder if there is a proper way to disassemble and eat a pomegranate in a polite society dinner setting.

I placed the coffee beans into the coffee grinder and placed the ground coffee into the coffee maker and poured the fresh coffee into a coffee cup for my coffee break with coffee cake. No Starbucks today, but that's ok.

Two chefs were talking, one said to the other, "Let's do lunch."

I needed to eat something that would stick to my ribs but I don't think the gummy bears worked.

He thought that he was hearing strange voices but then he realized that he was in a Chinese restaurant.

Licorice used to be one color, black. Today it is black, red, purple, green, blue and there seems to be 40 or 50 feet of it in a bag mostly under the brand name 'Twizzlers'. While all taste good, the black seems best. I like the old black hard sticks of licorice which are no longer around; that's progress?

A kiwi is a brown fuzzy Chinese fruit with a green sweet edible interior and is grown in California and surprisingly Italy, small kiwis are called pee wee kiwis.

I ran into a friend dining alone and eating a giant steak. I asked him "Are you eating that alone?" he replied, "No I'm eating it with mashed potatoes and peas."

I ate lunch at a junk yard, naturally I ate junk food.

She was a cook named Blanch who fell behind in her car payments so they garnished her wages.

They told him that she was a tomato, I was a vegetarian and I liked tomatoes especially if she was a New Jersey tomato.

He was in a wonton mood so he went into a Chinese restaurant and ordered soup to go.

Sucrose, lactose, sucralose fructose so many sugar substitutes what's wrong with plain sugar?

He was always unlucky he always got the short end of the chicken wishbone, he finally gave up eating chicken.

Two chefs were arguing and things started to escalate they eventually got into a stew after a while one chef started to stir things up.

He loved strawberries so much that he married a strawberry blonde who had a strawberry mark, he kissed her until he was strawberry bushed.

He used to be a masher but as he got older he became a couch potato, his dog was named Spud.

He was always unlucky when he ate at a Chinese restaurant he got a Chinese misfortune cookie.

My doctor was Indian and I was a cook so I curried his favor.

I went to a Chinese restaurant for take-out food but there was a sign on the door that said, "I'll be back, C.U. Soon." That's how I learned the name of the owner who was C.U. Soon.

Her coffee was very strong, she denied it but I had a hard time removing the spoon from the cup.

A pilot needed a carbohydrate rush but his favorite Italian restaurant was 200 miles away so he hopped into his plane but about 110 miles enroute he had second thoughts but at that point he was pasta point of no return.

I had an hour to kill so I ate a pomegranate, after that I spent another hour eating an artichoke that my wife cooked, when I got done I was still hungry, maybe I'll eat a crab next I still had some free time.

When he dropped a donut on his crotch he began feeling crotchety.

He was a cook with a lot of experience he was well seasoned.

He was upwardly mobile and when he was invited to an exclusive roast he looked forward to it but he was disappointed because when he got there overdressed it turned out to be a cookout with barbecue beef.

He was a city boy and he got hungry on the farm, but they gave him good advice they told him not to touch or eat any road apples.

He was poor he couldn't put on the Ritz but every morning he put jam on a round cracker.

Growing up I ate a lots of rhubarb made with apples and oranges, it's an acquired taste, I never expected it to come in handy but when I played baseball and a rhubarb broke out I was always first in line.

He was a role model at a bakery.

I worked at a bakery and I used to say, "Don't stop me now, I'm on a roll."

In high school he used to work in a produce department at Good Deal Supermarket in Irvington, New Jersey it must have made an impression on him because he married a girl named Romaine.

He spent one night at a round table looking for a square meal.

He wanted a rump roast for supper but he made the mistake of backing up against a hot stove.

I was feeling low, life was boring I was in a rut even my car was in a rut, now I'm out of a rut and in a pickle. How do I get out of a pickle?

He was a cook he liked to savor the flavor and he used savory to make his meals even more savory.

He worked at a knitting mill so he was used to scarfing down his food.

It seemed as if I was on a yo-yo diet I would gain 10 pounds and lose five, then gain five pounds and lose six pounds, up eight, down six, in the end I lost one pound success at last.

I had a Porter house steak and I've never been to his house, in fact I never ever met him.

In the asylum he wanted to be a naval destroyer so he hit an orange with a sledge hammer.

Everything is organic today especially produce and fruit there are organic apples, bananas, carrots, tomatoes, peppers, peaches, etc. How can I tell they all cost more but they all look the same, if I pay more will I live longer? Does organic taste better than inorganic, I've been accused of having no taste at all.

The can said best if used before it goes bad. In some areas they would say, "Before it goes bad, I'd best use it."

He said that he was in an outreach program he drove around in a car and ordered food at the McDonald's drive-thru and he reached out of the window.

He not only indulged he overindulged now he is overweight and needs to underindulge. Just food for thought.

The chef was having a lot of pressure and psychological problems, things got worse when they caught him smoking the oregano.

He wanted to order a Jewish meal but he suspected something about the restaurant wasn't kosher.

He lost so much weight that he was awarded the no-belly prize.

He was a devil when he went to the butcher shop he demanded his pound his flesh.

I was in the desert and a thirsty man approached me and said, "Water, water." I gave him some water and he washed his bifocals, and said, "I can see clearly now the rain will fall, eventually."

Two potato chips, male and female, were at a dance the male chip said, "Do you dip?"

I ate my hotdog with relish or I relished my hotdog, either way it was delicious.

He went to a dude ranch out west the only thing that they used on the salad was ranch dressing.

He was eating at a fancy upscale Chinese restaurant when he ordered a hamburger, French fries and a coke accidentally on purpose.

He was a stranger in New York City everyone knew it when he went into a delicatessen and ordered a pastrami sandwich on white bread and please hold the pickle.

I ate two moon pies and for some strange reason my trousers kept slipping down.

At our annual Thanksgiving dinner, my mother told me to, "Stop gobbling your food."

I went into a restaurant and ordered a melted cheese sandwich, toast and a cup of coffee. The sandwich tasted great but when I left the restaurant I was set upon by two rats.

I ate at a diner and I dined at a restaurant and we pigged out at a buffet.

In the north the waitress said, "The cook will be with you in short order," down south the waitress said, "The cook will be with you directly."

I had eaten a galumki and a pierogi but I didn't know what a frondorki was then I learned that it was the key to the front door.

They said that I was rich and that everything was handed to me on a platter, I pleaded guilty, I told them that the platter came in handy at supper time.

Of all of the chefs, Jack was the consummate consumé cook that consumers loved to consume because it was delicious and so consumable. But Jack was too consumed in his work so he went to Disneyland where he acted Goofy, it seemed Dopey but he was Happy.

He felt uncomfortable so he wanted some comfort food, he had heard so much about it on the cooking shows, after all they were all making 'comfort' food, so he went to a restaurant but could not find comfort food on the menu. What was it? It couldn't be on the menu because the prices made him uncomfortable, so he went home and cooked hot dogs and beans and he felt comfortable.

Pete complimented the restaurant owner who gave him a complementary meal. Pete was profusely complimentary because it was the first complementary meal that he ever received. It turned out that he was the 10,000th customer and it could be a long time before that happens again, then again he thought about signing up for food stamps but he made too much money, that's show biz.

I bought some cottage cheese that wasn't made in a cottage it was made in a factory in Philadelphia. I was on a cottage cheese diet and I worked at home in a cottage industry, even though I lived in a brick house. How much cottage cheese can you eat? On my next diet I'm going to spit out anything that tastes good, that'll work.

The sculptor had carved many statues at courthouses in several states and he was always working. He was invited to a Thanksgiving dinner one year and the host asked him to carve the turkey based on his credentials.

A chef bought a French cookbook but he made little progress on the menus he said he needed more time to digest all of the pages

After the crime occurred the police grilled the barbeque chef for two hours. The barbecue chef got mad and he did a slow burn. A judge fined the chef and garnished his wages for money he owed.

I ordered a beef steak sandwich and since I was from New Jersey I asked for a big slice of the delicious New Jersey beef steak tomato. The tomato slice was so large that I said, "Where's the beef?" The restaurant owner said, "What's you beef?"

He was a cook and he rarely got mad but when he did he did a slow boil.

I had heard about bouillon soup, I heard that you used a bouillon cube so I bought one and to be on the safe side I dropped a one ounce ingot of gold into the boiling water and it tasted rich.

I was mad when I went into the restaurant, I ordered baked chicken, I told the waiter that I had a bone to pick.

I had a half of a case of envy, a friend told me about a fancy French restaurant that had ambiance. When I entered it was dimly lit and I looked for the ambiance but couldn't locate it. I asked the snooty waiter who frowned and asked me if I was gauche, I told him that I was Hungarian and I tried to act blasé. I wish that I knew more French, when I leave I'll tell that snooty waiter, bum voyage wasn't I a bon vivant?

He went into a fancy French restaurant and had difficulty reading the French menu so he asked the waiter what he recommended? The waiter said, "May I suggest the Poulet Flambé." The diner said, "What is that?" Reply, "Burning, burnt chicken."

An alien went to McDonald's and everyone was curious about what the alienate? He said that the Big Mac and fries tasted out of this world, what else?

The police swooped down on the produce department because Miss Tomato said that Mr. Celery was stalking her and it made her nervous. Mr. Lettuce had been stalking her but he turned over a new leaf.

She had an affection for confection or was it a sweet tooth? If she kept it up one tooth may be all that is left and worse diabetes may loom in her future. So she cut back on Snickers bars, Mars bars, Reese's pieces and even Coco Puffs and she is as sweet as ever and perhaps for a long time, but she still sneaks in a chocolate bar once in a while.

The lady complained that the fish was not fresh. The fish dealer said, "Are you kidding lady, the only way that this fish could be any fresher is if you were on the fishing boat and barbecued it on deck or ate it raw, look lady, it's moving."

As my friend left he said, "Let's do lunch sometime." I didn't have time to explain that I don't eat lunch. I could do breakfast or supper a lot easier because lately I get up late. While I'm not antisocial I'd much rather eat at my home with my wife and I can watch TV. I don't do supper, I eat supper, yes I do. I don't do a lot of things, but if pressed I do do supper. Lately I get a lot of takeout food I never feel taken and I don't have to figure out how much to tip. I don't have to tip myself that's my tip of the day. If you decide to take it or leave it it's yours to do or not to do, without question.

Someone told me to "Go forth and be fruitful." After some thought I went to the produce section and picked up one pound of apples, two pounds of peaches, a bag of cherries, and a bunch of bananas, my mind is at ease, fruitful at last.

You can throw out a bad apple, if it's true that one bad apple spoils the barrel. You can't have a barrelful of fun if it's filled with bad apples, it's even too late for applesauce, keep an eye on the apples or they'll be rotten to the core.

I went to a Dairy Queen for an ice cream sundae and the employee inside was using the multiple head blending machine to mix up a couple of milk shakes. She said, "Hello, this will only take a minute, I'll be with you in two shakes."

The cook said, "I'll be with you in short order, perhaps I can join you in an extra large cup of coffee unless you prefer tea for two. I confess that I have a few things on the back burner coming to a slow boil. I have been working my buns off trying not to act like a hotdog, but I'm still on a roll. I think that I know what side my bread is buttered on and I'm not trying to butter you up, if I did I'd be toast. All of this is just food for thought. I have an aversion to food clichés that are overdone.

His name was Roquefort and he came from France where he was a big cheese, one thing that could be said for Roquefort he had excellent taste.

I'm not anti-pasta, but I am pro-volone.

My doctor told me to cut down on sodium, but I took his advice with a pinch of salt.

I ate supper with a chess champion. We had a checkered tablecloth and it took him twenty minutes to pass me the salt.

He abandoned his diet; he is now considered a deserter.

A gentleman is a person who knows that a tomato is a fruit, but doesn't make a production number out of it, and never puts a tomato in his fruit salad just to prove a point, after all he is a gentleman.

The veterinarian recommended a stable diet – oats and straw.

I ate at the same restaurant for the last six months, one day I got my own coat back.

I found out that 80 percent of people die of natural causes, so I cut back on eating natural food.

Her name was Patty and whenever she went past McDonalds she had an overwhelming desire for French Fries.

The food at the Chinese Restaurant must have been good, all of the Chinese truck drivers ate there.

I found a new diet, I just eat what I can't afford.

She wanted to kiss me before she ate but she was afraid to spoil her appetite.

Recipe for gypsy chicken soup. First, steal one chicken.

"Fish and visitors smell in three days." *(Benjamin Franklin)*

If you eat enough watermelon you will eventually succeed.

My watermelon joke is pitiful.

Obesity in children is a real problem today, they just installed industrial strength see-saws in the local playground. During a weight mismatch the skinny kid was catapulted 30 feet away.

I'm getting older, I went to the Havre de Grace Seafood Festival, unfortunately I quickly pulled a mussel.

McDonalds has a new sandwich made entirely from chicken lips. It's called a Mick Jagger.

FRANKENSTEIN

Frankenstein had bad luck, he married someone who turned out to be a witch and now there's trouble brewing.

Frankenstein and his wife went to a carnival and made 300 dollars starring in a one night side show.

Igor helped put Frankenstein together, but he was under qualified his work was only sew sew.

Frankenstein went to a doctor's office he complained that he felt run down, the doctor treated him with electric shocks, but he still felt tired. Evidently the doctor failed to charge him enough.

Would kids be interested in eating beans from a can labeled 'Alien Beans' that tasted down to earth?

I was watching TV and they asked a young boy what he wanted to be when he grew up, without hesitation he said, "I want to be either a brain surgeon or a garbage man."

"Frankenstein I don't mean to pry but what is that bolt on the side of your neck?" Reply: "You know it's always something if it's not one thing it's another. I used to have screws but one day my wife said, "Frank, she called me Frank for short, she always wanted me to be Frank you don't seem to have head screwed on right." That was the day I switched to the bolt."

FRIENDS

Visits always bring pleasure, if not the arrival, the departure. *(Portuguese Proverb)*

You have to hand it to him, that's the only way that he'll pick up a check.

My friend said that now that he enjoys trouble, he's happy nearly every day.

I wanted to see things your way, but I didn't have glasses with your prescription.

I said that I could see the handwriting on the wall and I began to worry. But then my friend told me that it was just graffiti.

His personality left a lot to be desired and he was not very likable. He decided to move to Hawaii, but it was three months before anyone said "Aloha".

An anarchist makes a poor house guest, even his manners are revolting.

Humpty Dumpty was a good egg but had a bad habit of getting upset too easily.

My neighbor was rude, lazy, stupid and conceited, but I still treated him as an equal.

My friend said he never wanted to be a conductor. I said, "You would never want to lead a band?" He replied, "It's not that, I changed my mind when I got an electric shock at the wall outlet."

My friend says that he was listening and that he was all ears. I said that I didn't remember calling you an elephant and you certainly don't look like one.

He was constantly finding a fault or faults in people which clearly indicated a career path in seismology.

Prayer at Weight Watchers Dinner: May all your friends be fatter than you are.

Whenever he lit a match he used to say "Ready, aim . . ."

I belong to a gun club, but I quit when I found someone rifling through my wallet.

My friends were called Socrates and Plato and now my views are more philosophical than they used to be.

Out west he was considered a tenderfoot, it wasn't that he lacked experience but he bought boots that were one size too small.

When he moved into the neighborhood the neighborhood moved out.

He was a good old boy but he was not old, he was originally from the old country. He was old fashioned, an old hand, a goodie but not an oldie, from the old school, who wore old style old clothes and owned an old English sheepdog and always had a good old time because his watch was given to him by his father.

Yesterday were you the same as you are today and tomorrow will you be the same as you are today or worse than the next day and how about the distant future will it be better than today or worse than yesterday. Please give me a straight answer, yes or no?

You were once beyond, removed, distant and far away but as I got to know you, you were nearby, near, next, adjacent and close but later we drifted apart and no matter where I looked for you near or far, high or low you were nowhere to be found around, that squares it.

Bob was eating a meal with his wife and had a mouthful of spaghetti when friends passed the table unexpectedly. With his mouth full he couldn't say anything, impatiently one of his friends said, "Why don't you say "Hello or something, why don't you spit it out?" That's exactly what Bob did.

Bruce was asked what his sign was, Bruce replied, "I was born under a pizza sign, five blocks from the hospital.

My friends said they were going to "Trip the light fantastic'. Fantastic means extraordinarily good, but exactly when did the light fantastic come to light, it seems archaic so it must have been light years ago. Perhaps it came from an old poem or song when some bright eyed writer alighted on an idea that came to light and saw the first light of day. The author must have been in a lighthearted mood to think that the light fantastic expression was a lights out idea, but who am I to make light of this surely all I wanted to do was to shed some light on it.

My friend said, "I stand corrected." At the time he was sitting down and I was standing. Correct me if I'm wrong but is it more correct for him to say, "I sit corrected." It seems more correct to me but then again I don't want to correct a wonderful expression that's been around forever so for now let's let it stand. Correct?

Two people of Slavic extraction were arguing, exasperated one remarked, "It seems as if we are Poles a part."

Pete was my neighbor but he wasn't neighborly as he could be. I wanted him to be a good neighbor since we had very few neighbors in our neighborhood. In our neighborhood Pete and I had the only neighboring properties, other neighbors were dispersed throughout the development. The nearby neighbors were more neighborly than Pete.

I finally put up a tall fence and proved that good fences make good neighbors, for Pete's sake.

My buddy always maintained that he was single by choice, he never mentioned that the choice was always made by the ladies that he dated.

He just left his girlfriend cold, he was an Eskimo in Alaska and it was thirty degrees below zero.

She tried to kill him with a look, but she was cross-eyed and an innocent man nearly died.

A friend is a person who dislikes the same people you do.

My girlfriend said that she wanted to take our relationship to a new level, as it turned out I moved from first to the third floor and she moved up four flights.

I invited a friend named Morris Code to a party. He replied, "I'll be there on the dot, but for now I have to dash."

GAMBLING

I'll bet you that I have quit gambling for the last time again.

I was at a carnival and a young man watched his date try to pick up a stuffed bear with a three fingered hoist mechanism. He spent four hundred dollars before he got a five dollar teddy bear, but was she happy?

The gambler went to the doctor and the sign outside of the physician's office was: Office Hours 9 to 5. The gambler didn't like the odds and left.

He told me that he would hate himself in the morning. I told him to sleep late.

He was a hard luck horseplayer who was on the merry-go-round of life but unfortunately he got a horse that limped.

I used to sell decks of playing cards to all of the big casinos in Las Vegas, but the sales pressure was much more than I could deal with.

Whenever I finally decided to roll up my sleeves I was wearing a short sleeved shirt. I lost my long sleeved shirt at the race track.

I saw still photographs where you could see that actually a horse that's running will have all four feet off the ground, that must have been the horse I backed because it looked as if his feet spent so little time on the ground.

He was frequently out and about until he went to the racetrack where he was out about 50 dollars.

He was close to death and the priest came in to give him the last rites and absolution, but the patient wasn't quite ready, he asked the priest if he knew what the power ball numbers were since it was up to 250 million dollars.

He was a card player and his name was Ace, he was lucky because he shuffled through life and dealt from the bottom of the deck. He was married and had a full house. His wife was a queen and one son was a joker. He did well until he was caught cheating, he lost to a black jack.

He was a card player who reached the pinochle of success.

I played cards with a guy named Patrick, I didn't like playing with him because he always seemed to have a Pat hand.

He played roulette and he placed several chips on different numbers his friend told him to cover his bets so he threw a towel over them.

I wanted some plants so I planted some seeds in dirt and watered them, when they sprouted they looked like sprouts and not plants the more they sprouted the more they looked like plants. After all of this work I was tired and hungry so I ate a bagful of Planters Peanuts, made sense.

That track announcer said that the horse won going away when I took another look it was still on the track.

I was somewhat embarrassed when a visitor said that I lived in a 'one horse town'. I told him that we didn't have a horse. We used to have a race track with lots of horses but that was years ago. Now we don't even have a pony but even with many dogs we can't put on a dog and pony show. We've made progress, instead of gambling at the racetrack we can now bet on the lottery, power ball and scratch offs, at a lot of small businesses all over town, we're diversified. From a practical point of view as a gamble the odds were much better at the race track and at least you got a run for your money.

I was in Las Vegas during a terrible lightning storm. I felt safe beneath a slot machine because I was told that it hadn't been hit in ten years.

In Las Vegas I lost my watch, my car and three thousand dollars, but I considered myself fortunate, I didn't lose my lucky piece.

Cities are different, New York City wants to reduce the pigeon population, while Las Vegas wants all the pigeons they can get.

"Have you ever gambled?" Answer: "I was married three times, wasn't I?"

I was in Las Vegas, I took a nine to five job, I liked the odds.

A log-stupid bumpkin wanted to have some fun with his friend, he said, "If you guess how many lottery tickets I have in my pocket, I'll give you both of them?"

Lady Godiva didn't win any races, but every horseracing fan said that she showed on a least one occasion.

"It is better to be lucky than good." *(Old Gambler's Saying)*

Gambling is a great way to get nothing for something.

My horse came from a long line of thoroughbreds, in most of his races he was at the end of a long line.

The horse I bet on was an excellent runner but it could never go as fast as the money I bet on it.

A Martian landed in Las Vegas and walked into a casino. His first words were, "Take me to the cleaners."

In the Las Vegas Casinos there are no clocks. I had my doubts about that, but I changed my mind because I lost all of my cash in no time.

GARDENING

I worked for a landscaper. I specialized in installing and arranging shrubbery but I had to quit, the work was too hard I used to go home feeling bushed.

Just because I work in my garden doesn't mean I'm involved in a plot.

My neighbor asked me after work, "Did you soil yourself?" I replied, "I sell potting soil and garden humus and soiling myself is an occupational hazard."

I used to sell potting soil and humus for the garden, all of my deals were dirt cheap.

Is it possible to kill a dandelion? If you dig them out, they are back next year if you spray them, they are gone but eventually come back. They grow very early in spring and very late in the fall and if you control them the neighbor's seeds fly into your yard, "Lion's tooth, they are as tough as a lion honestly, no lyin'."

A gardener used fertilizer and peat moss on his celery, but I like mine with cream cheese and olives.

GHOSTS

Can you communicate with a ghost? You can as long as he speaks clearly in English. You have to use hand signals with foreign ghosts.

Momma and poppa ghost wanted their children to follow in their footsteps but that was a tall order because they didn't have any footsteps.

This condition was a blessing in disguise because they never got off on the wrong foot.

I took a picture of a ghost, he must have been insincere because I could see right through him.

A young spirit wanted to play football but couldn't get into the lineup. The coach told him that he didn't have a ghost of a chance.

Two ghosts fell in love and got married but their mother-in-laws always haunted them. Again, and their children were nothing to look at.

Will we ever colonize Mars? Reply: "That's mission impossible there is no intelligent life there. But then again how is that any different than Earth except for Albert Einstein?"

He was a sentimental ghost he always like to visit his old haunts.

He was a homeless ghost he couldn't hold a job and had no visible means of support.

A ghost was unemployed for 26 weeks, he wasn't a failure, and he just couldn't scare up a job.

A ghost went into a tavern, he was a big spender. He said "I'm buying a round of boos for everyone."

I think that I'm in love with the Statue of Liberty the last time that I saw her she said that she was still carrying the torch for me.

I fell in love with a beautiful ghost but one night she just disappeared, to this day her memory still haunts me.

He was a ghost with a grudge he was mean spirited.

As a young ghost he was abducted, more precisely he was spirited away.

GOLF

I was watching a funeral procession when the lead driver in the hearse slowed down as he approached a short section of road that passed through a golf course, at that moment an out of breath golfer knocked on the hearse window and said, "Do you mind if we play through? I just hit it stiff and I'm on a roll and I don't want to lose my momentum, I'd be eternally grateful."

While I was golfing I was hit in the head with a golf ball. After the stars cleared a man who couldn't talk approached me with four fingers in the air.

A golfer had four of his children as caddies because his wife wanted him to spend more time with the children.

His golf game knew no bounds, he was always in the adjacent fairway.

He loved golf he said "That it suits me to a tee."

When I watched golf they said that, "You play for show and you putt for dough." I had a hard time getting to the green I didn't mind putting for dough but you can't if you're still in the fairway or the one next to it, no joke, to a serious golfer.

He played golf, sometimes he was on and sometimes he was off. He had an on again off again game he was like that with practically everything.

As a golfer Tom was above par but he longed to be below par, that was his goal. First he wanted to get down to par because being at par was very good but being below par was exceptional. Tom's wife had other ideas she thought that Tom was barely up to par and almost never above par and she was dead set about him being below par. Tom kept hacking away at golfing. He was hooked on it, but he rarely got down to par and no matter how often and how long he practiced he knew that he would never be below par. He maintained that it was just a slice of life for an old duffer.

A golfer was on the scaffold to be hanged and his last request was, "Could I get in a few practice swings?"

The less you hit the ball in golf, the better you are.

I always replace my divots, but since they are so large I feel worn out after the ninth hole

My future wife and I hit it straight off on the first hole.

Everyone, including my wife, thinks that when I play golf I'm just out enjoying myself and having fun. If they knew the aggravation, tension, degree of disappointment, and frustration that I experience, perhaps they should come along and have some "fun" too.

A beautiful lady asked me if I had played around lately. I told her that I hadn't touched a golf club in five years.

Pencils at a golf course have no erasers. I got an eraser and reduced my golf score by ten strokes.

GOSSIP

People will listen more attentively and believe you quicker when you whisper a rumor.

In many beauty parlors the nature of the gossip alone will curl your hair.

An apple and gossip are similar, they are both better when they are juicy.

GOVERNMENT

Senator, I have trouble answering your question because I can't recollect the exact detail of my relationship with the contractor that

I recommended and then got the lucrative contract, but I do recollect that I saved 15 percent on my GEICO car insurance.

Ask not what I can do for my Country, but what my Country can do for me, is that correct? Or ask how much my Country can do for me and not what I can do for my Country, or how can I live in the country and not what I do to move to the country? I'm so confused.

I make a motion to table a motion to cut down noise and commotion, and don't get the notion and begin a promotion to stop all emotion or slow down all motion on the motion.

A small country wasn't worried about a brain drain, no one was smart enough to be missed.

She has an income tax figure, the IRS is after her for not filling out her form.

The government motto in Washington is to eliminate waste no matter what it costs.

Alexander H. Stevens, a southern senator, was the smallest senator at 80 pounds and less than five feet tall. A large western senator said that he could swallow him and never know that he ate anything. Stevens replied, "In that case you'll have more brains in your stomach than you have in your head."

Graffiti - Mafia: Organized Crime. Government: Disorganized Crime.

HAPPINESS

Santa Claus made all of his deliveries at Christmas, but when he was done he was left holding the bag.

My flashlight batteries were low so I took a dim view of my surroundings.

There was laughter in the air or was there an air of laughter?

Jim always wanted plenty, enough was not good enough it was short of plenty. Jim wasn't satisfied with adequate he wanted plenty, good and plenty. Abundant was good but abundant wasn't plentiful enough. Luckily Jim lived in a time of plenty and plenteousness so he got his fill of plenty, such a large amount of plenty that he was plenty full.

Some cause happiness wherever they go, some cause happiness whenever they go.

HEALTH

How could you be so stupid and live to be so old? Reply: "I tried to take good care of my health all along."

He was so heavy that when he stepped on the bathroom scale an alarm went off and a sign popped up saying 'No Wide Loads and One Person at a Time'.

He bought a small bottle of charisma pills but he swallowed ten pills with no result. In hindsight he thought that he should have purchased the pills in a quart sized bottle.

I didn't have a case of the jitters but I had at least a cigar box full.

The EPA has issued four hundred pounds of regulations eliminating carbon dioxide from the atmosphere, soon there will be no trees, no cars with combustion engines, and no people, mission accomplished.

He wanted to put iron into his backbone but he was out of his element.

I told the nurse that I didn't know what to do with an enigma she was hard of hearing and gave me an enema.

I read my prescription bottle and it said shake before suing so I took up dancing and I did the twist before swallowing the liquid.

My friend walked down the street chewing gum, he wanted to prove that he could do it.

He was undecided if he was fearful of the fearful storm and he feared that his fearful headache would leave him with a fearful expression so he scared up a brave smile with happy results.

He wasn't just rich he was filthy rich, he just didn't like taking a bath.

I had aches and pains and I was sorely tempted to stop exercising.

He was overweight, he preferred to be called well rounded.

I had a cold and had a hard time breathing but when I got in a traffic jam I really felt congested.

He was a consumer, he had consumer credit and bought consumer goods he was a part of the consumer society with all of his consuming, actually he was a consummate consumer who died of consumption or coughin' too often.

He was a life guard at a pool he liked diving into his work.

He was the picture of health but all of his pictures were unflattering.

The total amount of my hospital bill was so outrageous, I sent them a letter saying, "I was there for only five days and your bill was so large do I own the hospital or am I leasing it for a year?

I used to be in bad condition but I conditioned myself to be in top condition, I was then in unconditionally good shape and evaluated my present conditioning condition and was satisfied with my conditioning unconditionally.

Everyone's selling fish oil, omega-3 fatty acids, it's supposed to be good for heart health and joint health. I read the label on the bottle and it said, "Supportive but not conclusive consuming EPA and DHA omega-3 fatty acids may reduce risk of coronary heart disease." As a youth I took cod liver oil but the fish oil now is anchovy, mackerel and sardine, the druggist at Wal-Mart said that they were quite similar. I bought a bottle and after a week I noticed an immediate improvement, I could swim farther and longer, dive deeper and see underwater without goggles, I even felt more comfortable in a school setting. Cod liver oil or omega-3 fish oil I guess people just like getting oiled.

I went to the drug store today to refill my high blood pressure medicine, the pharmacist said, "We can refill it but you will be 20 pills short. Come back later, by then the delivery truck will be here." I said, "Listen if you guys don't get your act together I'm going to stop being sick."

I guess I'm getting old, my wife and I celebrated the New Year at home. I had rye, and my wife had whole wheat.

He looked pretty frightening, a pharmacist hired him to stand in front of the building to make people feel sick before they went in.

My neighbor drank a quart of prune juice every day and his personality changed completely, now he's a regular guy.

Health insurance is similar to wearing one of those hospital gowns, you only think you are covered.

If you want to look thin quickly, pal around with heavier people.

I intend to live forever, so far, so good.

Sickness: Ill, pill, bill, will.

I'm nearsighted and I needed my glasses to locate my reading glasses.

He used so much saccharin and Sweet & Low that he developed artificial diabetes.

I told my buddy that I had just visited my doctor. He asked, "Which doctor?" I said, "No, he's really a board certified physician."

A new antibiotic is so powerful that you can't take it unless you are in perfect health.

Most of my doctor's patients backed into his office. My doctor did not let anyone get away without a shot of antibiotics for every ailment.

Sign in health food shop window: 'Closed Due to Illness.'

"Never miss an opportunity to relieve yourself; never miss a chance to sit down and rest your feet." *(King George V)*

"First rule of vacations: Take half as many clothes as you planned, and twice as much money." *(Anonymous)*

Try our herbal remedies – you can't get better.

"If a man stops to ponder over his physical or moral condition, he generally discovers that he is ill." *(Johann vonGoethe)*

HOTELS

They say that when he was young that he led a sheltered existence but when he got older he spent a lot of time in a shelter.

A hotel hired a skeleton on Halloween night to open some hotel room doors, he had a skeleton key.

He worked at a hotel and every morning he went around knocking at the guest doors, he became so good at it he was a rousing success.

My apartment was so small that I felt that I was living in close quarters.

At the hotel he signed his name anonymous but that caused a stir, while he wanted to remain anonymous people became very curious about his true identity. Things got desperate so he took desperate measures he changed anonymous to Mr. Smith and no one cared. There were twenty Mr. Smiths in the same hotel as well as ten Mr. Jones.

It was a very fancy hotel, you had to take a shower wearing a tie.

In a manor of speaking, a man's home is his castle.

HUNTING

The game warden called the hunter a poacher he said that he caught the hunter, red handed, poaching eggs over his campfire but in this case instead of a fine, they shared breakfast together. Justice was served.

An explorer was paddling in a dugout canoe up the far upper reaches of the Amazon River when from a distance he heard the incessant beat of native drums and he commented to his native guide, "Bruce I don't like the sound of those drums." Bruce replied, "Not to worry that's Horace the youngest son of the Indian chief and he always wanted to play the drums. Well today his father Maurice let him but Horace has had only three lessons so he should improve, based on the sounds he's bound to sooner or later."

A hunter shot an elk. He knew it was an elk, he recognized the membership card in the man's wallet.

"The Constitution preserves the advantage of being armed which Americans possess over the people of almost every other nation where the governments are afraid to trust the people with arms." *(James Madison)*

HUSBANDS

"You say that you have a late husband, when did he die?" Response: "Oh, he didn't die he's just always late."

The beautician's husband gave her a permanent wave and she hasn't seen him since.

My husband gets plenty of exercise. Last week he was out four nights running.

"You say that your husband is departed, when did he die?" Response: "Oh, he's not dead, one night he went out for a pack of cigarettes and he just departed."

Sheiks have their own problems. By the time they stop kissing their last wife good night, they've got to kiss the first one good morning.

A husband said to his wife, "How can you blame me for our martial problems, I'm never home?"

If a married man expresses an opinion while he's all alone in the middle of a forest, is he still wrong?

Behind every successful man is a surprised woman, behind her is his wife, and behind his wife is a surprised mother-in-law.

Her late husband appeared relieved at the funeral he had a faint smile on his face.

KNOCK, KNOCK

Knock, knock.
   Who's there?
Little old lady.
   Little old lady who?
I didn't know that you could yodel.

Knock, knock.
   Who's there?
Cows go.
   Cows go, who?
No, cows go moo.

LAWYERS

Court Talk: "Were you alone or by yourself?"

"Are you the defendant's mother?" Reply: "I am." Question: "How long have you known him?"

Lawyers: "How many times were you shot?" Reply: "I can't remember being shot before."

Since her husband was a mouse and a rat she hired an exterminator rather than a divorce lawyer.

A person in debt went to a bankruptcy lawyer but couldn't figure out a way to pay the lawyer.

The judge said to the lawyer, "I want an explanation and I want the truth. The lawyer replied, "Well which is it Your Honor?"

Your Honor, I do not want to distort the truth until I get more evidence.

My friend told me that he wanted to call his lawyer but he could not decide on what to call him.

I felt honored when the judge thanked me.

Thomas Jefferson worried that the courts would overstep their authority and instead of interpreting the law they would begin making laws as an oligarchy, the rule of the few over the many.

He was a lawyer with a questionable interrogatory.

My attorney asked me if I had an air tight alibi for the night of the crime. I told him at that time I was submerged in a submarine off the coast of Japan. Which was a watertight alibi, close enough.

Before he was a lawyer he worked as a part time carpenter to pay for college. His work experience came in handy since he was good at fabricating evidence.

He was not above the law but he was beneath contempt.

Judge: "Has the jury reached a verdict?" Reply: "Yes we have your honor we find the defendant too stupid to convict." Judge: "The defendant is free to go simply."

Judge: "Bailiff is the jury still out?" Reply: "Yes, Your Honor, they are either sleeping or out shopping."

Judge: "Did the jury reach a just verdict?" Reply: "Your Honor we just finished arguing, I mean deliberating, just before lunch but we couldn't decide on an empty stomach, we were just about ready to give up when just after lunch one juror changed his mind just in time to prevent an injustice."

He dated a lawyer, he told her that he was courting her so on their next date she brought along a can of tennis balls and a tennis racket.

I went to a cookout where I saw a prominent judge sitting at a picnic table, I said, "Your Honor may I approach the bench?"

May I conclude that we have concluded the discussion? Based on the conclusions we reached you are included in the all-inclusive agreements, assuming that you agree with the agreements? If you disagree you can choose to be excluded and in that case just forget about it as if nothing happened, and that concludes it, conclusively.

He wanted to be a member of a jury, he didn't like his job he liked sitting around all day listening to tall tales. None of the prosecution or defense lawyers wanted him because he seemed far too anxious, and kept repeating, "Me, me, me."

An Indian became a top lawyer he was called the suing Sioux.

A lawyer was paid with seven bottles of whiskey, but he complained that he could not make a case out of it.

"Have you ever been a witness in a suit like this before," asked the lawyer. The witness replied, "No, the last time I wore a pink outfit."

Someone walked into a bar and shouted, "All lawyers are jackasses." A customer jumped up and said, "I resent that scurrilous remark." The bartender said, "Are you a lawyer?" Reply: "No, I'm a jackass."

An honest lawyer died and they were taking up a collection to bury him. A politician came by and asked, "What was the average contribution." It turned out to be $10. He donated $100, and said, "Bury ten of those scoundrels."

The lawyer petitioned for a new trial based on newly discovered evidence. He said, "I was unaware that my client had uncovered an additional source of funds; that is, one thousand dollars, to be precise."

"It will be of little avail to the people that the laws are made by men of their own choice if the laws are so voluminous that they cannot be read, or so incoherent that they cannot be understood." *(James Madison)*

"The difference between truth and fiction is that fiction has to make sense." *(Mark Twain)*

The lawyer was lying at death's door, that close to death and still lying.

Saint Peter wanted to sue the devil, but that was difficult because he couldn't locate a lawyer in heaven.

"I cannot exactly tell you sir, who he is, and I would be loath to speak ill of any person who I do not know deserves it, but I am afraid he is an attorney." *(Samuel Johnson)*

LOSERS

Where is beyond? How far do I have to go to go far beyond my destination? I lived beyond my means, at times was I beyond hope and paid a psychic to speak to someone from beyond. I've spent a lot of time contemplating the beyond, but I'm afraid that all of these matters are beyond my comprehension.

He obligingly obliged to be obligated in an obligatory manner, he was formerly a delegator now he's an obligator.

Since I hadn't been anywhere it was hard to make a comeback.

He went to the orgy and complained about the cheese dip.

The door to your new office has the word 'Men' painted on it.

You have an amorous meeting with your wife and your self-winding watch stops.

I bought a book about cowards, but the book promptly fell apart. Cowards aren't the only ones with weak spines.

LOVE

Since she began wearing a girdle I suspected that there was more to her than meets the eye.

A girl asked her boyfriend if he really loved her she asked, "Would you die for me?" Pressed he replied, "I have what you call an undying love for you."

Two fuller brushes fell in love, but they had a falling out and the male got brushed aside.

In Australia two shoes fell deeply in love they were soul mates.

It's time to get a new boyfriend when you are tired of seeing him. If you are in love you are never tired of seeing your husband and if you are single and in love you want to see more of your boyfriend.

My mother said, "I'm doing this because I love you." I said, "Mom can you spread it around a little because there's only so much love I can tolerate."

He knew that this time it was real love, they ate at Burger King and he shared his tasty French fries with her and he was more crazy about her than French fries.

I love every inch of you, if you were taller I suppose I could love you even more.

He loved a meteorologist for two weeks but on one weekend it started to wane.

She was an acquaintance until we got better acquainted, now she's an old flame whose flame began to flicker.

He was a man among men he was also a man among women which was convenient.

She liked him because he had a familiar face but she dropped him like a hot potato when he tried to get too familiar.

He told his date that he had feelings for her but she objected because she thought that he was doing a little too much feeling.

He was properly dressed from head to toe when he met a girl whom he argued with and they went at it head to head and toe to toe but later he asked her and they danced cheek to cheek and now they see eye to eye.

He wanted to trifle with her affections but he received only trifling results, it was a trivial pursuit.

He loved her but she resisted his advances, but it became cloudy and overcast and his ardor began to wane.

When I met her she bought sunshine into my life when one day when she visited me and she raised the window shade.

She liked pigeons and he liked pigeons they had a lot in common when they dated they cooed at each other. They were kooky enough to get married or was it a coup?

He met a lovely woman at Weight Watchers, he soon fell in love and told her, "I want to see less of you in the future."

They accused him of being craven but what he craved most was affection.

She used to work in a cotton field and now I cottoned to her.

He said that she was the object of his affection but she objected. She didn't like being treated as an object and found his actions objectionable, but things improved after he brought her a giant diamond where money was no object.

I found cupid's bow you know how careless cupid can get.

Grace received perfume as a gift, she loved perfume and when she put it on she just had an air about her, she said, "It was Heaven Scent."

I used to do a lot of swimming when I rubbed my girlfriend's back I told her that I was doing the backstroke.

I forgot that I was suffering from amnesia but I used it to my advantage as a pickup line I would say to a beautiful lady, "Don't I know you? You look familiar, are you?"

He was courting a young lady and he treated her like a queen but she ran up king sized bills and he lacked the jack to pay for them but he and an ace up his sleeve until he got caught double dealing and the queen left the trailer court with a broken heart.

He said that she was becoming, but he did not tell her exactly what she was becoming.

Marvin said that Marsha was beautiful beyond compare. Is that possible, I questioned that? Compared to what? No doubt Marsha was beautiful and even intelligent but if you are hungry how does that compare to a pizza, a hamburger and fries or a hot dog at the ball park, maybe not. Perhaps if Marvin shared these things with Marsha she would even look more beautiful by comparison.

Tim's family was well connected but he had no connections and had difficulty connecting with anyone especially people of the opposite sex, as it was he was disconnected. Desperate he contacted a matchmaker with connections who connected him with strange as it may seem a girl from Connecticut. He's been happily married for six months while his married friends are becoming disconnected.

She fell in love with a lumberjack he split and lumbered off and now she's pining away.

He was a tennis player on the rebound, love meant nothing to him. He had a lot of tennis partners but none that he could court seriously. He was hoping that some tennis skirt might catch his eye. They could get married and have a ball together forever.

My buddy said that he was looking for some old fashioned loving, so I introduced him to my grandmother.

I always wanted someone to love and to hold, but after I met you I changed my mind.

Her idea of a romantic setting was a ring with a diamond in it.

LUCK

I heard that he ran out of luck. Why couldn't he just walk away from it, running just speeded up the process.

Houdini was the greatest escape artist who ever lived but he never met my Uncle Sly, who escaped the draft, never picked up a check, dodged traffic and escaped marriage – that's talent.

A black cat crossed my path but I wasn't worried, I don't get out on a path too often I usually follow the straight and narrow.

What a day, my brakes failed, my business failed, my headlights failed, my plans failed, my courage failed me and I failed my math test. On the bright side I realized that I was a success at failure.

Tom wanted to comprehend so he took a comprehensive test to test his comprehension but much of the test was beyond his comprehension, it was incomprehensible. Since he determined that he wasn't a genius he decided to rely on luck, but like everyone else he works 9 to 5 waiting for his ship to come in, as luck would have it he lived in North Dakota.

She bought a magnetic proof, shock proof, and water proof watch, but now it's lost.

My friend told me that he got really lucky last week. He said that he found his car in the Wal-Mart parking lot.

There was a tribe that couldn't read or count, if a man in the tribe was handed a four leaf clover would it bring him good luck?

He was hoping for a lucky stroke, sad to say it was his rich uncle's.

I'll say I'm lucky, I won the million dollar lottery on the day after my divorce became final, Bingo!

Lucky? He found a sea shell and when he put it to his ear he heard a busy signal.

MAGIC

The crowd was disappointed when the low budget magician pulled a gerbil out of his hat. The rabbit left this cryptic message, "Hare today, gone today."

This magician claimed to be the greatest magician that ever lived. I put him to the test, I said can you make my debts disappear or the ring around the bath tub?"

The low budget magician couldn't afford to make an elephant or building disappear, what was worse just before a show someone stole his magic tuxedo coat, his top hat and rabbit and he had to improvise. He pulled a gerbil from a borrowed derby, his baton turned into plastic flowers that needed watering, he asked a chicken to peck a card, and for a finale he went into the audience and made 50 dollars disappear.

Something happened that I didn't expect. I never suspected the unexpected and was surprised when it happened. Had I anticipated the unexpected I would have been better prepared to achieve my original expectation.

MANAGEMENT

In Japan years ago management training personnel had a lot of buttons on their shirts and as you gained experience and performed well, a button was removed when the trainee lost all of his buttons, he was ready to join management.

He called in his crack management team to brainstorm a problem after four hours all they got was a headache.

The head of the company was so dull that after a two hour uninspiring meeting we called him the chairman of the bored.

He was in charge of a large lumber company he was referred to as chairman of the board.

I was in charge of the people in the basement, I was a low level manager.

When someone ordered me to do something I wanted to do the opposite I used that to my advantage as a supervisor, when I ran into someone like myself I told him to do the opposite and it ended up that he did what I wanted him to do and he never guessed it.

He liked to make wise business decisions so he opened a spaghetti restaurant, he was so proud that he used his noodle.

He cooked all of his meals in a microwave he wanted to be a micro-manager.

He was the middle son of a middle income family who in his middle age became a middle manager in a weight reduction business. He led a middle class life with a middle class wife and had a son in middle school. Politically he was neither left nor right he was comfortable in the middle. This saga begins and ends where else but in the middle?

I used to have an important job. I was a plant manager, unfortunately, all of the plants died.

My boss asked me just what I could do that no one else could do. I said, "I can read my own handwriting."

My boss fired me because he said that I lacked communication skills. I was speechless, I didn't know what to say.

There is no real reason for it, it's just company policy.

My boss wanted to show me the door, but I told him that I had seen a door before.

A person in charge of a zoo is referred to as a zoopervisor.

I asked my secretary to take a letter. She picked 'K'. The next time I asked her to take a letter that I had written, she was gone for three days.

The company wanted to hire an expensive out-of-town management consultant. Then it dawned on us. "Hey, why don't we try to foul it up ourselves? Great idea."

Now that I'm the boss I'm considered thorough, when I was a non-supervisory employee, I was considered slow.

You are qualified for a position in top management, but you don't qualify for an entry level position.

I almost never found anything that I've put into a safe place.

I was lazy and filed most of my paperwork under 'miscellaneous'. This section was so thick I could never find anything.

MANNERS

I wanted to join an exclusive club but I was told that I was excluded.

In a manner of speaking he was well mannered because he was taught manners, so he never acted in a capricious manner it came naturally because he once lived in a manor.

I was a salesman and I asked a lady if I could help her. She said, "Oh no I'm just looking." Reply: "What a coincidence I married a looker."

Some gangsters have impeccable manners, they even get time off for good behavior.

The English landowner said, "Jeeves, draw my bath." The butler replied, "Yes sir, I believe I can sketch it from memory."

I'm leaving, don't bother to show me to the door. Host: "Oh, it's no bother."

Two of the two biggest lies in the world. A host who says, "Must you be going?" and "What's your hurry?"

I showed him the door, but he said he knew where it was.

"Excuse me! Do you know what time it is?" Reply: "Sure I do, thanks!"

"Mr. Jones told me to tell you that he's not in." "Fine, tell Mr. Jones that I didn't call."

You seem to have everything, except manners.

MARRIAGE

My girlfriend threw me a kiss once but since she wore glasses it missed me and hit a young man standing next to me. They will be married in two months.

They had been arguing and his wife gave him the silent treatment for a week which he gladly accepted with a long sigh of relief and contentment.

He could read his wife like a book, unfortunately that book was a horror story.

He bragged that he was the boss at home, he said that only yesterday he had words with his wife. Later I found out those words were, "Yes Dear."

His wife never stopped talking, day in and day out. One time her husband lost his voice for five days and she never suspected anything.

His wife drove him to drink so he saved a lot of money, because he didn't have to take a taxi and he saved time because he didn't have to ever walk to the nearest bar.

Since married they are sticking together through thick and through thin. She was thin and he was thick.

He always longed for connubial bliss but he became apprehensive when he read that ignorance was bliss.

You three make a great pair if there ever was one.

The bride looked stunning but the groom just looked stunned.

To his wife, "Darling I'm dying and my estate is worth $500,000. Wife: "John you're more important to me than money. By the way does that 500k include the house at the seashore and the yatch?"

The bride wore a lovely gown and train which fell to the ground when she walked down the aisle.

A father announced that any man marrying my daughter will get a nice cash gift from me. A suitor took another look at his daughter and asked, "Just how big is the gift in dollars?"

Always marry a florist because the more he goes to seed the brighter his future.

I went to a Chinese wedding and waited outside for the bride and groom to come out to get into the limousine. When the service was over the happy couple came out the door but had a hard time reaching the car, so much rice was thrown it was nearly six inches deep and the couple kept slipping and sliding.

We were married 24 hours ago but it seems as if it only happened yesterday, how time flies?

She couldn't stand her husband so she remained seated and she had even more problems standing him when he was drunk.

Dear you need only say one word to make me happy, "What is it?" "Adios."

His wife told him that she had given him the best years of her life. He replied, "I suppose there's little hope for the future then."

Tarzan, "Jane before I met you I was a swinging single."

Jane: "Tarzan you said that we would live in a high rise." Tarzan: "Sorry Jane, I misspoke I meant to say a tree house."

When I married I did not know that my wife was a medium, now she's an extra-large.

No one gave her a bridal shower so she was relieved when she was caught in the rain before she was married.

My friend told me that his wife made him what he was today. I know now exactly why he was broke.

My mother's sage advice was to save my hay, I might marry a horse someday.

It was a cowboy-cowgirl romance on the ranch. He popped the question and the marriage was technically a Western Union.

Since he decided to get married he hasn't had a single thought.

He wanted to marry his girlfriend, she looked beautiful and was intelligent but she turned him down. She said that she was even more intelligent and beautiful than she looked.

He never got any credit so he decided to marry the girl at the bank.

She dated him for seven years, she said he did not like being rushed into marriage too quickly.

She married a gemologist, he fell for her when she told him that she was a diamond in the rough.

She wasn't much to look at so she married a man who wore really thick glasses.

When he carried his bride over the threshold he fell for her and with her at the same time.

My wife said she needed a new compact so I bought her a new small car.

I argued with my wife while fishing, but then I lost debate.

My wife and I harmonized well so we always made beautiful music together.

He said that he had been married for 30 years and that they were the happiest three years of his life.

I married a girl named Carlotta, her father was a used car salesman.

He was a fireman dedicated to his work he even married an old flame.

She had emerald eyes, ruby lips, golden hair and teeth like pearls, she married a jeweler.

His wife was named Bubbles and he always bought her a bottle of bubble bath.

My wife loved dogs, she used to bark at me.

I had a good job and I made a lot of money and I wanted to bring home the bacon, but I married a lovely Jewish vegetarian and I had mixed feelings about it.

My wife said that she wanted a baguette so I bought a thin loaf of French bread to make her happy. I needed to brush up on my French, she really wanted a ring with a gem in it, who knew?

A mechanic wanted to put some spark into his marriage, for his wife's birthday he gave her a set of jumper cables.

My wife and I had been married a long time and she said that we needed to spice up our relationship so I bought her a case full of McCormick products including oregano, red pepper, thyme, dill, curry and chili pepper.

She was the second mate on the sailboat, she had no official position but she was the captain's second wife.

The grammar school teacher wanted to marry above her class so she married a college professor.

At age 30 she was asked to marry five times, twice by her father and three times by her mother.

She wanted a big wedding, she bought a wedding dress, rented a wedding hall, bought a wedding cake, hired a band for the wedding march, and got a wedding ring. One month later she wanted a divorce and has the wedding blues.

He said that he loved being outdoors, he loved the great outdoors, he wasn't always like that but his wife caught him fooling around and threw him out.

Two square dancers were married when they left the altar they sashayed down the aisle.

She had a page boy haircut, her husband insisted that his home was his castle.

Two dance instructors got married, at the church she waltzed down the aisle wearing a smile.

She was only five feet tall and she married a professional basketball player, she said that she always wanted to marry someone that she could look up to.

He wanted leave his wife a message but his pencil had no tip so it was pointless.

She married a midget and then complained that she married someone beneath her.

He received the most humiliating punishment, a tongue lashing from his wife.

Mike was a divorcé and his ex-wife was a divorcée they were both divorced but very little actually separated them.

John was happy go lucky and single but people commented that despite being in good shape that somehow John was incomplete. Hearing the rumors John decided to get married and now everyone says that he's complete but others say that he's finished.

Mary said, "I demand an explanation!" I replied, "Give me a minute I'm trying to think of something that may appeal to you, is it remotely possible that you would be interested in the truth because the truth is so bizarre. OK, if you really want to know I was in a space capsule circling the earth at the time in question. That's my story and I'm stuck with it. What do you mean you don't believe me, have I lied to you since last week?"

Mabel said to her husband, "Say, just what are your good qualities, they seem to elude me?" "Au contraire my pet, let me count the ways. I am fit as a fiddle, sharp as a tack, quick as a bunny, busy as a beaver, hungry as a wolf, bald as an eagle, faster than molasses in January, brave as a lion, contented as a cow, hungry for applause and happy as a lark, shall I continue?" Mabel, "Enough already, I can't take any more you forgot to mention modesty." Husband, "So I have, how did I miss that?" Mabel, "You have so many admirable qualities if you had any more you could be a one man zoo?"

His wife treated him like a dog and kept him on a short leash.

Mary came from a well-to-do family and they spent a lot of money to make her refined. She was just fine before she became refined, did she become refined in a refinery or was she just refinished? The fact that her father owned a refinery did not enter the picture at all. When Mary married, she married Jim who was unrefined or partially refined but Jim was just fine because he was a millionaire.

Her name was Precious she was married to a jeweler, he thought of her as a diamond in the rough but he knew that she had a few flaws.

Slim was a novice pool player who racked his brain on how to improve. He was always behind the eight ball what he needed was a cushion. Once in a while, on cue, he hit the ball off the rail and pocketed it. But his future was not in a pool hall idling away his ill spent youth, his chances for success were slim. Slim was so slim that he opened a chain of weight loss studios with himself as a role model. On cue he married an overweight widow who was a millionairess. Fat chance, she was a cutie.

We were married by a justice-of-the-peace and I haven't had any peace since then.

She thought that she would marry in the winter because her boyfriend said, "It will be a cold day before I marry you."

She's been to the altar so often, she got ordained.

If you're married two great places to hide money at home is in a sock that needs darning or under the vacuum cleaner.

I became apprehensive when my blind date showed up in a wedding gown.

She wanted to change her name to his, so now they call her Bartholomew.

After we were married, I apologized to my wife for being late for our wedding. She said, "Well you're just in time for our divorce."

Her mother arranged a match for her daughter and the mother refereed the entire match.

She was working like a horse while looking for a groom.

The bride was priceless, but her father still had to give her away.

At a redneck wedding does everyone sit on the same side of the church?

My friend had a real problem. He was out of a job, his wife had kicked him out, and his parents would not let him back to stay at their house again.

I told my wife that when I get old I don't want to be dependent on a machine or be in a vegetative state. With that remark my wife unplugged the TV set.

She was asked to marry dozens of times, but she finally told her parents to stop pestering her.

When my wife gave me that strange look I realized that I must have been enjoying myself at the office party.

Wife to neighbor: "My husband is lazy, shiftless, selfish, greedy and unreliable; but have you ever heard me say anything bad about him?"

When I bought a waterbed, my wife and I started to drift apart.

She thought of a new way to frighten a bachelor. She sneaked up behind him and threw handfuls of rice at him.

MEMORY

He could not get her out of his memory but then again he had a very questionable memory.

He had a photographic memory but he ran out of film.

"I hear and I forget, I see and I remember, I do and I understand." *(Confucius)*

I was at a weekly dance in my hometown when a young lady asked me, "Do you always come here?" I answered, "I don't remember coming here twenty years ago."

I had amnesia for as long as I can remember.

"Did you forget you owed me ten dollars?" Reply: "No, but give me time."

I hate Indian givers on second thought I take that back.

MILITARY

The Colonel had a major problem when he received a letter marked private in the general mail.

My best friend and old army buddy, Neal, lives in Lynn, Massachusetts. Lynn is an old blue collar city with a rhyme associated with its name, a rhyme familiar in New England but unknown elsewhere. No offense intended this is it: "Lynn, Lynn the city of sin, you never go out the way you went in."

I was an old soldier but the only thing that faded away was my brown hair.

In the army they told me that "One dull pencil is worth a thousand sharp minds", which is excellent advice if you have a bad memory. Even if you write it down and don't forget anything what have you lost, just throw the note away and be about your business?

When I went into the army I wanted to become a sniper but the sergeant said I'm afraid that your chances look like a long shot.

He was in the army too long whenever he ate a meal he attacked his food.

We used females to man the defenses and man the guns, they wanted to defend us to the last woman, how manly?

In the army I complained of feeling light headed and the sergeant put me on light duty so I replaced all of the burned out light bulbs in the barracks.

When I put on my army work clothes I felt fatigued.

He had an explosive personality so they kept him out of the Ordnance Corps.

He came from a tough army when if you were less than a sergeant and fouled up you received corporal punishment, what did majors receive?

He wanted to retreat but he was already too far behind his own lines that he would have had to leave the country, to retreat any further he could receive an extreme caution under cover medal.

They could not prove that the army officer was lying but there didn't seem to be a colonel of truth in what he said.

I was a Boy Scout and I had 10 matches all of the other boy scouts tried to outmatch me.

I was sent to an outpost it was a strange place someone had removed all of the posts.

He said that when he was in the army his position was overrun, he explained that it wasn't by the enemy but no one ever cut back the brush or mowed the area.

He was a big shot at the firing range.

He had an entrenching tool and he dug a trench four feet deep but the sergeant said that it wasn't deep enough so he had to retrench.

He was retired from the army but had to be vetted for his new job.

He was a point man in the army when he was in the barracks on fatigue detail he was in charge of sharpening all of the pencils and pointing out improperly made bunks.

In the hospital they put me into a semiprivate room the patient next to me was an army private first class.

He used to be a paratrooper and when he left the service he worked his way into an important position in the lucrative defense industry after 30 years he received a golden parachute at his retirement.

Tom looked like a ripe avocado but was not suited for the Marines, while he had a rough exterior he was yellow on the inside.

As a child Max slept in a bunk bed, he joined the Army and slept in a bunk bed and his brother was in the Navy and slept in a bunk bed or a hammock on a ship. When visiting friends Max bunked with them. This story may be true or it may be pure bunk.

One coup is enough you have to be crazy to have two coups.

Since early childhood an Indian brave named Geronimo wanted to be a paratrooper. He always wanted to be considered a part of the airborne troops. After rigorous training they told him that when he jumped out of a plane to shout 'Geronimo' he asked "What is this some sort of ethnic thing, why not call out oops, or help or even horse manure?" The instructors convinced him that it was tradition and shouted with a sense of pride and esprit de corps, out of a spirit of pride he shouted Geronimo as he jumped. He like hearing his own name he was used to it besides it was not easily forgotten because he loved himself, and it was something that he could remember for a long long time.

Jack joined the paratroopers, something that he always wanted to do. He was well suited for his work, so well suited that they nicknamed him 'Jumping Jack'. While he was the best he was different, whenever he jumped he didn't say 'Geronimo' he said, "Uh oh!"

Some people will wear only new clothes, others will only wear clothes once or twice. If you come from a big family the younger children get hand-me-downs so that he youngest child often ends up looking like an uncolor – coordinated little hobo. My friend Max wore hand-me-downs, the problem was all he had was older sisters and it took me a while to get used to Max in a dress but he turned out OK because as an adult he became a Marine. I know that Max was a Marine because I saw him in a dress uniform. Then I remembered everyone in the military has a dress uniform while that may be news to you it's old hat to me and I'm used to it and the order, "Dress right dress," is a military term.

Army food is tasty. I can still taste it after twenty years.

I wanted to see the world during my military service, I joined the navy but was assigned duty in the submarine service.

Fort Hood was so big that when you get a one day pass you can almost make it to the front gate to go to Kileen.

MODESTY

They told me that he was so successful that he was bigger than big, now that's really big. I've had big moments, big aspirations, big times, big thrills, big dinners, big hopes, really big successes and big disappointments but I never had any occasions where any outcome was bigger than big. Big deal!

I told them that I didn't want anything, I wanted nothing and they had no trouble complying with my request, after all what is nothing? It's nothing to talk about or practically nothing. You can't make a big thing out of nothing and twice nothing is still nothing, which may be something to think about but not for long.

He started out in obscurity and now he's mired in oblivion.

MONEY

He needed to borrow 1500 dollars towards a used car he got his trigonometry teacher to cosine.

I had an unorthodox stock broker who wanted to parlay my small gain into an initial public offering. Then he recommended a small Swiss cheese company, being a savvy investor I thought that his latest proposal had holes in it.

Nitric acid decomposes a scrape of counterfeit gold, while a real gold scrape remains intact.

"Everything has its limit – iron ore cannot be educated into gold." (Mark Twain)

In case you wanted to know back in the 1700's in England: four farthings were worth one pence, 12 pence were worth one shilling, and 20 shillings were worth one pound. Plus, the guinea – a slightly larger coin than the pound was worth one pound and one shilling.

"He who is not contented with what he has, would not be contented with what he would like to have." *(Socrates)*

A banker was learning to swim after five minutes his instructor said, "Can you float alone?" The banker replied, "I don't make it a habit to lend money to strangers."

He was very successful during his lifetime unfortunately when he died he was just two dollars short of being a millionaire.

At his company he was the employee of the week, worker of the month, and employee of the year, but if you left him some money you would have to watch him every minute.

Someone was using the change machine to count change at the supermarket. I heard that they charged six percent to count the money. I get only one percent all year on a better money market account. Why not hire unemployed people to count the change part time, that way we can get hope and real change.

People tell me that with cell phones and computers that watches are obsolete now. I like a watch, out of habit I like to know how late I am running or walking. My wife gave me a watch for Christmas and I was grateful and I told her that there was no time like the present.

The crook put his stolen bills in the refrigerator ice tray and covered them with water, he thought that no one would look there and he could get his hands on cold hard cash quickly.

A panhandler asked me for a Kennedy half dollar, I asked him if he preferred to be called a bum or a panhandler. He replied, "I'm neither, I'm a coin collector down on my luck."

What's the latest dope on Wall Street, or am I looking at him?

My friend asked me if money talked. I replied, "I'm not sure but the last time I saw my money I thought I heard it say, adios."

Trying to look rich kept him poor.

I was told to save some money for a rainy day but we've had so many rainy days lately which makes it difficult to pick the proper day to spend it all.

Is this coin valuable? If I hold the coin long enough will it be worth more? Answer: It doesn't look valuable but if you plan to hold it long enough you may want to think about putting it down from time to time.

Some people want to eliminate pennies from change this idea is senseless.

I got a new 100 dollar bill at the bank it had a black strip down the middle, a picture of a feather, an inkwell and a watermark with Benjamin Franklin's likeness when you hold it up to the light, it would cost a million dollars to counterfeit it.

I received my company shares in the mail and I kept them safe in my house but the company went bankrupt so I ended up as a stock holder and I put the stock into a picture frame and its now on my wall.

He was a man of substance until they caught him with an unknown substance.

He heard about the expression waste not want not, but he was wasteful by nature and was frequently wasted. Even his stomach was a vast wasteland, at work he was in charge of waste management.

He suffered from want, he wanted everything and he just couldn't get it.

He wanted to get rich so he developed a strategic strategy that was so good that he called it a gem of a strata-gem.

He wanted to make his money to stretch but all of the paper money was made of paper and linen and he couldn't stretch a buck so he solved the problem, he wrote rubber checks, and they bounced.

I got a bill in the mail it said this is the last warning again and again and again. I said, "Thank you, thank you, thank you."

I had a roll of money until I got rolled. Now someone else is rolling in my dough.

He had a lot of loose change so he lined his pocket with pocket change but he soon lost it all when he couldn't pocket any balls in the pool hall.

It was a sunny day and I wore dark glasses, I sat down on a bench at a busy section of Central Park and I drank hot coffee from my thermos, out of a tin cup. By the time I finished I made eight dollars.

Everyone wants to be number one but there is only one number one. You can get rich being number two or even number three or four. You can't count on success, sometimes no matter how hard you work it eludes you, but you're ok as long as long the mafia doesn't have your number.

He told me that he was considered nouveau riche I asked him if had hit the lottery or what? He said that he found a five dollar bill in an old book. I told him that reading pays.

I noticed that I received a notice in the mail a notice that had previously remained unnoticed because it escaped my notice. I acknowledged the notification and I notified them that I was ignoring it.

If you have an abundance how many items does it take to qualify as an over-abundance.

I dropped some change on the sidewalk when I visited New York City everyone helped me, when it was all over I think I made an extra 75 cents after I counted it all.

I asked a prospector what his prospects were, he was prospective? He said, "The prospects are good for me to prosper and become prosperous. If I become prosperous it bodes well for the prosperity of my posterity, but I've got to get off of my posterior to improve my prospects, and if I mind my own business the future could be golden, and the more gold the better my prospects prospectively speaking."

As a baby Jack played in a playpen. As a young lad Jack loved to play, he was playful actually full of play and he played until he was played out. Jack had a playhouse and spent lots of playtime at the playground with his playmates. Jack hoped that if he played his cards right and he had a level playing field he could become a success, and a play by play account of how that happened would take too long, but Jack is rich and Jack has plenty of jack.

We were really poor, when I was young our house was broken into by burglars and they left several new items.

It was the type of gift that after you removed it from the box you keep checking the gift box for the present.

A fool and his money are invited to, and throw the best parties.

Things are rough today. Money doesn't buy as much as it did when I didn't have any.

Inflation is really bad today. They caught a guy giving away one dollar bills and he was arrested for littering.

My extensive frozen assets consisted of two ten inch pizzas, three chicken pot pies, and two TV dinners.

I left my wife at the bank and kissed my money goodbye.

They were so rich they had an electrician come in every morning to plug in the toaster and juice machine.

When you make a 911 call in Beverly Hills you have to give three personal references before helps arrives.

MUSIC

Press 1 for English, press 2 for Spanish, press 3 for answers to common questions, press 1, 2, 3 and 4 simultaneously to hear the 'Flight of the Bumble Bee'.

I used to play trumpet in a band but I got into an argument with the band leader and I left on a sour note.

He was good at dancing and they called him Twinkle Toes but I never saw him Twinkle and if he was on his toes, was he a ballet dancer?

Evidently the public has a high regard for musical incompetence.

Bagpipes were invented in Iran and brought to Scotland by the Romans.

"Did you blow your horn before the accident?" Response: "I played the trumpet for four years in high school."

Dr. Stradivarius said that "I feel as fit as a fiddle this morning."

A violinist kept fiddling around until many of his bills came due, now he has to face the music.

Was Elvis surprised by his immense success? Answer: "He was not only surprised, he was 'All Shook Up'.

I wanted to do the hokey pokey but I was a poor dancer and a slow learner, the instructions confused me. I flunked the hokey pokey test so I wasn't invited to the next two weddings, was it my fault that I had two left feet?

Jerry Lee Lewis was in California, near San Francisco, when a minor earthquake hit the area. The quake lasted for two minutes. When asked what happened Jerry Lee replied calmly, 'A Whole-Lot-A Shakin' Goin'On'.

Johnny Cash was driving his wife June when he was pulled over by a state trooper for erratic driving. Suspecting alcohol the trooper asked him to walk a straight line to see if he was impaired, but Johnny refused. Finally June asked him to obey the troopers orders Johnny relented when he said, "June Because You're Mine I'll Walk the Line."

Little Richard was minding his own business eating a 'Tutti-Frutti' ice cream cone when he was approached by a group of four lovely fans, they were 'Long Tall Sally', 'Lucille', 'Jenny Jenny', and last but not least 'Good Golly Miss Molly,' when he saw Miss Molly he said 'She's Got It' and 'The Girl Can't Help It' so now we're going to 'Rip It Up'.

Johnny Cash beat up 'A Boy Named Sue' when he went to court he was 'Busted'. He said 'I'm In The Jailhouse Now' and he added 'I Got The Folsom Prison Blues'. In jail I'm trapped in what seems a 'Ring Of Fire' and 'If I Had A Hammer' I could break out and there would be 'Peace In The Valley', once more.

Frank Sinatra met a lovely lady he said we are 'Strangers In The Night', 'Let's Take It Nice And Easy' 'Everybody Loves Somebody' so let's dance 'Cheek To Cheek'. I think about you 'Night And Day' if 'Anything Goes', 'Don't Blame Me', because 'I've Got You Under My Skin', 'All Of Me, Why Not Take All Of Me?' 'I'm Going Out Of My Head' because 'I Don't Stand A Ghost Of A Chance' but 'It's Been A Long, Long Time' and if we marry it will be 'The Good Life' and 'Nothing But Blue Skies' from now on.

What did Elvis Presley say when his girlfriend wanted to dump him? He said, 'I Can't Help Falling In Love With You', 'I Can't Stop Loving You'; 'Have I Told You Lately That I Love You?' 'Don't Be Cruel' 'Well All Right Okay You Win' but right now 'I'm All Shook Up!' You are just a 'Hard Headed Woman' so 'Little Darling' 'It's Now Or Never' but I guess 'It's Over' and me and my 'Hound Dog' and 'Teddy Bear' are checking in to 'Heartbreak Hotel' tonight so for now 'Let It Be' so long 'It'll Be A Blue, Blue Christmas Without You.'

Tony Bennett met a new flame and said, I was a 'Stranger In Paradise', but 'Because of You' 'The Best Is Yet To Come' now 'I Got The World On A String' so now 'I'm Steppin Out With My Baby' and I treat her 'Tenderly' but we broke up and 'I Left My Heart In San Francisco' but 'Just In Time' I went to Las Vegas and went from 'Rags To Riches' and now 'It's The Good Life'. When I remember 'Your Cold, Cold Heart' and the 'Shadow Of Your Smile', 'Who Can I Turn To?'

A famous violinist received a letter from a budding female violinist who asked for an audition, the violinist agreed and he listened to her with his back to her as she played two violin selections. When done she said, "What do you think?" The famous violinist said, "Perhaps you should consider marriage, my dear."

'I'll Be Home For Christmas' it's a 'Silent Night', 'Let it Snow' but 'Baby It's Cold Outside' and 'I'm Dreaming Of A White Christmas' now it's a 'Winter Wonderland' and 'All I Want For Christmas Is You', I think I hear 'Jingle Bells', look it's 'Rudolph The Red Nose Reindeer' we'll 'Rock Around The Clock' and Merry Christmas.

He was musically inclined he sounded better when he played his trumpet on the side of a hill.

A minister asked Elvis a question about gardening. He said, Elvis what type of mulch should I use around my sanctuary? Elvis replied, 'Sanctuary? Sanctuary mulch'. The minister said, "Gee! Thanks a lot Elvis."

They started a band at the Smucker's Preserves Company and every Saturday night they had a jam session.

He was a fresh water fisherman who sang in a barbershop quartet, he had a bass voice.

He was instrumental when he started his own band.

She used to be a part time belly dancer but she got tired of it, she had a bellyful of dancing because she kept getting bellyaches, after eating and then dancing.

I took lessons at the Fred Astaire Dance Studio and they wanted me to 'Begin the Beguine', I thought that I could waltz through it but I pulled a muscle doing the hokey pokey.

I met Mick Jagger and he started getting smart, so I told him "Don't give me any of your fat lip."

I made a mistake when I tried to walk past a conga line at a dance, I got a kick out of it for my efforts.

He was an excellent violinist but he had the bad habit of fiddling his time away rather than face the music.

He attended the accordion concert, as a grand finale 100 accordionist played 'Lady of Spain' despite requests to the contrary.

He had a dubious musical distinction. He was the first chair in the kazoo band and was famous for his version of the 'Flight of the Bumble Bee' which always received a seated ovation.

He used to play a kettle drum but his mom needed the kettle to make peach jam.

Two Indians came to Las Vegas for the entertainment they wanted to whoop it up. Ten Navajos joined them and they had a whoop-de-do.

My brother used to listen to stereo radio and stereo music all the time he was one of those stereotypes.

He wanted to start a choir in his church but everyone who volunteered sang off key which made the choir hard to acquire much less inspire.

He liked rock and roll, he went to a rock concert but when he left and got to the parking lot he got rolled.

I don't eat a lot of salsa but when I used to dance I liked to dip.

He was a union man who worked for scale, and he made musical instruments, not full size but ½ scale and when he finished with pianos he used to practice the scales on it.

He was a rock singer he wasn't much of a singer but he was a roaring success.

No matter how sophisticated that a rap song is it will never be a rhapsody.

They weren't a real rock band they were a shamrock band they were from Ireland.

A dance instructor spent a week in Florida to get a tan but at home in New York within two weeks he said "Where did my tan-go?"

I took dancing classes in high school and I was coming along ok until some wise guy put on a record of the 'Saber Dance'.

He wanted to do the hokey pokey but he didn't think that he could leg it out or put his left foot in.

She was a dancer for a very long time but she was not fully aware that she was on her last legs.

I found a book on origami with an attached song the words were, "You got to know how to hold them, know how to fold them." (What else?)

He was a musician who lived in the country, he had a fireplace and before winter he always bought several chords of wood.

Fred Astaire was never better than when he danced Gingerly.

The master of ceremonies hit the microphone and said, I'd like to make an announcement, "Rock and roll is here to stay." What a revelation, it was something that I could identify with it. Last week a kid threw a rock at me and the next night I got rolled.

The violinist was a gambler who didn't like modern music he said that he was going for baroque.

While he was an orchestra conductor he disliked facing the music in his private life.

Sam went to Australia and bought a digeridoo but he had a tough time checking it in as baggage on the airplane going home, but it was easy to spot on the airport luggage carousel. When Sam got home he blew into it and got diddly squat after some practice his wife accompanied him in a duet, she played the bagpipes every once in a while, their son would jump in on the drums creating a trio, of course the neighbors were upset. The trio was called the 'Way Down Under Trio', they got an occasional gig as background music in horror films when the director wanted to raise the dead.

They called her a canary in a dance band but she's a canary that flew the coop because dance bands with a canary are hard to locate nowadays. She wasn't much of a singer but now she is an excellent tweeter.

He was of Greek origin and when he was in the Army he fired a bazooka at tanks when he got out of the Army he played the bouzouki.

Many years ago I was working part-time in a produce store in Hollywood, California when Carmen Miranda danced in and bought 80% of the fresh fruit, apples, pears, pineapples, oranges and bananas. She said that she just flew in from Brazil to make her next movie and that she was thinking about a new headdress and had not decided on exactly how it will look but it had to be at least three feet tall. Carmen said that she planned to work on it in a couple of days because her present headdress was so heavy that she had developed a headache and her neck was getting sore. Carmen said that she loved fruit and as the headdress ripened she didn't throw it away she ate it.

He wanted to sing in the Alps but his echo proved that he was a far cry from having a good voice.

Joe had questionable voice it was one of those group voices the bigger the group the better he sounded. Joe had to be refrained from singing a refrain. Joe's singing instructor nearly quit the profession because Joe never improved. No one could discourage Joe. He took a trip to the mountains and one evening he sang and when the echo came back it frightened him so badly that he stopped singing on the spot.

Bob lived in an isolated town out west and every Fourth of July there was the big yearly parade. Nearly everyone in town participated in it, the police cars, the town fire truck, the clowns, the high school band and the war veterans. So many townspeople participated in the parade that when they marched down the middle of Main Street there were only a few people in town left to watch the grand, wonderful and joyous spectacle. The hot dog vendor nearly went broke due to a shortage of customers.

I was told to keep my sunny side up, which I remember as a lyric from an old popular tune. It is good to have a sunny side but a lot of people have a dark side which is best hidden undercover. I always like to walk on the sunny side of the street but I prefer riding in my car, sunny side up eggs are good if you don't have to worry about cholesterols that clog your heart. Whenever I keep my sunny side up you're looking at my bright side and not my dark side because as an aside I'd like to get everyone on my side.

As a composer I always wrote verses easily, but I had trouble with the chorus. None of the girls would go out with me.

Sign on music store door: Bach at 2. (Often Bach Sooner).

His mother wanted her son to play a musical instrument, so she decided on the bagpipes. She figured if it didn't pan out, and he played badly, who could tell?

I was fortunate to be playing my bagpipes at two in the morning because for some strange reason my neighbor came pounding on my door.

She sang with her eyes closed so she would not have to witness the guests suffering.

That was no piccolo that was my fife.

I was put on hold on the telephone and while listening to the background music, two thoughts crossed my mind. First: The orchestra sounded as if they were busy trying to get somewhere and could not tell when they had arrived; and Second: They were busy playing until somehow stumbled across a melody.

"Anything too stupid to be spoken is sung." *(Voltaire)*

A man walked into a bank carrying a viola case. Being an ex-musician the bank guard knew that the case did not contain a weapon but, he was afraid that the customer might take out the viola and play it.

I watched a symphony in Bermuda, it was great until the musician playing the triangle vanished.

The conductor had more fun than you could shake a stick at.

NEIGHBORS

My neighbor knows everything, he told me "That only ignorant people are positive." I said, "Are you certain of that?" He said, "I'm positive."

My nosy neighbor asked me, "How do you do?" I did not want to incriminate myself and replied, "What do you think I do?

It was rumored that my neighbor talked to himself but how would I know, I'm never around when he's alone.

NUDISTS

I was visiting a nudist colony and that the only thing that the members were wearing was a smile and an occasional apology.

I had to quit my job at the nudist colony, I was barely making ends meet.

A nudist is a person fully undressed for nearly every occasion, formal and informal.

She was so lovely, in the nudist colony everyone wondered what she would look like fully-clothed.

A young nudist couple decided to break up, they were seeing too much of each other.

A successful stripper has to get the audience clamoring for less.

He belonged to an exclusive nudist colony, at dinner all of the men wore ties.

The biggest problem in the nudist camp was that she was a bleached blonde.

He joined the nudist colony but had to quit within one week because he couldn't make a living. After all, was it his fault that he was a pickpocket?

Are nudist camps in cold climates clothed for the winter?

OCCULT

I wanted to go trick or treating at Halloween completely wrapped in a white bandages but my Mummy said that I couldn't because the old Geza wouldn't approve of it.

Just because your boyfriend acts like a wolf at Halloween doesn't make him Wolf Man.

A priest specialized in driving out demons, kept gaining weight because he failed to exorcise enough.

Wolf Man was afraid that at midnight he would turn into a wolf, he had a minor problem, most guys are wolves 24 hours a day.

OPTIMISTS

An optimist is a guy who lights a match before he bums a cigarette.

If my blood type could be B-negative does that make me a pessimist by definition?

PANHANDLERS

A panhandler knocked at a door and asked a housewife for a piece of cake, he told her that it was his birthday.

A panhandler asked a passerby for one dollar, who replied, I don't give money to tramps." The panhandler handed her a card and said, "In that case see me in my office at the address shown."

Harrison was approached by a panhandler who said, "You know that it is better to give than to receive." Reply, "I'm so happy to hear you say that and I agree, in that case why don't you give me a dollar and I'll be on my way, and thank you in advance."

I realized that the blind beggar, with a tin cup, could actually see. When I questioned him he said, "You're right, but it's my brother's day off, I am just filling in for him, temporarily."

PERSONALITY

He didn't know what's what about this or that and because he liked to chit chat his work output was so-so, so he could never become a member of who's who by and by.

"Always do right; this will gratify some people and astonish the rest." *(Mark Twain)*

"Nothing shows a man's character more than what he laughs at." *(Johann vonGoethe)*

"Remember that there is nothing stable in human affairs; therefore avoid undue elation in prosperity, and undue depression in adversity." *(Socrates)*

"A liar is not believed even when he tells the truth." *(Aesop)*

She was a little rough around the edges since she had tomboy traits, so her mother sent to charm school, now she has so much charm she has enough left over to put into a doggie bag for her girlfriend.

He was an imperfect gentleman, I don't know anyone that's perfect.

I wanted to feather my nest but I was stumped. Where could I get the feathers since I don't hunt. I've heard of feather merchants but I never met one, so that was out. If I could only find those birds of a feather that flock together I'd be tickled pink.

He was stubborn beyond reason, he got all or nothing, rather than half of something.

I wanted to climb the ladder of success while it seemed that some other people got there on an elevator and lottery winners get there on a rocket.

I always wondered if I would be somebody and then I realized, "Hey, you are somebody but not a special somebody. I didn't know anybody who could help me be that special somebody, that everybody wanted to know because as the song goes, I ain't got nobody."

I never realized I was out front until someone kicked me from behind.

He seemed to be reserved sort of a hard-boiled egg but things are looking up because he's finally coming out of his shell.

They claim that he had no personality but on closer inspection it was discovered that he had a personality deficit.

Real Baltimoreans pronounce fire as 'far'. At Christmas they know that the three wise men were actually three Baltimore firefighters because they had come from a 'far'.

I looked through binoculars from the wrong end, everything looked so small and far away, I got a new perspective on my situation.

The receptionist on the telephone asked me to leave my name and number. I told her that I was a convict incognito, but that I would give her an assumed name and that I had a ten digit number, but that I was really number one. I told her that I got her nervous when anyone had my number, conditions being what they were.

I don't object to you disagreeing with me as long as we do it my way in the end.

I just didn't fail, I failed in front of everyone, I wish that I could succeed under similar circumstances.

If your actions make others feel important you're on your way to success.

I cannot find the proper words to describe the candidate before you, words fail me but he is never out of his depth and he has the energy of an experienced elderly worker.

Can I count on you to be counted on or are you a no-account that can't be counted on? The proper answer really counts in many countless uncountable ways and you can count on that, or do you teach arithmetic and can't be counted on at all?

If you have all the answers can you lead a questionable existence?

A conflict prevented the scheduled conflict resolution class from meeting.

All those with low self-esteem and would like to lose weight may attend the dual purpose meeting here next week, please gain entry through the double doors at the back of the building.

If it wasn't for bacteria some people would be uncultured.

I used to burn my bridges behind me but I ran out of wooden bridges.

I had an unlimited amount of excessive exuberance until someone said, "Cool it."

He was superficial deep down.

While he had no class he was at the head of his class.

He sucks up information so fast, he is like a vacuum cleaner with no bag.

His name like acid reflux comes up a lot.

He was very active as a member of the moose lodge but we couldn't get him to slow down to do anything.

His moral compass was more like a gyroscope.

The last time I shook his hand I lost my wallet.

He had lived a very dull life but he was cheered when he found a box of crayons and decided to write his memoirs.

They erected a statue to honor his accomplishments to his surprise it was only three feet tall. They said that they ran out of money.

Every person over forty is responsible for his face. Abraham Lincoln once said of a proposed cabinet nominee, "I don't want him in my cabinet, I don't like his face."

Everyone said, "You have spunk" but I just didn't know how to get rid of it.

When I thought that I had no problems I was told that I was the problem.

I lived in an average house on an average street in an average town. I went to an average high school, had an average job with average pay and then I won the state lottery and while I have no job I'm living a well above average life style and I only bought one lottery ticket.

He rarely went anywhere with anyone or anybody, but he didn't worry anyhow and didn't care anymore about anything anyway but he realized that he had too many anys.

He was a marked man. Someone put an X on the back of his coat using a piece of chalk.

He was overweight, I suspected that he was a turkey because in the summer his wife applied suntan oil on him using a turkey baster.

He was very colorful. He had brown hair, hazel eyes, white teeth, a pink tongue, a green shirt, grey pants, white socks, and black shoes, but for some reason he was feeling blue.

She couldn't make up her mind, she never let facts interfere with her judgment.

He was a measurable success, he was six feet tall and weighed 200 pounds.

Did he tell the truth, he was accused of going too far but some said that he didn't go far enough, so far he was far from deciding how far he had to go to be known far and wide as the person closest to the truth.

He had a large nose he was a prominent figure in his community.

He had a keen sense of smell a keen sense of humor, a keen sense of judgment but a dull personality.

He knows how to keep a secret but he liked to gossip so he couldn't keep his word about his silence.

I told him that I was concerned about his concerns concerning a bill but I told him not to concern himself unnecessarily and that a solution would arise that would be best for all concerned.

He wanted to rearrange the deck chairs but someone turned the tables on him.

He wanted to be considered to be one of the crowd so he joined a crowd going by but no one knew who he was, it was the wrong crowd.

He could never follow any organized group he was a born straggler who struggled to cure his straggling.

They said that he was ready willing and able but he was especially Able because that was his name.

Someone reported seeing a giant white figure in the Himalayan Mountains, the figure had a very large stomach, they named him the abdominal snowman.

He had a sterling character he thought that problems always had a silver lining 92.5% pure.

He was a symbol of success but then again he was always symbol minded.

He used to be an overdog now he's an underdog either way he is dogging it.

He was a stranger in town but what was even stranger was his strange expression which struck everyone as strange as strange as it seems. He even had a strange friend and at night they were strangers in the night. Does all this strike you as strange?

He said that he wanted to do his thing but he wasn't sure of what his thing was. I told him if he did anything or something that he might be right since anything and something are a part of everything and his thing was somewhere in the spectrum of everything. He was confused and changed his mind and did nothing.

I lost my temper and my friends and I kept looking for an hour and finally gave up. I finally calmed down ready to start again but this time I said, "Don't make me lose my temper."

She was like the moon she told me that she was going through one of her phases.

She was a Valley girl from California she said that "It totally was like gnarly or whatever, ooh."

He was usually cool, calm and collected but when he sat on a block of ice it had a chilling effect on him.

While he did what he pleased he didn't please anyone since he caused displeasure but he did have a pleasant personality and he was pleasantly rich which was pleasing to his girlfriend.

Her name was Pepper but she was the salt of the earth.

He said that he was nosing around, what was he a dog? A nose is an organ of smell sometimes I can smell things that I can't actually see, it's a sixth sense. I don't mind people snooping around as long as they don't turn up their nose where there is a risk of drowning in the rain I've even put money on the nose as everyone knows.

I began groping for something under the bed so I began feeling low.

Curiosity got the best of me but my best was never good enough so I didn't have anything left over.

He was a bright prospect at night he walked around with a flashlight.

He felt like a lion who liked to dress up and go out on the town he was known as a dandy lion.

She repulsed his advances what else could she do he was repulsive.

I was asked if I was positive I said "I was negative at first but now I think I'm positive, but I'm not positive I'm positive but I have a positive attitude and I'd like to give a positive feedback positively but I'm definitely not negative.

He had a grin from ear to ear his nickname was 'big mouth'.

Roughly speaking he talked rough, acted tough, roughed up people and lead a rough and tumble existence, he got a lot of rough breaks especially in golfing where he spent a lot of time in the rough but he was used to it and could tough it out.

He was born in the cellar so he was low born but he wasn't always low born he was always treated like royalty and he felt like a king until he ended up in court.

My boss said that I was his right hand man but I was left handed so it was right that I left but I knew that I had the right stuff right off because I was right minded and always demanded the right of way rightly or wrongly what else is left to say, right.

He wanted to be responsible but he had been irresponsible for so long it was a hard habit to break.

He was a chemist with a sharp wit whenever he was criticized he always had a retort.

He was self-propelled that explains why he never got anywhere.

They told him that he was born to the purple but it was cold and he was so cold he started to shiver and his lips began turning purple, maybe they were right.

He used to be chalant but he decided against it now he's nonchalant.

When he rested his mind he didn't disturb anything, it had been resting for many years.

He wasn't entirely always appropriate but lately he was somewhat misappropriated.

He was touted as a model of decorum but little did they know that he was rotten to décor.

I lived on the tenth floor naturally I had high expectations.

When he won he did a war dance, when he settled with someone he smoked a peace pipe, when his head got cold, his wig kept his head wam, but no matter how you fooled him he couldn't be buffaloed and he always felt at home on the range.

He swore at me in a cursory manner.

Considering everything he was consistently inconsistent his selective consistency was the hobgoblin of an intelligent mind.

I was wide awake with a clear conscience but I could make unconscious decisions about unconscionable topics which came in handy because I liked being conscientious and didn't want to be conscience stricken.

I just couldn't conform, I was a nonconformist, I didn't feel comfortable conforming but after my Catholic conformation I began getting used to conformity so now I'm a conformist, which is more acceptable and easier on me.

He was asked to complete the questionnaire, someone had filled about one half of it and left town, so it was lucky that he happened by but I don't know how useful the information would be unless they were analyzing split personalities.

He was so lazy that his self-winding watch stopped.

He examined himself and found himself wanting but then again he always wanted something.

He said that he had a point of view but as far as I was concerned he missed the point completely.

He told me that he had a plan, I didn't fully realize how stupid his plan was until he told me. I told him that he had to do his planning and carefully plan for a plan, I told him to revise his plan because I planned to read it.

I see your point of view but not your viewpoint.

He said, "I've got your number." What did he mean? I didn't have a number, what am I a convict? My days are numbered, I have a telephone number, I can sing a little number, people have done a number on me, just exactly which number is he talking about, can he be more specific?

He knew that he was native to the area but he was unaware that he was indigenous, he was original but not as original as most of the plants that were indigenous as well as native.

He wasn't a first class nuisance but even as a second class nuisance he could be easily promoted and if he gets any worse and bothers more people he could become a public nuisance.

She was kidnapped by a group of youngsters we suspected that when they asked for a case of lollipops as a ransom.

The suspect was shy and clammed up but eventually he came out of his shell.

Sam led an exemplary life people used him as an example, some people made an example out of him, he exemplified an exemplary life, he was the personification of exemplification. Sam got tired of being an example he wanted to be the exception and ultimately exceptional but he needed someone exemplary as an example.

He had low self-esteem and he felt that he was of no consequence, he had an inconsequential job with inconsequential pay consequently he considered a positive change. He now works for a vending company and said that he can handle change and even counts on it.

Tom lived a very dull life, every day was the same as the next, wake up, shave, eat, go to work, come home, watch the evening news on Sunday he went to church. Tom purchased a diary to chronicle his activities, he filled out the first page and used ditto marks on 260 pages, on 52 pages he entered "Went to church." For Saturday he lied on that page to spice up his life by lying.

Harry was very confused he said that he was often discombobulated so he tried to get his life in order and thought that if he had been discombobulated he would improve by being combobulated, but didn't know how to go about it.

Bob fell out of favor into disfavor, out of grace into disgrace out of order into disorder, out of honor into dishonor, out of interest into disinterest, Bob was into and out of a lot of things.

Charlie liked to doodle and was a member of a doo-wop group. Charlie was a doofus who bought a doo hickey and who wore doo-dads he didn't do a lot was his last name Doolittle, anyway he was a doozy.

Sarah embarrassed easily over and over and one day she couldn't take it anymore she said, "I'm tired of being constantly embarrassed from now on I'm just going to be chagrined.

Thomas had always been doubtful so doubtful he was nicknamed Doubting Thomas. He was always skeptical and that progressed to doubtful and even doubly doubtful. He was always reluctant to take a firm position even when pressed he would say, "Doubtless you say it's true but I'm beginning to doubt it without a doubt."

It wasn't that he was always a bad apple in his defense he said that he had started at the bottom of the barrel.

He wanted privacy so he got an unlisted number in a location between two area codes, all he could do was call out.

Dave wanted some advice so he went to an advisory service to be advised where he talked to an advisor who gave him bad advice so he was worse off than when he started, advisedly so.

People used to say, "Don't get excited." Why not? Usually excitement is associated with something good such as hitting the lottery, but it can lead to nervousness or tension, which are bad. Tension results from being too intense I can remember being intense in the Boy Scouts, but that was nothing to get excited about.

People said that he was 'as tough as nails'. Years ago they used to use wood as nails and later nails were made of copper or brass and not steel, but tough as nails may not hit the nail on the head, I just don't think they nailed it or him. I used to drive nails into masonry or wood and a lot of them bent, how tough were they? This one's a nail biter and hard to nail down. I even knew of a baseball player who tried to steal and he was nailed at second and thought that was tough. I may go to my grave without fully understanding what tough as nails really means but don't put a nail in my coffin just close the lid.

My doctor couldn't figure out what was wrong with me and said that I must have a nervous problem, what nerve? Just because he couldn't help me he said that I was the cause of the problem. He said that I was a type 'A' person similar to a racehorse, a type 'B' person was like a plough horse. What if I got impatient waiting for a McDonald's hamburger or impatient in the express checkout line that wasn't conclusive proof that I was nervous. To make matters worse my wife told me that I was impatient too often. I was starting to get upset. People were getting on my nerves. Maybe I am nervous. What to do? I wanted to start a fight with someone but the other guy was much bigger, that's when I lost my nerve, now I'm as cool as a cucumber.

I was dreaming about the old West, I put on my chaps and my pardner and I moseyed over to the corral to cut out cayuses and break a passel of broncos that we lassoed with our lariats. When complete we put on our peacemakers and sashayed past the calaboose and visited an old friend on Boot Hill when I awoke I watched a John Wayne Western on TV and went out and bought a Roy Rogers sandwich for lunch, back to reality.

Roy said that the was doing his thing I didn't know what his thing was. I had heard of a thing-a-majig and a thingumabob so I asked Roy, "How are things going is there anything in particular that you plan to do? Instead of nothing Roy replied "Whatever I do is my thing and it could change from day to day." Roy said, "It doesn't mean a thing if you don't have a thing." As things are I plan to do something but if I don't then nothing would be my thing, have I missed anything?

She had a magnetic personality and attracted men who had the mettle of steel.

My trash man was really distraught when I bought new metal trash cans that were pre-dented.

PICKUP LINES

In all modesty, besides me have you seen anyone here that you like?

Just to be indifferent I tried acting normal.

POLICE

She dated a policeman, he always held her for further questioning.

Large inflatable toys were stolen, police were looking for burglars out of breath.

He was so crooked he couldn't think straight.

This pickpocket was really good, he picked my pocket on a trampoline.

A crook couldn't decide whether he preferred being right handed or left handed. His friend told him that crooks have more success being underhanded.

The police caught a mime stealing some items, they told him that he had the right to remain silent, the mime put both hands in the air.

A guilty policeman copped a plea.

The detectives were sloppy at the crime scene they removed the body without a trace.

He was a questionable subject that the police called the subject in question, when they questioned the subject in question he gave evasive and a questionable answers, no question about it.

When the police discovered that he had a record they made him play it.

He was a full time exterminator and a part time detective, these two pursuits complimented each other because he was very skilled at bugging telephones.

He was a private eye, when he used both eyes he charged twice as much.

Sherlock Holmes took a glass of distilled water and stirred in two teaspoons of Kool-Aide and said, "Watson I believe I've found a solution."

The policeman collared a dishonest minister.

He sold blankets during the day and was a part time detective at night he had a talent for undercover work.

A spy was extremely cautious when he ordered a bowl of alphabet soup, he suspected that he letters spelled out a hidden message. After 15 minutes of intense scrutiny he deciphered the message, it was, "Eat your soup it's getting cold."

Watson and Sherlock were long time friends, one day they were reminiscing and Watson asked, "Sherlock do you remember the school we went to when we first met?" Sherlock replied, "Elementary my dear Watson, elementary."

Someone stole truckload of Kleenix, they questioned the usual suspects but there wasn't a tissue of evidence connecting them to the crime.

There was a car accident at a traffic light in town and a crowd gathered. One of the crowd commented that there was a kerfuffle at the scene. A policeman arrived and said, "This is a fine kettle of fish." I wasn't sure what a kerfuffle was and it's relation to a kettle of fish. Besides I had never seen a kettle of fish. I saw a film where they made bouillabaisse in a kettle on deck of a French fishing ship, but that had fish, shellfish, vegetables and saffron (if they had it). Since I lived in a city along the Chesapeake Bay perhaps it all made sense, a somewhat fishy commotion.

The police said that he was a person of interest but he was an uninteresting person. I suspect that he could be a suspect if the police developed more specific interest in him, evidently the suspect was innocent because the police lost all interest in him, they became disinterested, interestingly enough.

The police wanted him to undergo a polygraph test to see if there was any truth to his alibi. After the test they determined that the technician administering the test was lying, it was so obvious that they didn't even need the polygraph. The suspect passed with flying colors.

I consider myself above the law. In my cash starved town I rented an apartment located above the police station.

The policeman said to the crook, "Are you going to come quietly or do I have to wear earplugs?"

The policeman told the suspect, "You have the right to remain silent." The policeman had no idea that he had just arrested a mime.

I know why they had trouble catching the one armed man in that old TV show, they didn't know how to handcuff him.

A policeman asked me where I was at eight. I told him, "I think I was in the third grade."

Stupidity is not a crime, you are free to go.

I was placed under house arrest in my mobile home so I just towed the home to a different state.

Judge: "Because you were joking in the court room there's an additional fine of $10, does that suit you?" Reply: "Judge, I call that extra fine."

The judge told the streaker to take a tablespoon of Windex every day, that will prevent streaking.

Firemen have a hard time extinguishing the fire at the circus. The heat was intense.

Injudicious comment when stopped by a policeman: You're not going to check my trunk, are you?

POLITICS

What can be worse than a pencil without an eraser or a pencil with an eraser that smudges the writing. Some erasers just don't erase, when I find a good eraser I'm afraid I may lose it. If you're confident use a ballpoint, but don't lend an eraser to a mafia type, he's liable to rub you out.

"There is no country in the world where the Christian religion retains a greater influence over the souls of men than in America, and there can be no greater proof of its utility, and of its conformity to human nature, than that its influence is most powerfully felt over the most enlightened and free nation on the earth. *(Alexis de Tocqueville)*

Senator I stand, corrected "I did not say that 'You were the oaf of office', I said, "Let's have the oath of office."

"Whenever you find you are on the side of the majority, it is time to pause and reflect." *(Mark Twain)*

George Washington was famous for his memory. All of his monuments were erected in honor of his memory.

A Congressman asked me by mail, "What is the most important thing that Congress could do to improve the nation, overall." I replied, "Meet less often."

A politician had a lot of pull but was stymied when a door at the mall was marked 'push'.

He was the court jester but the king didn't find it funny when the jester was caught fooling around with the queen.

Some people have a talent for remembering names this is a handy talent and useful in society and in politics. I tend to remember faces and I often remember people that I have seen years before. Sometimes I don't even know my own name. Someone asked me, "What's your name" and I said, "I don't know I'm not myself today."

No one ever erected a statue or monument to a critic or a committee, or a government agency.

My local politician must have been in show business because whenever I asked him a question he tap-danced around the answer.

Representative: I don't want to allocate existing money to give to someone, I want to give the money to someone and then figure out a creative way to tax you to pay for it all.

He had a future in politics whenever he played golf and the ball was in a large divot he kicked it out. He wanted to improve his lie.

I asked a hypothetical question and I got an indecisive incomprehensible questionable answer.

He's a natural born leader, his brother was a caesarian.

Politicians hand out taxpayers money with reckless abandon, what do they care it's not their money, and yet they are buying votes because they are nice guys. Even Santa Claus hands out presents only once a year. Let's get politicians to wear Santa Claus outfits when they get into a generous mood.

He was an arsonist who had no friends even his language was inflammatory.

A newspaper reporter wanted to get an unusual story, so his boss told him to interview a parrot that kept saying that he wanted to be a politician. After the interview he asked the parrot if he could quote him on his remarks?

The great President Thomas Jefferson could read and write in English, French, Greek and Latin and now his face is on a nickel, but I suspect that he had a sixth sense.

Many of the revolutionaries in France were not only disgusting they were revolting.

I was in Russia and I turned my bicycle upside down and spun the front wheel forward until it finally stopped, when I spun it in the opposite direction how was I to know that I started a counter revolution.

I didn't have a firm position on the proposition, at first I was in a seated then standing position but I wanted a new position on the proposition that wouldn't be an imposition during a transition at least that was my supposition, what's your position?

He brought order out of chaos, calm out of disorder, it was easy for him he used to be an orderly.

He was a politician and a consistent jogger so he decided to run for office.

Bill heard that politics was corrupt he lobbied an uncorruptable politician trying to corrupt him and couldn't, but Bill had his suspicions because the politician bragged that he could say, "For me?" in eight languages. He was on the anticorruption committee but didn't pursue anyone because they were too big to fail and jeopardized future campaign donations.

Mark criticized a politician with some disparaging remarks, the politician replied, "I'm not going to dignify those remarks." Mark replied, "I don't want you to dignify my remarks I want you to ratify or clarify them."

When you have a house divided, you can end up with a lot of rooms.

I was stumped in the argument so I wanted to use an analogy but I was told that an analogy is not proof, how about a simile but could like and as do it? Perhaps a syllogism, but I was weak on deductive reasoning so I did what all good politicians did to win an argument I made something up and lied, as if I knew what I was talking about.

My neighbor asked my political affiliation he said, "Are you left or right" I said "My parents, were left and I started out left, but as I grew older I drifted right. There was a period where I was in the middle and an independent but eventually that left me. It all depends on the candidate sometimes I'm left and sometimes I'm right, but I'm not always right because the candidate would not do the right thing, so what did I have left. Comment: "So you are left, right". I said precisely right.

I was upset at being frustrated. How could I take out my frustration, actually I didn't want to take it out I wanted to suppress it. I was unfilled, dissatisfied and thwarted and I can't remember the last time I was thwarted. I was weary and exasperated although I was familiar with exasperation as long as it didn't lead to frustration. To solve the problem I avoided the acts that caused the frustration and I added some variety which was the spice of life, and spice makes things easier to swallow.

The political incumbent was recumbent and couldn't stand to make a speech, at that time. Later when he could no longer stand lying down and he attended a political convention and made a speech that got a standing ovation and he said, "I couldn't take this lying down."

During the 1948 election Thomas Dewey asked his wife, "How would it be to sleep with the president?" After his loss his wife said, "Tell me Tom, am I going to Washington or is Harry coming here?"

"Suppose you were an idiot, and suppose you were a member of Congress, but I repeat myself." *(Mark Twain)*

Politician: My opponent deserves to be kicked by a jackass and I think I can fill that bill.

My Senator never gave a straight answer, unlike water passing through a filter, he never made himself clear.

"Rome had Senators, now I know why they declined." *(Mark Twain)*

My politician was a part-time ventriloquist, he could lie without moving his lips.

"You replace Monsieur Franklin?" asked the minister. "I succeeded him", was Jefferson's reply, "No one can replace him." *(Thomas Jefferson)*

Introducing a United States Senator: "And now, here's the latest dope from Washington."

POLLUTION

They held a track meet in Los Angeles. One athlete threw a javelin into the smog filled air and it's still up there.

POST OFFICE

My post office box at the post office doesn't look like any box that I see normally. Although I check it regularly I get mail there infrequently. Despite the fact that the post office box is the smallest offered the yearly rental keeps getting larger soon to reach 100 dollars yearly. The post office must think that good things come in small packages.

When you mark a package 'fragile' that guarantees that the post office department personnel will not drop-kick it into the delivery truck.

A blacksmith told a knight of the round table, "Hey, you've got mail."

Sometimes because of mix-ups, foul-ups, lost mail, and other delays, by the time I received my car registration through the mail the vehicle registration had expired.

Stamps are getting so expensive that college students are thinking twice before writing home for small sums of money.

PSYCHIATRISTS

If two light beams going in the opposite direction meet do they cancel each other?

I liked history but my psychiatrist told me not to dwell in the past.

My psychiatrist said that I had a split personality, I was so mad I was beside myself.

I could not afford to go to a psychiatrist so I did the next best thing, when I got a haircut I explained my problems to my barber who listened attentively. He told me that he couldn't solve my problems in one visit but he said if I came back every two weeks by the time I was dead all of my problems would go away, what great advice, he also told me to keep busy.

He suffered from a compulsion and took compulsory college courses which led to a doctorate. Now he treats other people with compulsions and says, "I know, I know, I know how you feel."

I was a disinterested bystander but the longer I watched the more interested I became until I became involved, I was so involved I became preoccupied and it became an obsession. The psychiatrist cured me of my obsession so now I'm a disinterested bystander again.

He said that he was stressed out he couldn't handle stress so he took stress pills during stressful situations which calmed him psychologically and lowered his stress level and now he's just worried about a relapse.

He had a clock that went crazy, it was a cuckoo clock.

He told the psychiatrist that he was an animal and then he came home from work udderly exhausted.

Doctor, you've got to help me, lately I have the feeling that I'm two different people, I'm beginning to feel as if I'm beside myself."

I saved back copies of 'Life Magazine', 'Reader's Digest', and 'Consumer's Report', almost as an obsession. I went to a psychiatrist and said, "Doctor you've got to help me, I have issues."

I was extremely surprised when after two years of therapy my psychiatrist finally spoke saying, "No Hablo Espanol?"

The psychiatrist told me to try to forget the past. I asked him, "Does that include what I owe you?"

I asked my psychiatrist, "When will I be cured?" He said, "Not until you run out of money."

The psychiatrist told his patient, "If it's not one thing, it's your mother."

Madness takes a toll, it's always good to have the exact change.

A psychiatrist will listen to you as long as you don't make sense.

"Doctor, this place is so busy, it's a madhouse." The psychiatrist said, "Nurse please refer to this as a mental hospital, we are all professionals here."

PSYCHICS

An elderly Jewish woman went to a séance where the gypsy contacted her dear departed husband Max. The woman asked, "Max how's by you?" Max replied, "Zelda I think I'm in a swamp in Louisiana."

The psychic gazed into her crystal ball and slapped her client. She said, "I see in my crystal ball that you have a date with my husband next Friday."

Great psychics can talk to the departed while drinking a glass of water.

I tried to predict the unpredictable but I never expected the unexpected that made the plausible implausible and I began thinking about the unthinkable to lead me to the think that I was trying to do, the undoable, now im pondering the imponderable.

Do psychics ever win the mega millions, if they did they could brag, "I only bought a one dollar ticket."

A psychic made a lot of predictions, once in a while she was correct.

Pete came home and listened to his answering machine and he had five messages, all the same, they said, "Hello, guess who?" he paid an unemployed psychic in his building to help him guess, no luck so far.

Alex was always quite quirky and frequently acted quixotic queerly enough. But what saved him was his humor because he wrote short funny quips some of which were clever which prompted quite quizzical looks. Alex finally capitalized on his clever funny quips and became rich when he managed to corner the market by selling his quips to be used as quick quirky messages in Chinese fortune cookies. They were so popular that Alex sold millions of them and lots of people waited for them and made important decisions based on Alex's sage advice which were quotable but quixotic.

In Arabia a gypsy who could read palms, went broke. She had no talent for climbing trees.

His psychic girlfriend left him before they met.

I didn't tell the psychic my name, I figured that she already knew it.

PUTDOWNS

Since I was easily pleased I used to like everyone and then you came along.

No I don't think that you're an idiot but I've been mistaken before.

If you agree to do it my way I'll graciously compromise and let you.

I loved him like a brother but everyone knows that my brother and I never got along.

You're not as obnoxious as people said that you were.

You remind me of someone that I'm trying to forget.

You look familiar, didn't I see your picture on a box of dog food?

Have a seat so that you can rest your brains.

How did you get a handicap placard? Was it for lacking good sense?

Let's play horse, I'll be the front end and you play yourself.

Maybe I'll see you next week. His neighbor said, "Thanks for the warning."

I was at a masquerade party and she was wearing a Marilyn Monroe mask. I said to her, "Have we ever met, you look vaguely familiar."

He had a deep voice and a low IQ to match.

Your work deserves a compliment if you ever did enough of it to compliment.

You remind me of my father before I ran away from home.

Your reputation precedes you, can you say anything in your own defense?

When I look into your lovely blue eyes I keep thinking that it's been a lovely evening before you arrived.

How nice to meet you, I thought that you looked a lot younger.

I didn't want to just take the insult lying down so I got up and asked him to repeat it.

I wanted to say nice things about you but I didn't want to get into the bad habit of lying.

In all honesty things haven't been dull since you were here the last time.

He wasn't exactly tall dark and handsome. No question that he was tall but the darker it got the more handsome he appeared.

When they made you they threw away the mold. By the way doesn't stinky cheese have mold in it?

I helped him out the same way he came in.

I ran into him again, luckily I was on my bicycle and not in my car.

Was your brother an only child?

I defended you, everyone said that you were a perfect idiot, but I said no one is perfect.

When I met you it was a memorable occasion you were someone who no one could ever forget.

Your personality leaves nothing, correct that, something to be desired.

Were your clothes designed by Ronald McDonald?

She was a hippie? Her clothes were unforgettable but then I remembered that the circus had left town and that the clowns forgot to take their outfits with them.

When you act normal you're different from everyone else I know.

It's so nice of you to come, I haven't seen you since the last time I saw you.

It was nice of you to come to the party, we were having a good time and then you rang the doorbell.

The instructor said that when you were absent from class we continued normally.

I distinctly remember the great pleasure I had the last time I said goodbye to you. I'd like to experience the same pleasure again as soon as I can.

Don't let my yawning give you the mistaken impression that I'm not listening attentively and hanging on your every word.

What a lovely hairbrush you have, I have one that's similar and I use it to scrub the commode after I use Draino.

It was a bad neighborhood I thought that my neighbor was a hood.

So nice to see you. I heard that you were in the neighborhood but you know how fast bad news spreads.

I told everyone that you were gone but not forgotten. No matter how hard we tried, here you are again, what luck?

I was going to call you but I couldn't find the appropriate words.

I'm speechless, your dress is stunning when I saw it I was stunned, it fits you like a potato sack, is the circus still in town or am I mistaken?

Men like you made this country what it is today, and you know what shape the country is in today.

I heard that you were in the neighborhood but I was hoping that you were just passing through.

You are not a complete stranger but you're close to being complete.

Your breath reminds me of that lovely day in spring when I made my first visit to the city dumps.

You look terrible, I hope that your widow is happy or at least relieved.

You look like a puzzle with the most important piece missing.

You walked in and when I saw you, I got the impression that you were the perfect finish to an extremely boring and dull day.

Your kiss seemed cold but slightly warmer than the last time I kissed my mother-in-law.

When I saw you I remembered that I had a weak stomach and was easily frightened.

It would be refreshing to hear an intelligent remark from you.

He is less dense than some of his competitors.

As long as I'm near the window let me help you out.

You're going to be missed around here but not for very long.

It is a pleasure to regard you as a former colleague.

No one is better unqualified for this position as you seem to be.

He performs well under constant supervision.

This person on a moped will go far.

As a pilot he spends a lot of time taxiing his plane on the runway, likes to fly low and slow.

He has a photographic memory but has run out of film.

After eating dinner I occasionally have nuts so I'm glad that I invited you.

You look as if you just returned from a zombie 50th year reunion party.

When I saw you, the theory that man descended from apes had new fresh and plausible meaning.

Would you allow me the pleasure of the next dance, I'm not sure that it will be a pleasure but if you're willing to take a chance, so am I.

I miss you a lot perhaps the next time I should take better aim.

You're welcome to come back if you promise not to stay so long.

I'd like to respond to your inane and tasteless remark but I can't bring myself to respond without considerable further thought. Why don't you get back to me in let's say five years. If we are both still alive, and by then perhaps, with the passage of time, I may have an appropriate response but if I'm lucky I may have completely forgotten you inane and tasteless remark, see you then.

You're welcome to come back if you promise not to stay so long.

"Let's meet as little as we can." *(William Shakespeare)*

You are not as dumb as you look, but then again that would be impossible.

If I agreed with you, we'd both be wrong.

I thought you were a pain in the neck, but now I have a lower opinion of you.

The topic of monkeys came up in conversation today, and your name came to mind.

Just because you have one doesn't mean you have to act like one.

As an outsider what do you think of the human race?

You are down to earth, but not quite deep enough.

I never forget a face, but in your case, I might make an exception.

He is a difficult man to forget, but its well worth the effort.

You're not yourself today, I noticed an immediate improvement.

You dress beautifully for a person who is obviously colorblind.

If you have a minute to spare tell me all you know.

Is your family happy or will you go home tonight?

You are as necessary as a fence around a cemetery.

I was looking at the animals at the zoo and somehow you came to mind.

For a minute I didn't recognize you, it was the most enjoyable minute I ever spent.

I know that you always feared success, but I know that deep down you had nothing to worry about.

I don't want to dance with a pretty girl, I want to dance with you.

She loves nature despite what it did to her; a peeping Tom reached in and pulled down her shade.

"What happened to your hair? It looks as if it could be a wig." Reply: "It is a wig." Response: "Really, I could never tell."

"Why do you sit there like an envelope without any address on it?" *(Mark Twain)*

I've heard so much about you, what's your side of the story?

QUOTES

"Against the assault of laughter, nothing can stand." *(Mark Twain)*

"Whatever you can do, or dream you can begin it. Boldness has genius, power, and magic in it." *(Johann vonGoethe)*

"You can't understand something if you don't possess it." *(Johann vonGoethe)*

"It is easier to stay out than to get out." *(Mark Twain)*

"This administration will be remembered in spite of ourselves." *(Abraham Lincoln)*

"Well done is better than well said." *(Benjamin Franklin)*

It's better to ring the doorbell than to knock on wood.

I was told that to be forewarned is to be fore armed. To be on the safe side the next time I was forewarned I hired a guard who was twice as handy as the average guard.

"Heaven for climate, hell for society." *(Mark Twain)*

"The secret of humor is surprise." *(Aristotle)*

"I cannot undertake to lay my finger on that article of the Constitution that granted a right to Congress of expending, on the objects of benevolence, the money of their constituents." *(James Madison)*

"I believe I have no prejudices whatsoever. All I need to know is that a man is a member of the human race. That's bad enough for me." *(Mark Twain)*

Pythagoras saw a puppy being beaten and with great empathy said, "Stop, do not beat it; it is the soul of a friend which I recognized when I heard it crying."

"There is no sadder sight than a young pessimist." *(Mark Twain)*

"Let us be thankful for fools, but for them the rest of us could not succeed." *(Mark Twain)*

REAL ESTATE

He was a real estate agent and he was happy with his lot.

My landlord asked me if I wanted a larger apartment, when I said yes, he gave me a putty knife and told me to scrape off all of the old wallpaper.

A Scot had a hard time finding an apartment. A friend advised him to leave his bagpipes home on his next apartment hunting trip.

I met a Texan who was rich and yet he said he owned only two acres of land – in downtown Manhattan.

He was a real estate broker and he met a beautiful lady who was also a real estate broker, they had a lot to offer each other.

I had new linoleum installed in the apartment kitchen, the installer asked me how I liked it, I told him that I was floored.

They say that he lived in a one horse town but when I was there I never saw a horse but I did meet a few donkeys and jackasses.

He was a real estate agent who specialized in subdivisions and on days off he lifted weights but the other agents said that he was overdeveloped.

He said that he felt like a beaver ever since the collapse in housing prices because his house was nearly under water.

She lived in an old house with old furniture that had the qualities of quaintness but she was in a quandary and questioned if the furniture was really quaint or just cheap. She wanted to quash the cheap connotation since the furniture was quasi antique at least that is what the lady at the Salvation Army store told her, but why quibble it was the quintessence of early Salvation Army, and that qualified as quaint, unquestionably.

I was looking for a house and I wanted to see a model home, but she wouldn't tell me when she got off from work.

The real estate business was really slow, the 'For Sale' sign needed repainting three times.

Our apartment was so small that whenever I ordered a large pizza we had to go outside to eat it.

RELIGION

A priest went to a psychiatrist who determined that he had an altar ego.

He was very religious and his job was being fired out of a cannon at the circus. Because he led such an exemplary life when he died he was canonized.

"If I cannot swear in heaven I shall not go there." *(Mark Twain)*

He told me that his wife was an angel because every day she was constantly harping on something.

A church dumped cases of that demon alcohol in a river where they had baptisms. Before baptism the congregation sang, "Shall We Gather at the River."

Eve complained to Adam, "All I do is cook and clean all day, you never take me anywhere, do you call this paradise?"

A wealthy church member was marooned on a Pacific island but he wasn't worried because he had been a large donor to his church and he was sure that they would rescue him shortly.

Sampson told a joke that was so funny that it brought the house down.

Not all of the animals in Noah's Ark came in pairs, two worms came in apples.

Noah was in trouble once the water rose he had forgotten to put two shovels on the ark.

Mrs. Smith had trouble sleeping in the hospital because of her strange surroundings. She hit upon a good idea to put her to sleep she wanted copies of her pastor's last ten sermons.

She went to the altar so often she wore a wash and wear gown.

He went to church early in order to get a good seat in the back.

At the bottom of Noah's Ark there was a sign which read "Do not remove this plug."

A new speaker system was installed in church, it was donated in memory of a church member who wanted to honor his talkative wife who passed away recently.

If God is everywhere is there any room left over for another God?

"Preoccupation with immorality is for the upper classes, particularly with ladies with nothing to do. An able man, who has a regular job and must toil and produce day by day, leaves the future world to itself, and is active and useful in this one. *(Johann vanGoethe)*

An angel received a telephone call in heaven. When she answered the phone she said, "Halo."

My wife will definitely go to heaven because she has lots of practice harping at me. No doubt if they have an orchestra there she'll be in the string section.

Moses was forced to take showers because whenever he took a bath he had the bad habit of parting the water.

There is no smoking in heaven, if there were it would be holy smokes.

They claimed that he was religious just because he tripped over his halo.

An hour before the company luncheon everyone helped themselves to a lot of the free delicious bean dips. When the pastor got up and said prior to the invocation, "Can I have a moment of silence please?" All hell broke loose.

If I don't end up in hell I'll be infernally grateful.

Sign on wet church floor: "Don't walk on water." The janitor just mopped the floor and had just placed the sign there.

When visitors heard that the country pastor had gone to the United Kingdom, they all thought that he was dead.

An Old Catholic priest was nostalgic for the days when the mass was spoken entirely in Latin. He wanted to give the current generation a taste of the past but his memory was somewhat faulty. He made the sign of the cross and said, "Dominic go frisk them."

There was only one opening for the Bible school studies. Job interviews were delayed until the minister's daughter finished her freshman college year.

The preacher had his work cut out for him. He put a twenty dollar bill in each of two collection plates, when the collection was over the total came out to be $34.50 in singles and change.

One good thing about religion is that if you are dedicated and believe enough you have a good idea of where you are going and look forward to it, if you are uncommitted is your future questionable?

In Biblical times when David and Goliath met, one bookmaker gave ten to one odds on Goliath. A bettor took the odds, he said, "It's a stone cold bet.

"Recognition of the supreme being is the first, the most basic expression of Americanism thus the founding fathers of America saw it, and thus with God's help, it will continue to be." *(President Gerald Ford)*

He wanted to sing with a church group choir so he inquired about joining.

I was forcibly impressed with religion at an early age when the preacher threw a Bible at me to get my attention as I slept through his sermon, was it the wrath of God?

She was a minister that lacked grace while dancing, but was excellent before a meal.

He said that he belonged to an orthodox church but whatever he did was somewhat unorthodox in his behavior, however he liked traditional food and he ate Burger King veggie burgers, occasionally.

He was a faith healer and he touched me for 500 dollars.

My car was dirty so I prayed for something useful, I prayed for rain.

They said he was a saint but that wasn't possible he wasn't dead yet but he had definite possibilities.

He was very religious, he smoked, drank and gambled religiously and he worshipped women, cars, and money.

I heard the Pope speak and I wondered if he was pontificating but I knew that he couldn't because Popes were humble.

He saw a cross but he couldn't tell what kind it was there was so many of them: Maltese, Celtic, Papal, Orthodox, Calvary, Latin, Greek, St. Andrews or Jerusalem actually he was crossed up and at cross purposes.

"He charged nothing for preaching and it was worth it." *(Mark Twain)*

Nathan was a substitute altar boy when the regular altar boy could not make it for mass they called on Nathan, he was an alternate.

Harry went to divinity school he didn't want to be a divinity but have the qualities of a divinity something difficult to do, but he did the next best thing he married a girl who was just too too divine.

Mary was somewhat flighty and often referred to as a ding-a-ling, a ding bat or a ding dong and she was sick and tired of being dinged. She said that ding-a-ling and ding dong didn't ring a bell with her.

Everyone congregated in front of the church they were the congregation. But a policeman came along and said, "I apologize but it's my job to follow the law and disperse congregations." But no one moved, out of desperation he pulled out 100 tickets to the policeman's ball and tried to sell them to the crowd that dispersed immediately and he still had 100 tickets left for sale.

Tom went to the priest and to ease his mind he wanted to make a confession in the confessional. The priest listened intently and when Tom was completed the priest said, "Stop wasting my time, I've got people with real problems, all you do is complain about unimportant things and don't come back until you are in dire straits, for you penance say "Amen to that."

I heard of a religious person who had an unusual way of casting out demons he used to do it on an exorcise bicycle.

Bob worked in the top of the roof of a church, he was inspired.

Two monks lived in a cloister for years but one of them began having second thoughts, he said that he was raised in the wide open spaces in Texas on a ranch and that the life of confinement was getting to him. He told the head monk that he had decided to leave because he had developed an advanced case of cloister-phobia.

When I was young a wealthy ex Polish count visiting this country said to me in excellent English, "Native Boy, could you direct me to the nearest supermarket?" I was never referred to as a 'Native Boy' wasn't that for people in Africa or on an island in the Pacific Ocean? I thought about it I grew up in New Jersey so at the time I was a native of New Jersey. I wanted to correct him but I knew that technically he was correct. I was hoping that he would not send in missionaries to save me from myself. I told (directed) him where to go and he left happy.

I saw a picture of a fakir in India lying on a bed of nails. While he appeared comfortable, I wasn't, I didn't get the point. I hope that sleeping on that bed was pointless and I hope that he was thick skinned, he must have made his own bed.

A novice newspaper reporter was assigned to visit a monastery to determine the mission of the monks. Curious she asked one of the monks, "Could you tell me something about your vow of silence?" The monk stared at her, took out a quill, ink, and parchment paper and wrote, "Are you serious, come back in about a year, I'm allowed a couple of sentences annually?"

I bought a hotdog at a religious convention. When I asked for change from a twenty dollar bill, the vendor said, "Change must come from within, my son."

A young lady made a play for an unmarried minister. She pursued him with a religious fervor.

Two men in black suits knocked on my door and asked me if I was interested in eternal life. I replied, "Who isn't, but for now I'll take a one year subscription."

"To humiliate a bishop the host brought a baboon dressed in clerical garb to a party. The bishop said, 'I did not know your Lordship had so near a relative in holy orders'." *(John Montagu Sandwich)*

"Heaven and Hell. I don't want to express an opinion, I have friends in both places." *(Mark Twain)*

A lady rushed into a church and said "Is mass out?" Reply: "No, but your hat is on crooked."

I was never very educated and knowledgeable concerning religion, but my wife got my attention when she started showing me what hell was like.

If your prayers aren't answered, the answer may be no.

Because he was more than satisfied with himself, the egotist did not ask God to make him an even better person.

The best sermons have wonderful openings and conclusions with minimal time in between.

Cod moves in mysterious ways, no wonder they are hard to catch.

One of the four wise men thought that he knew a shortcut to Bethlehem, he never made it. He was the least wisest of the wise men.

Things were really tough, I met a Mormon with only one wife.

Brigham Young could have had only one wife who owned 25 wigs.

W. C. Fields was spotted reading a Bible on his death bed. When asked why, he replied, "I'm looking for a loophole!"

My church will accept any denomination as converts, but they particularly appreciate converting one hundred dollar bills from people in a charitable mood.

Did Moses wander in the desert for forty years because he didn't want to ask for directions?

"The greatest charity is to enable the poor to earn a living." *(Talmud)*

"When I hear a man preach, I like to see him act as if he were fighting bees." *(Abraham Lincoln)*

He was not very religious, he waited for the hearse to take him to church.

A man died and got on an elevator. The elevator operator asked, "Smoking or non-smoking?"

A preacher wanted to energize his flock, he said, "Bad times are coming and there will be a weeping and gnashing of teeth." One old church member jumped up and said, "Wow, am I lucky, I have no teeth."

The last time she sang in church, 50 people got up and changed their religion.

RENTING

I had a lot of antiques, one chair was 1776. The table cost a few more dollars.

When I was single I wasn't as neat as I could be in my apartment. You could imagine my surprise when I came home only to find everything neatly rearranged. I found a note that said, "Now that's better," Bruce. I guess the burglar had pity on me.

My bathroom was so small I could only brush my teeth up and down.

By the time the landlord arrived to check on a faucet leak, our kids had learned to doggy paddle in the basement.

Are exit signs on the way out?

RESTAURANTS

Sign in restaurant window: "Eat Here and You'll Never Eat Anyplace Else Again."

Restaurant loud speaker: "Will the owner of a red convertible with yellow fenders and pink satin seat covers go to the parking lot. The parking attendant wants to see what you look like."

A restaurant was so crowded that one sticky fingered customer put the silverware into someone else's pocket by accident.

I ate at a Chinese restaurant and found my doctor's address in my fortune cookie.

I was in an upscale restaurant and I asked the waiter what he recommended. He took one good look at me and said, "You should wear a blue silk tie with your grey suit, and by the way don't eat the chicken tonight."

I went to an inexpensive restaurant and I developed a muscle pull trying to get the three foot tall pepper mill to work properly.

ROASTS

Roasts Preview

The chances of being called upon to be a master-of-ceremony (MC) is perhaps one in a million. The MC is recognized by his peers to be at the top of his craft or profession by the audience. The audience is made up of seasoned, talented, experienced and frequently well-to-do individuals who have been around the block, been there – done that people who are slightly jaded, world weary, and who are looking for something out of the ordinary in order to enjoy themselves.

The MC of a roast needs to be creative, witty, outright funny and frequently outrageous in his remarks to get and hold the attention and interest of his audience who have just finished a meal and no doubt had a few drinks. The same old, same old, worn out lines just will not cut it to do the job needed to enable the audience to leave talking among themselves about the delightful highlights of the roast. I have included a few examples that might be helpful, merely to jog your thinking if this extremely remote heady distinction ever befalls you.

General MC Introduction Discussing Honoree

It is a dubious thrill to be master of ceremonies this evening. I want to thank in advance, all of the upcoming speakers now clinging to the dais for their lukewarm and tepid pronouncements. Before we proceed I'd like to recognize his lovely or intelligent wife, Barbara. They have two great boys, one is an honor student at the local reform school, and the other one isn't.

Exactly why are we here tonight? We are here to honor this man. Can you think of anything that he's done to deserve this honor, other than outlasting his ex-contemporaries, but as long as we are here anyway let's give our honoree a brief subdued hand to make him feel welcome. Speaking about hands, I know that a lot of you would like to get your hands on him. After all, he owes everyone in the audience some money, but on the bright side, no one has lost any interest on the money because, with the possible exception of Guido, no one ever charged him any interest. Back to the topic at hand, and to make a short story long, our honoree is here to be feted. He is wearing shoes, isn't he? I can't see under the table. Speaking of under the table we all know how he made his very minimal fortune and that he needs to pay me back the ten bucks he borrowed from me last year, but enough reminiscing. Let's have a big hand, better yet, both hands for our guest of honor, XXX. Let the festivities begin.

MC – Some Recognition of Dignitaries

As I look around the room tonight I see a lot of extinguished people who honor us with their presence. By the way, if you have any presents, please leave them at the front door with Nunzio. I would like some of the questionable dignitaries to stand, if they can, for an extremely brief suppressed round of applause.

Introduce Dignitaries

It's nice to see these old friends. Frankly to be candid, in several instances we thought that you were dead. Speaking of the devil, our next speakers will warm your hearts with their somewhat incomprehensible speeches.

MC Introduction - Sample

It is a singular honor to be chosen as the master-of-ceremonies on this auspicious and less than gala event. I can't explain how it all happened. I was minding my own business, loading dice as usual, when I got this phone call saying that it was my lucky day. Evidently two guys in the pool room unanimously elected me to host these festivities. You know that the last time I got lucky I spent two years in the army. What happened to the other under qualified would-be MCs, did they leave town? They always were available for freebies of any kind . . . oh well. After what I was handed, I decided to make lemonade which brings me to our next speaker, Max Swartz, who will no doubt delight you, eventually, with his subdued eloquence. Max, did your wife say that you could be here tonight? Let's hear it for Max folks.

MC to Honoree – General Remarks

Many people wanted to attend this evening, but could not make it because of the great distance to be travelled. Even now, your close friend, Sam Horowitz, is next door in the go-go bar, but the arduous trek would be too taxing on his new pacemaker. Many of your other very close friends have written me with lame excuses which only acts as a testament to your underwhelming popularity and magnetism. A few of your acquaintances telephoned me to beg off by saying that they were making other arrangements for this evening; in one instance to attend a viewing of a friend who had a valid reason as to why he couldn't be here. I'm surprised that we have as many people here as we do so let's have our next speaker come to the podium and fabricate more of his positive exploits.

MC – Extra Introductory Remarks

As master of ceremonies I'm not here to bore you, heaven knows that many of our eminently qualified speakers will excel in that endeavor. So with that old cliché, without further ado, let me introduce our first speaker, the almost wonderful, Sam Sampson, who will mesmerize you with his oratory, fasten your seat belts. Let's hear it for Sam.

MC to Next Speaker

The next speaker is a dear and close friend, of mine. I've known him for two or perhaps, three days, not counting the hour we spent in the pool room around the corner, where he beat me out of five bucks. How about a big hand for Max Maxwell.

MC – Brief Introduction to a Typical Speaker

As master of ceremonies it is my purpose to make excuses for the earlier questionable speakers as well as to inflate the talents of our next speaker, Bob Schneider. By the way he requested me to remind you that Bob is spelled with one 'o'. Let's hear it for Bob. Is he sober?

Is this man worthy of being honored? There are many other human beings superior in every respect, where are they?

SALES

He was the number one doormat salesman but he had to quit, people started walking all over him.

They told me when I started as a door to door salesman that I would be a success if only I could get my foot in the door. After several weeks all I got was sore feet, plus a few orders, mostly - Get Out!

She wanted to buy expensive soap as a gift. The saleslady asked, "Do you want that scented?" Reply, "No I'll take it with me."

A salesman submitted his travel expenses to the company accountant who broke out laughing hysterically. The accountant asked the salesman if he wanted to publish the expense account as a science fiction novel.

The bicycle salesperson was a spokesman for racing bikes with narrow tires, which he pedals all day long. He said that he became an environmentalist when he fell off a bike, got up and began recycling.

My predecessors made a lot of money when this country broke away from England, they had developed a revolutionary new product.

I sold diet pills for a living which had no future and only a slim chance at a promotion.

I worked in a men's clothing store and I started at the bottom, I sold socks.

A businessman had a hard life, he used to wear tight shoes, the most pleasure that he had was at night when he finally took his shoes off.

In Lancaster, Pennsylvania if something is too expensive they say that the price is too 'salty'. If they can buy an item at a lower price it not only calms their minds but helps lower their blood pressure.

This guy was tough when he started out he was a fresh egg salesman, now he's just hard boiled.

I'm always here except when I'm not, in that case I'm somewhere else, probably over there. Where do you want to meet me here, there, somewhere or anywhere?

The incentive for Christmas shopping starts earlier every year. In a local store an owner put up a Christmas tree on 5 July, he said "Why wait until the last minute?"

He worked at a men's clothing shop where he sold a lot of suspenders to elderly gentleman in the afternoons and he had a few belts before lunch.

He was no salesman, his personality was so abrasive he couldn't even sell sandpaper.

He was a sponge salesman who was absorbed in his work.

I was a Fuller brush man until I had a brush with the law, then I sold encyclopedias until computers cut me out of business now I sell crystal balls to gypsies. I think I can see a future in crystal balls.

He bought a microwave and it was under warranty but when it stopped working he called the 800 number to inquire about the warranty the customer service representative said that his fears were warranted.

I got a good buy on my fire extinguisher, I got it at a fire sale.

There was a sign above the Wal-Mart customer service desk it read, 'Many Happy Returns'.

The furniture salesman wanted too much for the wooden counter so I made him a counter offer.

My insurance salesman said that he wanted me to have full coverage so for Christmas he sent me a pair of long johns.

He bought a very expensive watch on time.

She didn't belong to any union but whenever she went shopping with her friends there was a lot of shop talk.

I used to nibble at my food when I was young, when dating I nibbled at my date's ear, but dating nibbled at my pay check. Now that I'm a salesman, I can't get a nibble from a prospect.

A salesman was provided a full complement of compliments to schmooze every type of customer when he retired he returned the compliments.

I received a concession and opened up a concession stand at a mall as a concessionaire, if I didn't make concessions on prices I would have gone broke but I was used to being a broke, bloke.

The salesman said that the more I bought the more I saved, so I kept buying until I was broke, but I saved a lot of money.

Ernest the salesman told me that the watch screamed wealth but I didn't hear anything if it did scream it was subdued after all how much of a scream would a watch make even if it was ticked off?

Send in your order while supplies last. I've heard that statement over and over again. Just how big is that supply and is it possible that they can make more or did they just stop making the stuff? Did you ever get the feeling that they have unlimited supplies? I'd like to hear an advertisement saying "Don't rush in your order we have enough product to last one hundred years, we may never be able to sell it all and if you are not 100% satisfied don't send it back. It could happen."

I sold a bicycle at a yard sale and the customer said, "Can you throw in something extra?" I decided to throw in an old pair of red socks, I just didn't care and I knew that my wife didn't give a darn about it.

I went to a close out sale to get a close up view of the merchandise, but it was so busy that I couldn't get close enough and I was concerned that they may close down the sale and close up the store since it was late and they had a closed shop union. I bought a sweater at a good price which I liked because I'm close fisted. Now I'm closed lip and closed mouth about the close out sale and am looking closely for another.

Harry received a sales letter and they asked him to respond. As a respondent Harry wanted to send a response, he was responsible and it was his responsibility to be responsive. Harry told them that he didn't want any, to buy their product would be irresponsible.

I thought that I heard opportunity knocking, but when I opened the front door it was a young girl selling Girl Scout Cookies.

The car salesman swore he was honest. He said, "I have to be it's one of the conditions of my parole."

The sales lady said that the new 10 speed blender would pay for itself in no time. The customer said, "Great, send it over when it's paid for."

I went to a yard sale to look for a used vacuum cleaner, I found one and asked the owner, "Does it work?" Response: "It sucks." I bought it immediately.

A budding entrepreneur produced a product for five dollars which he sold for four dollars. The only reason that he didn't go broke immediately was that he was a lousy salesman.

I bought a five hundred dollar telescope. My wife said, "They saw you coming."

A salesman asked a lady client if he could help her. She replied, "Oh, I'm just looking." The salesman replied, "What a coincidence, I married a looker."

This store was so exclusive that when I wanted to spend $30 the salesman went outside to check the contents of the dumpster.

I was a salesman in Alaska. My boss wanted me to get used to making cold calls.

Some magazines are just loaded with advertising inserts many of which just fall out, often on the floor, or need a careful search to locate and tear out with at least one so well hidden it manages to elude me. There should be a prize for the magazine that contains the most inserts, maybe the "Stuff It" award.

SENIORS

The husband of an elderly couple, who had been married for 55 years, referred to his wife in endearing terms such as: sweetheart, dumpling, sugar, honey and darling. When questioned, the husband confided that he had forgotten her name several years ago.

As I got older burning the midnight oil meant staying up after 10 p.m.

A couple married for 50 years wanted a divorce. The judge said, "Why did you wait so long?" The husband replied, "Every year her coffee kept getting weaker and weaker." After some reflection the judge said, "I'll have to throw this case out based on insufficient grounds."

I always wanted to live a long time but on the other hand I disliked growing old.

I used to be a Boy Scout until I got hit over the head with a heavy handbag by a little old lady, who refused my helping her crossing the street.

They sold a 99 year old man a reverse mortgage he looked like a pretty good bet.

He was a senior citizen and he loved a challenge that he could sink his teeth into, unfortunately he left his teeth soaking in a container with Polident next to the bathroom sink.

He was getting older and received a rocking chair as a gift but no matter how hard he rocked he couldn't get anywhere.

I don't know why they called him 'Pop' his wife never had any children. Just because he had grey hair he was 'Pop' and I know for a fact that he had quit drinking soda in order to lose weight.

Bob was getting older but he wanted a life of adventure, he was adventurous and adventuresome but he married an adventuress so now he's too busy making money to keep her happy and his adventuring days are over but his last adventure might involve a bold undertaking.

I think young but I suppose that I'm considered chronologically old although I hate to admit it. Funny little things are happening lately, one young lady asked if she could open a door for me, a young man said, "Can I help you with those packages, mister?" While courteous I somewhat reluctantly resent it, saying to myself, I don't need any help, I'm capable. I never needed any help in fact I would help older people from time to time. The ultimate shock came in the Wal-Mart parking lot, I was loading groceries and a somewhat front toothless elderly lady pulled up in her car and said, "Are you leaving 'Pops'?" I wanted to tell her, do I look as if I'm from Boston and a member of the Boston 'Pops', but I didn't? I told her, "I'll be leaving just as soon as my rider shows up." With that she drifted off impatiently leaving me holding the bag, nice old lady at that, she could be someone's grandmother.

A reporter asked George Augustus Moore why he was so healthy at age eighty. Moore replied, "It's because I never smoked or drank or touched a girl until I was eleven years old."

My grandfather smoked for forty years. We tried to get him to quit, but he wouldn't. One day he was walking across the local highway when he was struck by a truck carrying a load of cigarettes. In the end, cigarettes did him in.

My doctor told my grandfather that he could go anytime and was my grandfather happy? He said, "Thanks Doc, I haven't gone in three days."

An old gentleman looked at a seagull flying freely in the sky and wondered, "If I were a seagull, who would I bombard first?"

An elderly woman nearly died of heat exhaustion near the beach in Miami, Florida. Fortunately an alert life guard had the good sense to unbutton her mink coat.

A lady is getting old when she orders a martini with a prune in it.

My grandma started to mumble when someone else's grandma yelled, "Bingo!"

I know a gentleman who could do the same thing at 90 as he could when he was 89.

An old man of 105 was asked how he managed to live so long, he replied, "I quit smoking last year."

A toast: May you live to be as old as your jokes.

A New Yorker visited Maine and asked an old resident, "Have you lived here all of your life?" Response: "Not yet."

One downside about retirement is that you have to drink coffee on your own time.

He was so old he was almost out of things to learn the hard way.

"The prosperity of a country can be seen simply in how it treats its old people." *(Unknown)*

He knew he was getting old. He told his grandchildren that when he was their age he had to walk all the way to the living room to change the TV channel.

You know you are getting old when you choose your cereal for the bran content.

"Your grey hair makes you look very extinguished." *(My wife)*

SHIPS

He was a sailor who drank a bottle of port during a storm, his philosophy was 'Any port in a storm.'

The sailboat was crewed by a crew, the entire crew wore crew neck sweaters and had crew cuts and they braved the cruel sea.

Someone used to say, "Well whatever floats you boat." I kept thinking what type of boat and exactly how big is the boat? To answer properly you have to know the draft of the boat which is the depth needed to float it. The next time I hear that expression I'm going to say, "Can you be a little more specific?" Besides, I don't own a boat.

A ship was foundering off the coast of Germany and the radio operator called for help, "May Day! May Day! We're sinking." No reply. Once again, "May Day! May Day! We're sinking." A German voice replied, "What are you sinking about?"

SHOW BUSINESS

I was watching a Western on television today, as is my want, and a cowboy came in from cow punching. After knocking out four steers he told the boss "I came to collect my time." The rancher handed the cow puncher a pocket watch.

He was a budding unemployed New York young actor who wanted to express himself so he shipped himself by United Parcel Service way off Broadway to the Millburn Play House in New Jersey.

The leading actor's next scene was at a lake where he was supposed to fish for bass. The New York actor had never fished before so the producer rehired the casting director to show the actor how.

She wanted to be a ballerina but she was a little too plump. Her hopes were dashed when she couldn't find a male ballet star capable of lifting her over his head because she was just too heavy.

Whenever he performed Hamlet a long line of theater goers were leaving not entering.

The actor gave a memorable performance, everyone said, "How can anyone forget a performance like that? I can't get it out of my mind."

I was watching a movie and I noticed that the female star didn't slap her boyfriend until he stopped kissing her.

I was watching television in England and I kept switching channels. I was certain that there was an English channel out there somewhere.

An actor loved himself so much that his telephone ring tone was sustained applause.

I was at Disneyland and began to wonder, where do all these workers go for a vacation?

Shakespeare's Hamlet was a tragedy especially when performed by a high school drama class.

He's an actor who comes from a long line of theater people. All of his parents, grandparents and great-grandparents were ushers.

He claims he was a method actor but no one could figure out what his method was.

I think everyone wants to be an entertainer nowadays. This guy owed me twenty dollars when I asked him for it all I got was a song and dance.

I told jokes on a ship called a superliner, actually I told one liners on a superliner.

The new comedian was quick, this was a real asset because he could outrun his audience.

The actor said that he was looking for the 'proper vehicle' so he rented a U-Haul truck.

He thought that he heard scattered applause from the audience but he was mistaken, it was an outdoor theater and the mosquitos were thick that summer.

She was very old and to celebrate her birthday they bought two birthday cakes, it took her twenty minutes to blow out all of the candles and before she did the candle light was so bright the cakes could have been used as runway lights at night to land planes in distress.

The only way that the actor could bring the house down was if he was a demolition expert as well.

An actor claimed that he would imitate turkeys, when he tried to get into show business he was rejected with the remark, "A lot of people can imitate a turkey." Rejected he flapped his arms and flew away.

He took the television channel changer down the block and pressed hard on the button, he said, "I'm not sure it works they told me that it was a remote control."

A New England fisherman wanted to supplement his income so he decided to become a part-time magician. His fishing profession crept into his magic act, during a card trick he would say, "Pick a cod, any cod."

The show had a happy ending. The audience was delighted to leave when it was over.

A magician was famous for sawing people in half. His son said that he had several half-sisters.

A magician asked a rooster to "Peck a card, peck any card."

SINGING

I sang in the fisherman's choir, they said that I had a bass voice.

She had an unusually deep voice that was nothing to brag about when she sang, maybe that is why her mother named her Mona.

As a soprano she got a lot of requests but she was determined to sing anyhow.

There was magic in her voice whenever she finished singing before a large audience as soon as she was finished the audience disappeared as if by magic.

Her singing was a moving experience twenty people headed for the exits and ten people headed for the restrooms.

I was at a variety show and I was in a hurry. I became nervous because the program indicated that the next singer was going to sing "The Stars and Stripes Forever."

He wanted to sing the refrain but he had to refrain himself.

Her voice was like a bird she didn't sing, she warbled.

I used to sing in my car when I heard a song I liked, I must have been a car tune artist.

My daughter sang a duet with our dog, it was a howling success.

Still involved with music Beethoven was decomposing in his cemetery grave.

Following her latest number she said, "And now what you've all been waiting for, my final song."

I get a lot of requests, but I sing anyhow.

SLEEP

I listen to a great radio program that's for people just going to bed or for people just getting up to go to work, I didn't know if I was included because I went to sleep two hours ago and I didn't fit into either category, I took a chance and listened.

I used to test mattresses, but I got fired for two reasons, laying down on the job and falling asleep on the job. I was just doing my job.

I had a hard time sleeping after my wife left me. She took the bed.

I was a very sound sleeper, when I awoke the next day I found a tag on my toe.

I wanted to quit work, but I said to myself, "Where else can you get this much sleep and get paid for it?"

I was so tired and what made things worse was that when I went to sleep I dreamed that I was awake.

When I was young I went days without sleep, fortunately I slept nights.

If it wasn't for my job I wouldn't get any sleep at all.

I was tired yesterday and I'm tired today which makes me officially retired.

I got a call at 2:00 a.m., when I got to the phone the caller asked, "Did I wake you?"

SMALL

How little is little, is it larger than tiny, larger than small, larger than minuscule, smaller than medium, or smaller than average. Small wonder I gave it a little thought, a very little thought.

He was a midget who was always short of breath, short sighted, short of cash, frequently short changed, short in the market, and short on luck. In short none of this deterred him because he was long on ability, and longer on talent.

He was a midget and he was feeling low, not low down just low.

I looked through my binoculars from the wrong end and everything looked smaller. I thought I was dreaming I got that far away look.

My town was so small that the dog catcher lost his job when he caught the dog.

Our town was so small you had to extend the town limits to eat a foot long hot dog.

My apartment was so small, I had very little room to complain.

SMOKING

I quit smoking, cold turkey, the day after Thanksgiving.

"Many man smoke, but Fumanchu." *(Old Chinese Proverb)*

It's not smart to smoke cigarettes in the rain, even if you don't in hail.

SPEECH

He was born with a silver spoon in his mouth, no one told him to take it out so it took him a long time to speak properly.

I'd like to introduce a man of wisdom, integrity, talent and manners but we couldn't find anyone like that, which brings us to our honoree this evening, what's his face?

Have you ever noticed that you never get a busy signal when you've dialed a wrong number? When someone I don't know answers a wrong number I'm tempted to say "Are there any messages for me?"

I found an old dictionary on a park bench. This made me happy but then again I knew that somewhere someone was at a loss for words.

Joe was mad at his neighbor and wanted to insult him thoroughly without mincing words, to cover all bases he purchased a thesaurus which helped Joe enlarge and concentrate on his vocabulary. This brought a satisfied smile to his face.

She said that she was fluent in many languages and could say yes in several languages, to prove it she said, si-si, ya ya, da da and qui qui. How could I argue with such overwhelming proof?

Someone will tell me something and then say "That goes without saying." Which gets me wondering, "Didn't I just hear him say that?"

He was fluid in three languages all of his words seem to either run together or overlap.

They say that he was a man of few words, it wasn't exactly his choice but his vocabulary was so darned limited.

A chatty neighbor developed laryngitis and I noticed a distinct improvement in the tone of his conversations.

His heated discussions were unenlightened so he kept everyone in the dark, besides his look was chilling.

He had a one-track mind and he was hard to side track, but a logical argument laced with facts could derail him.

I was an after dinner speaker because I was tongue tied at lunch.

I tiptoed through the minefield to get the explosive information that he had.

I could have been a great after dinner speaker but I didn't have the heart to disturb people who were sleeping soundly.

Prior to the speech the speaker placed his watch on the podium, things were going great until we had a temporary power failure when the lights went on, his Rolex was gone.

He was from the South and they told him that he was loquacious. He replied, "Well shut my mouth!"

My bombastic speech got me kicked out of the Ordnance Corps.

I couldn't comprehend the incomprehensible so I unscrewed the unscrutable.

I used to be garrulous but since I met you I'm at a loss for words.

I used to be ponderous in my speech but things have improved since I lost weight.

I used to be verbose until I ran out of verbs.

Do I like your speeches? I should say so I taped every one of them and whenever I can't sleep I play one and before you know it I'm out and it's time to get up, and I feel refreshed.

We missed your weekly speech but in your absence a guest speaker delivered a truly excellent speech but we're still happy to welcome you back.

Are these things black: ice, cow, eye, list, mail, sheep, smith, bottom, comedy, economy, hand, knight, magic, shirt and pudding? How black is black? Pitch black, black hole, black as coal, jet black, a witch's heart, black marked, black shirt, or black belt, black is so popular I thought I'd shed some light on it. Maybe no one likes dark humor.

Toast to a type of 'A' person: "May all your traffic lights be green, may you be first in the express checkout lane, may all bank tellers be waiting for you, may you be the only customer at Burger King, may you avoid traffic jams, may you find your keys and glasses immediately and may I end this toast."

They said that I could have more but the more I got the more I wanted, there's no end to more, need I say more?

If you hear loud snoring you know that your speech is a tad too long or uninspiring or both.

He was the ventriloquists' ventriloquist, he only threw his voice while drinking a glass of distilled water.

I'm allergic to bee stings I don't know why, we have a lot in common whenever I spoke I was accused of bumbling.

For fun my wife wrapped duct tape around my wrist to see how hard it was to get free. At that moment I got a call on my cell phone. I said, "I can't speak now I'm in a bind, actually I'm bound up at the moment."

The blacksmith spoke quite loudly he actually bellowed at his customer.

I told her that I wanted to have a couple of words with her, those words were 'Hello' – 'Goodbye'.

People often say "That boggles the mind." I never ran into a boggle so I looked it up and it means astonished or confused or baffled. How do you unboggle a mind is there a tool to wrench your memory? No one says "I'm so boggled" they say "I'm so confused." For now we are stuck with boggle.

I don't want to overdo this introduction so let me introduce last but least Joe Jones.

He was expecting to be accepted but he was dejected when rejected. He couldn't use his acceptable acceptance speech so it went without saying.

To do or not to do that is the question or is it, do be do be do?

He never stopped talking he just couldn't cut a long story short he had a talent for making a short story long.

He used to make candles for a living but he also waxed eloquent.

Back in the Revolutionary War era of the United States, a famous politician introduced a lady, Mrs. Paine, at a social function he said, "One never knows pleasure until you know Paine."

If you are not talking why do you keep saying that you are not talking. Can we talk about this?

He used to be a sheet metal worker perhaps why when he made a speech it was riveting.

I made off the cuff, off the wall, off the record, off hand, off key, off line unofficial comments, I was criticized for being off track only too often.

I used to be tongue tied but since the witch moved in next door I'm now spellbound.

I was a pro and I had a debate with a con we argued the pros and cons of the argument, but I couldn't be conned I was an old pro, professionally speaking.

I told him an amusing story but he said that he was, "Barely amused," I told a jolly joke, he said that it was semi-jolly; I followed with a humorous joke he replied that it was somewhat humorous; next came a hilarious joke and he laughed hilariously for a big finish I told him a killer joke, oops! Services will be held on Saturday at 11:00 a.m.

He spoke excellent French and he was looking for a job where he could parley his talent.

During a speech Winston used an exclamation in order to make an exclamation point.

Harry was always undecided, at best he gave an emphatic maybe. He liked maybe yes, maybe no, Harry maintained that he was not wishy-washy, shilly-shally, hit or miss or straddling the fence. He said that he was positively, definitely ambivalent and undecided. He said that he was neither hot nor cold on any topic. The local college wanted him to teach a course in assertiveness.

He said that, "I swear I don't know any curse words."

Joe said, "I don't know what to say I'm tongue tied." Joe didn't appear to have his tongue tied. Come to think of it I can't remember seeing anyone with a tongue that was tied. I knew that they tied the tongue of a race horse. I've seen them doing it and while it looks strange, horses have a long tongue which flops around when they are running and I was told that a horse's tongue may block his throat while running and affect its breathing. I began to understand that if you were somewhat hoarse you could be a little tongue tied, but that doesn't excuse all of those other people who are stretching the truth.

I used to be careless and would say things like, "Close enough for government work." But close enough was never good enough. I progressed to roughly correct but I never like roughing it. I moved on to almost correct but almost fell short. I was told, "You need to be precise." But I soon learned that to be on top I had to be exact or exactly correct this really paid off especially at the race track when I cashed in an exacta ticket.

I'd like to thank the distinguished member of the committee who presented me with this dubious award. There are a lot of people that made me what I am today. First of all I'd like to take more than a moment to thank my parents, where would I be without them? I'd like to thank my wife who was dumb enough to marry me. Then there are my neighbors, I'd like to mention them but I can't stand them. I want to give a shout out to my parole officer who has been kind enough to look the other way when I strayed. Almost finally I want to thank the village idiot who makes me look smart by comparison. Last but least I want to thank the audience who needs no thanks.

I am positive that a double negative is a no no. You should accentuate the positive and negate the negative. Sam used the word negative so often they called him negatorious a word that does not exist but reserved especially for Sam.

Tom delivered a rabble rousing speech, there just happened to be a lot of rabble around at the time. It's hard to gather a large crowd of rabble together since most of them are not professional people who are usually ruly while rabble are, by definition, noisy and unruly, as a general rule. Once the rabble were aroused and after their excitement calmed down, they dispersed and pursued their own interests which were generally uninteresting, mundane and extremely boring, after all what can you expect from rabble?

I needed to go farther but I could not go any further the further I went the farther I wanted to go. I wanted to further my education but I lacked the money to pursue it farther. Need I go any farther or is this far enough?

I work for a collection agency, I came by and came about hoping that you would come around and come across with some cash that you had recently come into. I wanted to come before but could not come down to come for and come away with what you owed until you came upon some cash, so please be forthcoming and don't let anything come between us because I don't want to come back and come to think of it my job is becoming routine collectively speaking, but I can't recollect when it's been more interesting.

Two murderers were scheduled to be executed on the same day. One wanted to give a speech before the execution. The second convict's request was to be executed first.

After that speech I feel refreshed and inspired. It's amazing what a short nap can do.

I really enjoyed the speech although I was sorry that I could not be there to witness my children growing up.

If you stand up you will be seen. If you speak up you'll be heard. If you sit down you'll be appreciated.

Our guest speaker could not be here this evening because of a conflict of interest. He did not want to come.

People could listen to his speech forever and his last speech was even longer.

I was so surprised to be nominated, I almost dropped my acceptance speech.

It's hard to exaggerate his accomplishments, but I'll do my best.

Ask me about my vow of silence.

Our next speaker will not bore you with a long speech. He can bore you with a short one.

"Please don't make a fuss over me. Treat me as you would treat any other brilliant speaker."

"Gentleman, you have been listening to that great Chinese sage, On Too Long." *(Mark Twain)*

When I want your opinion, I'll remove the duct tape.

I gave a speech about dandruff because I was asked to talk about something off the top of my head.

Thank you, after that tremendous welcome, I can hardly wait to hear what I have to say.

He sounded as if he took speech lessons from Gomer Pyle.

By the time he said, "To make a long story short," it was too late.

If it goes without saying, let it.

Someone talked me out of joining the debating team.

"It usually takes me more than three weeks to prepare a good impromptu speech." *(Mark Twain)*

His occasional flashes of silence improved the discussion and the conversation.

This organization believes in free speech. Have you ever paid a speaker?

I was told that there would be between 5 and 500 people here tonight, they were correct, 15 people falls within that range.

I gave a speech and was asked to tell everything I knew in 10 minutes, so I decided to speak slowly.

"Eloquence is essential in speech, not information." *(Mark Twain)*

SPORTS

I was watching people shooting baskets at a carnival and no one was winning a prize. Wilt Chamberlin and Michael Jordan showed up to shoot free throw shots they just missed the kewpie doll by one shot. The concession owner said, "Too bad you guys were so close, would you like to try again?"

You want to be where the action is going to be and not where it was.

What do you mean that there's something wrong with the cannon shell. It looked good when we fired it.

I can always find unimportant papers but important papers elude me when I need them most, I know they are around here somewhere.

I made a specific attempt to be ambiguous but I had a hard time explaining my position specifically.

A naked man hit the lottery, he said that he was on a lucky streak.

A basketball player thought that it was okay to bounce a check, wasn't he on the ball?

He was a jogger but he began to run around with a bad bunch of friends.

Two cowboys visited a zoo and came out with tattered clothes and scratches all over their body. One cowboy said, "I thought that lion dancing was supposed to be fun."

This is a lovely duck decoy that you've been carving. "How long have you been carving?" Reply, "Ever since I was a whittle boy."

For two weeks we searched desperately for signs of big foot or his foot prints. We were at our wits end, the TV battery was running down, the food supplies were running low, and it began to rain, so we decided to go over to Michael Jordan's house, we heard that he wore a size 18 basketball shoe, close enough.

Based on my doctor's advice I began to work out with a dumbbell, but then I thought that I could get someone who was a real dumbbell to work out with me.

He was the finest slow ball pitcher in the major leagues. The baseball took two minutes from the time it left his hand and crossed the plate. One crafty hitter turned the tables on him when he had enough time to remove a bag of potato chips, secreted in his jersey, he ate it, hit a double that scored a run.

His sailboat sank, that doesn't occur very often it just happened once.

I love fishing and all of the equipment associated with it, the lures are so beautiful and well-made that many fisherman collect them without realizing it. While I fish a lot less I got to the point that I released all of my fish because I did not want to hurt them, reduce the population, and allow the next fisherman a chance at catching the same fish. This calls to mind an old standby. I was out of bait and lures so I took a picture of a worm and put it on my hook, I caught a picture of a fish, it worked.

I heard that you wanted to lift a dumbbell, so you did a pull-up.

I wanted to prove a point and determine that if I dropped a balloon full of water and a marshmallow out of my third floor apartment which of these would strike the ground first? I couldn't finish the experiment because the guy I hit with the balloon was hot on my heels.

I was swimming underwater and I hit my head, I wanted to cry because it hurt but I said to myself, "What's the sense if I began to shed any tears, who would know?"

When I was young we played a game where I was a hostage. I sent out a message in invisible ink describing my whereabouts to my friends so my dog got the message out but none of my friends could see the message it was a blank piece of paper. I was a hostage for a week and if it wasn't for my peanut butter snacks I would have starved to death.

One summer two corn chips were carrying on a conversation by the side of a pool when one suggested, "How about going in for a quick dip?"

She said that she liked sports but she concentrated on fishing – fishing for compliments.

My hearing was so good that I could hear a pin drop everywhere except when I went bowling late at night.

I wanted a pair of running shoes and I was shocked at how much they cost as much as several hundred dollars. How much does it cost to make running shoes overseas? Someone's running off with the money and I'm not getting a run for mine.

A karate expert told me that he had a black belt in dancing.

The gun control laws are getting out of hand, let's hope they don't outlaw shotgun weddings next.

A father told his wife that he would take his five year old daughter to the zoo. When they returned that evening the mother queried the daughter, "How was the zoo?" Reply: "I liked it Mom, and Daddy was really happy when a horse paid ten to one."

He had to quit bowling his mind was always in the gutter.

When I went to the pool the lifeguard told me I was going off the deep end.

A bum wanted to make a name for himself, he had spent so much time in the gutter bowling was in his future.

I was unfit to be an exercise instructor.

He did not like anything related to exercise. His doctor said that he needed to exercise so he devised a strenuous workout as follows: go downhill, beat around the bush, push the envelope, crack a smile, jump to a conclusion, and poke around, that should do it.

Swimming pool announcement: "Will the lady who lost her bathing suit please come out of the water, we've found it."

I was lost while hunting and I finally found an old farmhouse and knocked on the door. I asked the elderly lady where I was? She said, "You are right here young man."

He was an honest chess player but was he surprised when his bishop got rooked.

He was a fierce competitor he almost drown bobbing for apples.

If you shake a leg and stretch your legs you can get a leg up. If you have a good idea that has legs you can get a leg up and if your idea fails you don't have a leg to stand on you may be on your last legs unless you start out on the right foot.

I came to the mouth of the brook, now I know why they call it a babbling brook.

He was a true pool player whenever he was faced with a dilemma he wracked his brains.

There was a discussion about soccer but they couldn't come to a conclusion they wanted to kick it around some more before they reached their goals.

I can row canoe?

He was an outfielder but he made a mistake when he tried to catch a bus.

I did an exhaustive study on exercise and for some reason I felt tired when it was over.

He used to practice marksmanship at a gun range but he wasn't suited for it, every time he fired a pistol his mind went blank and his eyes were blank, one good shot followed by two blanks.

I was a New York Yankees' fan and I went to a baseball game down South. I don't know how they knew that I liked New York but they said, "Drop dead Yankee."

She was a dashing figure which was apparent when she ran on the track team.

Since I went first I got the jump on the ski jump and when I won all the skiers jumped me.

He used to be a roller derby star but it had a negative effect on his work habits, he just wanted to skate through life, he just couldn't get serious.

He played for Washington, he was an old baseball player who was washed up and washed out on the same day, and hung out to dry.

He was a boxer who was losing badly and his corner wanted to throw in the towel but they were short of towels, especially a clean one, it was a dirty fight.

A midget got into a fight with a basketball player and kept kicking the player in the shins the basketball player had to stoop to conquer.

He used to time track races for years but had to quit when his expensive stop watch stopped, he just ran out of time.

They told the tennis player that he had an easy job or that he had a racket, he said that he didn't want to make a racquet about it.

I bought an outboard motor I hadn't planned on using it indoors.

I used to be a waiter at a restaurant and then one day a large basketball player came in so I had a tall order on my hands.

He was a boxer with very few victories he went into a revolving door and lasted only three rounds.

He was really fast he outran his shadow but at night sometimes his shadow beat him depending on where the light was coming from unless there was no light which delighted him because things were even.

He got into a row on the rowing team, they accused him of being rowdy.

The knights carried him to his grave on his shield. He was short and his shield was large but not big enough to save him from that cannon ball, but he was warned everyone said, "Duck."

He was very slow. How slow was he? He was so slow that while in South America he lost a race to a sloth he lost by a full minute.

He was a punter for the New York football Giants and every day that he practiced he got a kick out of his work.

He was a professional basketball player who decided to retire. His farewell speech he summed up his feelings when he said, "That's the way the ball bounces."

He was a fisherman which came in handy when he joined the debating team.

He was a pitcher during the season and a bartender off season. Whenever he pitched he uncorked a fastball at least ten times per inning.

He was a failure as a soccer player they said that he had nothing on the ball.

He was a body builder and entered contests and loved to pose, whenever he had to pose he did it automatically, it was a reflex action.

Al Kaline was a great baseball player whose name was condensed as Alkaline but his great personality neutralized any acid comments.

Mary was a fisherman's girlfriend, he liked her because she was alluring.

Mohammad Ali had a cat he said that it was an Ali cat.

When the New York Yankees lost the great Mickey Mantle they were dismantled.

Bob went to a baseball game, got hungry and wanted to eat a hot dog. When he found out about the price he commented that he could buy an entire pack of hot dogs at the supermarket for less. With this knowledge his appetite was curbed and he remarked "I don't want to pay for the ball player's million dollar salary out of my chump change pay." Bob said that at the next ball game he's going to make and take two peanut butter sandwiches and a pack of Twinkies.

I always wanted to be at the front of the line. As luck would have it whenever I went to say, Wal-Mart or the supermarket I was at the end of the line. To complicate matters friends would ask "Are you being up front with us?" I'd reply, "How can I be, I'm not used to being up front I'm always at the end of the line." To get away from it all I decided to change my luck so I went fishing at a beautiful lake, but after 10 minutes it dawned on me. I said, "Hey! I'm at the end of the line, again."

Two knights in shining armor were looking around scheduled for a jousting tournament later that afternoon. It was a cold day and the court jester, as a part of his job description, came out to warm up the crowd. After handing out blankets he proceeded to tell several inane king, queen and country, jokes and a smattering of dungeon jokes that everyone had heard before, because the jester wrote his own material. None of the jokes worked, it was a tough crowd, they were all low class and acted like a bunch of peasants, what else? Turning to the knights the jester told the old 'knight on a dog like this' joke that the knights, as a hazard of their profession, had heard often before. One knight said, "Gadzooks Jester, jousting is a serious business and nothing to jest about – to horse!" The jester said, "As soon as I get my bag of tricks I'll be with you in jest a minute."

The moderator asked the yoga instructor, "What's your position?" The yoga instructor said, "Well I have a lot of positions so I'm not too bent out of shape with any of them. I don't want to stretch the truth and jump to a conclusion. Then again I may change my position if I'm inclined to do so as necessary. That's my position until and unless I change my position is that answer OK, you know, I'm flexible?"

He was a Russian basketball player his first name was Rimsky, he was really good at foul shots.

A blowhard was bragging about how strong he was. I can lift and press 300 pounds and curl 150 pounds. A bystander spit on the ground and said, "Can you pick that up Sampson?"

A fisherman dreamed that he was on a lake in a large motor boat with a gorgeous voluptuous young lady. "How did he make out?" Answer, "Great he caught a six pound bass."

He met her during a 10K race, eventually they ran off together.

They held the first international marathon race in China, but problems started to surface. After about 20 miles many of the runners started to hit the wall.

I wanted to be a runner in high school, but couldn't decide whether to be a sprinter or a cross-country runner. As my endurance improved it helped me in the long run.

I feel sorry for some college football players. They can run, jump, kick and tackle, but they can't pass.

I watched the Boston Marathon and two runners approached the finish line; one runner was dressed as a chicken and the second wore an egg costume. I said, "This could get interesting? Will I finally have the answer?"

The little league coach told the player to stay on third, but his mother wanted him to come home immediately.

When I want to see a baseball game in the worst way, I take my wife.

The economy had taken a dip, many chief executive officers could only afford to play miniature golf.

There's a new sport, I spent an hour watching two silk worms racing. Too bad they ended in a tie, eventually.

I was accused of not pulling my weight, no wonder they let me go from the tug-of-war team.

I bought aftershave that smelled like chlorine, at work everyone thought that I had a swimming pool.

I caught a fish in Texas that was so small, it only took three men to throw it back into the lake.

The sports fan was an intellectual giant and you know how the Giants are doing lately.

I actually ran for my high school, I did not plan it that way, but I was late and the bus kept continually eluding me.

"Your parents raised a few dumbbells, were they weightlifters?"

Water floats my boat.

I'm a jogger and I overslept, now I'm running late.

I got over my fear of high hurdles.

I could kick myself for not taking karate lessons when I was young.

If we are already here, why is it we sing "Take Me Out To The Ball Game?"

My friend was the punter on our high school football team. I met him recently at the 50th class reunion and asked him how he was doing. He replied, "Oh, I can't kick."

STAMP COLLECTOR JOKE:
A stamp collector asked a lovely lady if she would like to see his stamp collection. She replied, "Philately will get you nowhere."

COIN COLLECTOR JOKE:
Someone asked a coin collector how he felt. The collector replied, "I used to be very good, but now I'm extra fine."

STOCKS

I was making money in the stock market until I ran into something called a stock market bubble which popped and the market collapsed so quickly that I ended up taking a bubble bath.

He was a broker and the longer I dealt with him the broker I got, he was one of those go for brokers.

He wanted to take a plunge in the stock market to get his feet wet instead he took a bath.

He was a retired paratrooper who owned a lot of stocks, when things began to look shaky he bailed out.

I bought some shares in a large company I felt comfortable about it because I was experienced, I used to be a stock boy in a grocery store.

He said that he was a stockbroker and I believed him but whenever I bought stock through him I ended up broker.

I just switched brokers today from stock to pawn.

Good news in the stock market today, my stock split, unfortunately so did my broker.

My uncle always told me that he had a seat on the curb, for years I thought that he was a big shot in the stock market.

My broker and I set up an all-encompassing program designed to meet certain investment goals over the next five years – with luck I'll get even again.

The latest dope on Wall Street is my brother-in-law. He bought shares in a meatball mine.

After the recent stock market debacle, how do you call your broker? "Hey cabbie!"

TIME

I have an alarm clock that tells jokes, it's laughable but the jokes are timely.

My watch runs only four hours a day, if it was in a strong union it wouldn't be part time. It would work at least eight hours a day.

It's hard to believe that at one time there was no lacrosse, soccer, television, credit cards, jogging shoes, roller blades, computers and its games, 10 speed bicycles, a tablet was aspirin, dope, pizzas, cell phones etc. How did we survive and were not bored? If you live long enough you'll make a future generation laugh and say "How old fashion, Pops?"

TRAVEL

I could never be a conductor on a railroad. While I had a one track mind I found that I was easily sidetracked, and everyone wants to punch my ticket.

As soon as I got off of the Orient Express I became disoriented.

I planned on taking a vacation. My travel agent asked, "Anywhere in particular?" I said, "Yes, but I want to get a round trip ticket and make sure that I come right back here."

I was nervous when I saw our airline pilot buying flight insurance.

Hotel Rule: Shine your shoes with a towel stolen from some other hotel.

I was lost and then I remembered, when lost follow the North Star, but no matter how long I looked at it, it I didn't go anywhere.

The main highway had a detour sign which disturbed me but as I kept traveling I noticed that the scenery on either side of the detour road was much nicer and much more interesting, I may take that road again.

He wanted to be an adventurer but he didn't like venturing too far.

On his vacation he saw all the scenery that he wanted to see but the area was so scenic that he couldn't avoid it. He saw so much scenery he said that it was obscene, he left the scene by the scenic railroad.

I have no sense of direction I thought I was headed south down the highway but I was actually headed east. The sun comes up in the east and sets in the west, but around noon its overhead and I can't tell which way to go. One of these years I'll get a GPS device that will tell me where to get off.

He was from Europe and visiting New York City and did not understand the English language very well when he asked for directions someone told him not to take abuse so instead he went by cab.

I looked into every nook and cranny I found several nooks but no crannies, what do they look like? A cranny was a small narrow crack, a hole or opening in a wall or a rock, who knew? After a careful search not a cranny in sight, anyway I tried to follow the dopey instructions.

He wanted to go thither and yon, he had heard about thither and yon but he didn't know where they were so he looked it up, thither is 'in the direction of that place' and yon is 'yonder or over there' so I went in the direction of that place over there so wherever I went was fine with me.

I was lost in a desert in Israel and was rescued by a big dog carrying a keg of seltzer.

My future wife loved to travel. She liked me particularly since I worked at a travel agency. Now that we're married I'm beginning to suspect she may have thought that I represented her last resort.

The quickest way to get a traffic light to turn from red to green is to search for something in the glove compartment.

I got lucky on my trip, the highway was open while the detour was being repaired.

I wasn't going anywhere so I decided to quit my job at the travel agency.

VAMPIRES

A vampire quit the acting profession. He could never find a part that he could sink his teeth into.

He used to be a vampire who got a job in a band while waiting for the next act to come on he really enjoyed it because the band had to vamp which was second nature to him.

WAITERS

On Menu: Special Today – No Desert.

The diner apologized profusely to the miffed waiter who had overheard a piece of the dinner conversation. The diner explained that he had said that his house was equipped with a dumbwaiter which was no reflection on him.

I asked the waiter if there was pig's feet on the menu. He said we don't let pigs walk on the menu.

I asked the waiter what did he recommend? He said, "I'm partial to licorice candy but it's not on the menu."

I complained to my waiter that my coffee was cold. He said, "That's understandable it came all the way from Columbia."

A snooty waiter saw a farmer who wore his napkin as a bib, he asked the farmer if he needed a haircut?

"Waiter, what's this fly doing in my soup?" Waiter: "How about that, not again, I guess we'll have to call the exterminator for the fourth time, at least he got rid of most of the spiders and other critters."

I just refused to take orders from anyone. Maybe that is why I lost my job as a waiter.

I was looking forward to a job at the restaurant, I just couldn't wait.

WEALTH

When I was wealthy I was intoxicated, since I went broke I was just drunk.

I began to cogitate an incogitable problem which left me in a six foot deep quandary.

He wore a black tuxedo with white socks or a pair of sneakers with a suit and a tee shirt with a tie, he was either filthy rich or he had no sense of style.

He made a fortune making submarine sandwiches he had a sign in the store window: 'Our Sandwiches are the Sub-standard.'

Tex used to be called an old coot but since they found oil on his small ranch and he became wealthy they now call him an old codger, if he keeps getting any richer he'd be called Tex the eccentric old millionaire.

WEATHER

I turned on a Spanish speaking TV station and they had a Mexican weather forecast "Chili today and hot tamale."

In Alaska a suspect was held by the police for questioning. The policeman said, "Where were you on the night of April to September?"

I was going to write a joke about snow but I don't think snow is something to joke about, do you get my drift?

How could I get his drift, I didn't know that he was drifting?

If a tornado dated a waterspout and they became serious would it be the result of a whirlwind romance?

He was a weatherman, his job was a breeze but when he was wrong he got a chilly reception.

I was so happy that my head was in the clouds but on second thought it was early in the morning and the fog had just rolled in.

He didn't realize how cold he was because when he looked at the thermometer it was in Celsius so he wasn't sure just how cold he was, he would have known if it was in Fahrenheit, he would have known the degree for certain.

She was a queen and they dubbed her the 'Goddess of Rain' but her reign was short lived.

A global cooling group debated a global warming group, the global warming group argument was hot and heavy but the global cooling group told them to chill out.

I couldn't find my ice scraper so I tried to scrape the ice off my windshield with my discount credit card. No matter how hard I tried I couldn't get more than ten percent off.

It was so hot that my date started fanning herself with a marriage certificate which was effective, because it put a chill in me.

I took my car out in the rainstorm, the weather man said that it was a driving rain.

The snow was so deep that muggers in Central Park were wearing snow shoes.

It was raining so hard for so long, that I saw a sparrow putting sandbags around his nest.

The air in Los Angeles is so bad that people were coughing outside of church.

WITCHES

He was a cowboy who complained to the witch saying, "I haven't seen you in a long spell."

A witch was a failure when she wanted to place a curse on someone all she got was a dizzy spell.

A witch became a famous mystery novelist all of her novels were spellbinding.

She wanted to become a witch but she had no talent for it, she even had trouble spelling in the English class at high school.

A witch had a price list, it was 20 dollars for a long spell and five dollars for quickies.

A witch wanted to give a man a hex but she picked the wrong man. He was a mechanic and he already had a set of hex head wrenches.

She was a witch but had to quit she was getting too many dizzy spells.

The witch wanted to put a curse on me but I swore right back.

WIVES

I wanted to change television channels but I couldn't find the remote my wife had put it into a remote location, it took me an hour to locate it.

They called him a stuffed shirt but he wasn't the problem, his wife always bought him shirts one size too small.

When he was single he led a colorful life, he had been green with envy, golden with wealth, red with embarrassment, yellow with fear, brown from the sun and often in the pink. Now that he's married his wife told him that everything was black and white.

In Australia he was a Mormon with ten wives when they divorced him he was decimated.

She was a part time ballerina when she was in the kitchen at home when she was 'en pointe' it came in handy to reach items on the top shelf.

My wife's name was Violet and as she got older she got a little shorter, she must have been one of those shrinking violets.

His wife was as pretty as she was when they were married, but he had very questionable taste when it came to beauty.

Ponce de Leon's wife said, "You went to Florida without me?"

His wife was a little tipsy and said, "Tonight you can do whatever you want." He sent her home to her mother.

I sold my twenty volumes of the encyclopedia, since my wife knew everything I didn't need them anymore.

I dressed my wife completely in leather and checked her in as airport luggage, and I never heard from her again.

Housework never bothered my wife, she did so little of it.

A husband asks his wife what she wants for her birthday. She said, "Oh, just something with diamonds in it." So he bought her a deck of cards.

Was my wife a bad cook? My cat had only four lives left and she cured the dog from begging at the table.

WOMEN

I told a funny joke to a seamstress, she was in stitches for quite a while.

My wife called her girlfriend and they were on the telephone for three hours. Each of them wanted to have the last word, perhaps they should take turns and have more free time during the day.

I wouldn't say that his wife was unattractive but he took her picture out of his wallet and replaced it with the picture that was in the wallet when he bought it.

Figures proved that some women spend a lot of time sitting instead of walking.

"Women are meant to be loved, not be understood." *(Oscar Wilde)*

"As long as a woman can look 10 years younger than her own daughter, she is perfectly happy." *(Oscar Wilde)*

His wife said she wanted a pair of satin underwear but her husband insisted that she purchase a pair that no one had ever used or sat in before

A spinster said that she had a dog that barked, a parrot that talked back to her, a fish that drinks, a turtle that's slow and a cat who comes home early in the morning, all the qualities of a husband.

She was part Indian and loved dancing but one very cold night she wanted to come home to a place where she could keep her wig wam.

She purchased a new pair of shoes, she said that these shoes were meant for walking.

She was drop dead gorgeous, strikingly beautiful, perfectly lovely, pleasantly attractive, uncommonly lovely, handsomely beautiful, ravishingly beautiful, stunningly beautiful, and breathtakingly beautiful and her sister didn't look too bad either she was awful pretty.

When she got out of bed she ran her fingers through her hair, for the rest of the day her hair never looked better.

While leaving the theater I walked behind a beautiful young lady when it dawned on me that I hadn't eaten jello in a very long time.

I was surprised to find out that my blind date was six months pregnant. Undiplomatically, I said, "What have you been doing lately? It may have been better if your ex-boyfriend had knocked you down instead of up."

She was only a moonshiner's daughter, but I loved her still.

She had a sunny disposition, but a shady past.

She was so well endowed, I could not step on her toes while we were dancing.

She wanted to play the accordion, but her arms were too short.

I walked down the street chewing gum, listening to music on my head phones and looking at all of the lovely ladies. I was multi-tasking at last.

The new French perfume was so provocative for men, it came with a brief self-defense booklet when you purchased a bottle.

WORK

I had so much work experience I was overqualified for retirement.

We were so busy at work every day that it was almost a scene of organized bedlam and chaos. Then one day we weren't busy and we didn't know how to handle normalcy, we just sat around looking at each other.

I used to work for a tire company but I was always tired. I woke up tired, I was tired all day and went to bed tired. Soon after I was fired I stopped being tired.

"Better do a little well, than a great deal badly." *(Socrates)*

I thought that my boss didn't have a sense of humor but I changed my mind when I asked him for a raise. He hasn't stopped laughing.

My boss wanted to pay me 500 dollars a week, I told him that I was worth much more because of my college degree and intellectual ability, I insisted on 2000 dollars every four weeks, he agreed.

A Texan was visiting Niagara Falls and bragged that his plumber in Texas could fix the overflow.

On my new job I was going gangbusters when the union shop steward approached me and hinted that I slow down because I was making everyone look bad. When I realized the error of my ways I slowed down and fit right in with the more experienced workers.

When my boss gave me a pink slip I told him that I didn't go that way and that I was happily married.

New employee's welcome to a new company: "We interviewed a lot of great candidates but we decided on you."

I thought that I had supervisory potential so my boss said that I could be in charge of all the mops, I was certain that I could clean up and be rich.

I saved a lot of time when I arrived late earlier than expected.

He was an airplane pilot that was a part time detective, both jobs complemented each other because as a detective he felt comfortable in disguise.

He was a plumber with a hobby of herpetology, these two pursuits fit perfectly since he used a snake to clean out clogged pipes.

Five little people in New York City roughed up someone making fun of their size. Is it possible the little people were actually elves who had been laid off by Santa Claus during the slack season. He let go elves with anti-social tendencies. Can we all just get along, that's the long and short of it.

I was in a dead end job, I wasn't getting anywhere and then it dawned on me, maybe I could get a job at a travel agency.

A man who made a living making and repairing watches and clocks walked into a doctor's office and said, "Tell me the truth doctor, how much time do I have?"

He made small ladies watches I guess he'll never make the big time.

He was so honest that he had to quit his job as an oil deliveryman, he never liked fueling anyone.

As a part time job I used to bag groceries at the local supermarket when I was in high school. Things were going along great until the day I got sacked.

I went to the company Halloween party dressed as a gopher, but I think that I made a mistake, my boss sent me out for more sandwiches and beer.

I was installing rugs for a living but things got sticky when one day my boss called me out on the carpet.

I had a low profile at work and my productivity was marginal but on the bright side when I took a week off no one missed me.

If I had any sense I wouldn't work in a perfume factory.

I used to work as a longshoreman but they kept docking my wages for union dues.

I got cut from the workforce at the scissor factory.

I broke a lot of cups at the china factory and my boss gave me a raise so that I could pay for the broken cups.

Jobs were tight, I took a pay cut, I cut my finger on my pay check.

I finally learned how to make fewer mistakes on the job, now I come in an hour late and leave an hour early.

I used to have a job as a night watchman but it was so dark there was very little to watch as far as I could see, but I did wear a watch with luminous hands that glowed in the dark so I never left work late.

A watchmaker and a gentleman who repaired clocks met and talked about business. It was a timely discussion.

I did not like the working conditions, I told my boss that the hours were too long. My boss straightened me out he said each hour still has only 60 minutes.

My boss did not believe in pay raises he kept saying we are just one big happy family, but I had to move into a cheaper apartment to make ends meet. If things get any worse I may end up living in a closet. It did not pay to be too happy.

He rarely made a mistake and he often bragged about it but that was very easy since no one ever saw him doing any real work.

I rarely do anything right the first time that would be too easy, if at first you don't succeed keep eating watermelon.

When did they stop building arks, it was good enough for Noah. I don't remember anyone building another one except in a movie, I guess it's time to barge on.

When I'm on the telephone I'm on hold and the music is busy, why don't they put the music on hold and get busy themselves.

He started working for the post office and it did not take him too long to be enveloped in his work.

He thought that he was a big shot at work. He was right after his boss fired him.

At work sometimes time went by so slowly, agonizingly slowly. If it went by any slower time would stand still. When I got home that evening in no time it was time for bed.

We were really hectic and chaotic at work, when we tried to straighten it out productivity tailed off.

I was assigned light duty but I was completely in the dark and wanted someone to shed some light so that there wasn't a shadow of a doubt about light duty duties.

Your applicant will have future potential forever.

I used to make pottery and put the mold into the kiln when the boss said that I was fired, that made me happy.

I had an inexhaustible supply of energy until I missed three utility payments.

I wanted to be a truck driver until I got railroaded.

I worked at Lipton's, it was a tea-riffic job.

I'm from England when I worked at Starbucks I found out that it wasn't my cup of tea.

He performs a lot of good deeds but right now we don't need good deeds we need output.

If you think something is impossible never criticize someone who is actually doing the impossible right before your eyes.

I can handle any job, I have no qualifications.

He used to lay carpet for a living but he had to quit after a week he found out that he wasn't that rugged.

Just because he scored low on his IQ test doesn't disqualify him for menial tasks.

If you are in a shop area and you want to look important carry a clipboard with a yellow legal pad on it, three ballpoint pens in your shirt pocket, a sharpie permanent marker and a stopwatch, you will get everyone wondering who you are.

I was a good plumber but I had to quit the job it was too draining.

I told her not to wear a bathing suit in the secretarial pool.

He excels when working alone, he used to be a bartender but he didn't mix well.

An electrician wanted to settle down and he married a girl who was a live wire.

I would jump at the chance to be a paratrooper.

He was a jewelry designer but he became jaded with his work.

He was a big gun at the Winchester rifle company until the day he got fired.

I worked in a laundry but all of the shirts were irrepressible.

When I was young I used to take lunch to my father. My father worked at a factory where they had a giant furnace that made molten metal which was poured red hot into a sand mold to make grates and other storm sewer parts; I recognized these storm sewer grates wherever I went. I always thought that my father had a great job.

He used to be a contortionist but had to quit he became too inflexible.

He was a criminal who had worked as a sponge diver near Tampa, Florida after three years of good behavior his criminal record was ex-sponged.

The farmer was not suited for farm work he was too industrious.

He was inducted into the sheet metal hall of fame.

His job as a chef was so easy they used to call him gravy.

He was a mortician, he had to make many grave decisions.

He was a bouncer at a bar, but everything he touched bounced, he bounced out of bed, bounced a basketball and bounced ideas but things went from bad to worse when his check bounced and he was bounced out of his job as a credit risk. Now he's on the rebound.

I was busy as a bee until my boss told me to buzz off.

My mechanic was Manuel, he read the manual for car repairs and he worked part time as a manual laborer for extra cash.

When I was a child I was handy with either hand, when I got a job and was paid I became ambidextrous.

I used to work at a hardware store and I bolted my lunch. When I left early I made a bolt for the door until my boss fired me unexpectedly like a bolt from the blue.

I used to sell rope until I became too entwined in my work.

She was destined to be an archeologist she spent forever digging through her old clothes.

As a child I liked to dig holes in dirt all over our back yard now that I'm an archeologist I don't dig any more, I excavate.

He was doing great as a dozer operator but one day he dozed off.

I asked the secretary if she could do filing, she said that her nails are always neatly filed.

I went to flight school so that whenever there was a crisis I knew how to leave in a hurry.

He was a plumber playing poker in Las Vegas, when he was dealt five hearts he felt flushed.

He got a job in flood control he was soon inundated with work.

He was a childlike architect he built his house entirely out of Lincoln logs.

He said that he used to be a big man in the market now he is the top dog at a flea market.

He was a level headed carpenter who was frequently inclined to lose his level.

I hired a brute I had a job that required brute strength.

He didn't like to work a lot so he got a job as a census taker so he only worked once every ten years.

He worked full time to get a job but in no time he landed a part time position, now he is working overtime to get a full time job.

His decision as a seismologist could not be faulted.

He was the key person at the key factory and the key to his success was to surround himself with key people who had a lock on the future.

He said that he was a stunt man but his friends were getting tired of his stunts.

He had been in so many dives that he became a submariner.

She got a job in a furniture refinishing plant and removed old varnish from the wood she was classified as a 'stripper' which was somewhat embarrassing since she was a regular church goer.

He was a civil engineer with a strange attitude he said "I am the king of all that I survey."

I went to a tailor for a fitting for a suit, he kept arguing with me about the color, the fit and the style, it wasn't that I disliked him but he just didn't suit me.

He worked in a bakery and he used to mix cake batter and stirred it with a wooden spoon to make it smooth and free flowing but after a couple of months he said that he couldn't take it any longer he was going stir crazy.

I cut down three trees that were too close to my house in my back yard but I could not figure out how to remove what was left, I was stumped.

They claim that he was a born ballet dancer he was strong good looking and always on his toes wherever he went.

He was a strapping young man, strapped for cash and he couldn't afford a car so he became a strap hanger until he became a success.

When I had a regular job I used to be paid, now that I'm at the top of the heap I get compensated, and as a lawyer when I win a personal injury case I even shared in compensatory damages as part of my compensation, how lovely?

He worked on the police force as a plainclothes man but he was unsuited for his job because he couldn't afford fancy clothes.

He was a coal miner who went to work in a coal mine every day but he complained that the EPA was hounding him, they claimed that he had a carbon foot print.

The husband and wife were trapeze artists in the circus, whenever he went shopping he told his wife, "I'll catch you later."

He wanted to be a teen age idol, he had a lot of experience because he was already used to being idle.

He was a career truck driver and he was in it for the long haul.

He was an exterminator and he never just left a job, when he was finished he bugged out.

He worked at the city dump unfortunately he had to listen to a lot of trash talk.

The new female employee was beautiful and her boss noticed that she was really on her toes, he was unaware that she was once a ballet dancer.

He worked at a factory that made cushions, he had a really cushy job.

I just couldn't concentrate about concentrating until I began to focus and the harder I concentrated the more unfocused I became and I lost my concentration I finally got a job in an orange juice plant and now I can concentrate orange juice.

I was a woodworker and made wooden counters the better I got the more counterproductive I was.

He worked at a bean factory all his friends asked him the same tired question, "How have you bean?" His standard reply was "Bean doing fine."

He worked at an aviary until he craned his neck.

He was a plumber he was told to sink or swim, in a kitchen he chose to sink, at the beach he chose to swim.

He was flippant about being serious he needed to take things more seriously in all seriousness he just wasn't serious minded all joking aside.

She was a seamstress she had a lot of stress and things were never as they seamed.

I had a skill and I got a job but I was told that it was an occupation; I got a telephone and soon it was a calling I made so much money it became a profession, now what?

He worked for the IRS whenever he got paid he looked at the money as revenue.

He belonged to a rock group but they never found any gemstones.

He was the king's plumber he repaired all of the plumbing, his work was so good that he always got a royal flush.

He used to sell rubber bands wholesale for a living, he wanted to be a physical therapist but his past caught up with him because on his first job with a lovely lady he started to rubber the wrong way.

I wanted to play it safe so I became a locksmith now every morning I get cracking.

He was a salesman who was a schmo and a schlemiel who used to schlep around selling shoes but he wasn't a schnorrer because he was good at schmoozing women so he was the top shoe salesman and well qualified for his job and he was not a schnook.

He worked in an open shop in the summer they left all of the windows open.

When I was a novice I knew very little, when I was an apprentice I started to learn, when I was a journeyman craftsman I knew my craft as a master craftsman I was even more crafty. Now that I know it all, I'm retired.

He was an electrician who said that he was overloaded with work and he felt increased resistance to it.

The trash man was always polite when he met a young lady he introduced himself by saying, "Hello, my name is Tom and I'm at your disposal."

He used to work in a factory that made sponges and he was absorbed in his work.

He worked at a plant that made many varieties of sandpaper but after about a year he had to quit because his wife told him that he was developing an abrasive personality.

Even though I carried a crowbar I didn't mean to pry.

He told the boss that he wanted a raise so the boss grabbed him around the waist and lifted him up six inches off the ground.

He worked in a clock factory he was never late he was always on the time but at work he had time on his hands.

He had an easy job, just to break the monotony every once in a while he took a work break.

He worked at a shirt factory for years he knew when to hold them and when to fold them.

The 911 operator was not suited for his job, when he answered a call he said, "What's your problem, turkey?"

They told me not to quit my day job, boy was I lucky I worked on the night shift.

My boss told me that his door was always open, big deal he never had a door so I could walk right in but I couldn't argue with him – he was right.

See you in a fortnight, now it's week by week, any day now, back in an hour, see you in a minute, just wait a second, yes! What can I do for you?

Everyone complains that they are overworked and underpaid while everyone wants to be overpaid and underworked, but all work and no pay that makes you the business owner.

Since I worked on a platform I brought a pair of platform shoes that was a step up.

He worked covering walls with plaster and plaster board but his wife told him to quit because he always came home plastered.

A plumber went to a city swimming pool on his day off and he went on the diving board but he was not much of a diver he was more of a plunger.

A plumber specialized in flooded basements he was the top plumber in the state, to cope with his specialty he even took snorkel lessons.

Santa was fat and jolly he was an all around good fellow all around.

He was very industrious he used to work with leather and he always gave it his awl.

He was avalanched with paperwork but he could handle it, he used to be a professional skier.

Phil wanted to drill post holes in his back yard but things didn't auger well for him.

He was a baker who liked to tell jokes but everyone said that his jokes were half-baked.

He used to be a basketball player but his basketball days were over but he was happy at his present job as a bouncer.

He couldn't focus when he worked he was careless, when asked why he wasn't accurate he said that he could care less.

Sheila worked in a factory that made woolen sweaters, their workers were a close knit group.

Pete worked in a ladder factory but his boss told him that in order to advance he should take an extension course in the evening.

Carl worked at a muffler shop where he worked very hard, every evening he went home exhausted. He complained to his wife that his work, by definition, was exhausting, his wife gave him a muffled reply, she said that her throat was tired.

Lee used to press clothes in a Chinese laundry but he was always held in high esteem.

Sidney worked for a large corporation and started out at the bottom delivering mail throughout the building, he got several raises but he wanted a more elevated position. To satisfy Sidney his boss gave him a job on the tenth floor and that made him happy.

Paul was a professional double dipper, he liked double dip ice cream, he liked double dip dancing, Paul was a double dipper at his job after he retired, and he even double dipped donuts. Paul was known as 'The Big Dipper' he was an astronomer.

A business owner needed to hire a stenographer so he hired a lovely lady midget he figured that she would be excellent at shorthand.

Ever since he was a little boy Tony wanted to be a carpenter, because he like working with wood, Tony didn't look like a carpenter and he had a lot of fun by asking people to guess his job. No one could guess his occupation except one old gentleman who nailed it.

Ray was short on intelligence so he worked in counter intelligence but it didn't pan out because he couldn't make intelligent decisions, his intuitive decisions were counter intuitive, now Ray works at a delicatessen, job description: counterman.

He was a gambler and a plumber, he was an excellent plumber but as a gambler he was a plunger which was also a plumbing tool with which he was very familiar.

He was a commercial fisherman who was enmeshed in his work, he considered his income as net profits, but he often worked for scale. Birds circling his boat made him fell gullible, most of his income came from a floundering business and all the hard work gave him even larger mussels. He used to brag but now he was clammed up, and he was once very generous but now he's shellfishly self centered. Now he's a charter member of a company with a fleet of charter boats fishing just for the halibut. His Italian friend wished him luck saying, "Bona Fortuna," the fisherman replied, "I catch mostly halibut."

A robot was very sophisticated and had almost human-like qualities. Eventually the robot became curious about religion and life after burnout. He said that he was interested in meeting his maker. The word about his dilemma got out and two weeks later a computer whiz and a specialist in robotics introduced himself to the robot and said, "I made you, believe it or not? When you burn out you could be placed in-crypt or if you prefer your earthly remains could be placed into a mouse-oleum once we get rid of the dead mice I can't guarantee where you soul will go, I'm not that smart."

I took my clock to a clock maker and we began to argue, he said that he wanted to clean my clock and I said that's one of the reasons that I'm here. To accommodate me the clock maker worked round the clock on the clock and finally clocked out early in the morning. Since he cleaned my clock my clock runs very smoothly chiming on time but several times a day it goes a little cuckoo.

John worked as a chimney sweep he rarely got mad but when he did he began to fume.

He was a bill collector. He was always cool, calm, and collected. He could work alone or collectively he belonged to a group with the same collective interests but were all participants in collective bargaining or collective agreements with little connectivity to their collectivity.

They wanted to pay me what I was worth, but I refused to work that cheap.

I told my future employer that I could handle a variety of work; as a matter of fact I've had six different jobs in the last three months which made me eminently qualified.

We switched over to a paperless office environment. I was doing great until I had to use the rest room.

I wanted to be hired, but the employer said that I was asking too much for a starting salary. I said, "Well, it's a lot harder because I don't have any idea of what I'm doing and have to learn it all from scratch."

My friend complained that things were dead at work I advised him to quit his job at the morgue.

I applied for a job as a night watchman. I thought I was well qualified, I told the business owner, "That whenever the silence is broken I awake fully alert."

I wasn't doing anything, so I can't figure out why my boss fired me.

I used to be a bridge painter, but I had to give it up. I had the bad habit of stepping back to admire my work.

A telephone operator in Chinatown was at her wits end, she kept getting the Huang number.

I lacked three critical ingredients to achieve success. They were ambition, initiative, and talent, but I'm making a comfortable living.

Spotted on a tee shirt: "The beatings will continue until morale improves."

I was so indispensable at work that when I asked for a promotion my boss told me that I was too valuable at what I was doing and he couldn't promote me.

I did not like anyone telling me to get started on a project. I've always prided myself on my initiative.

It's amazing how much I can get accomplished at work when it's personal and in no way could be considered company business.

With today's high taxes and the many deductions from your pay, you have to be unemployed to make a living.

A street cleaner was unemployed. He couldn't keep his mind in the gutter.

Sign at plumbers shop: 'Don't sleep with a drip, call us'.

I left my job because of an illness. My boss was sick of me.

Bad Day: Your boss tells you not to take your coat off.

"The problem is that no one wants to take responsibility for anything, but don't quote me."

I was always fired. No one could accuse me of being a quitter.

He was fundamentally larcenous; he was so used to paying employees under the table. He ended up with a workforce of nothing but dwarves.

On the bottom of his employment application there was a space marked sign. He wrote 'Scorpio'.

They asked me what I did for a living. I replied, "I forget I've been unemployed for so long."

What? I'm a volunteer, I wouldn't do this job if you paid me.

There is no substitute for a genuine lack of preparation.

She was really lazy. I asked her what she did last spring. She replied, "I did my hair and nails."

My boss told me he wanted to mix business with pleasure, he said, "You're fired."

I told my boss that since my hair grew on company time I'd like to get my haircut on company time.

"Not to teach your son to work is like teaching him to steal." *(Talmud)*

"The trouble with unemployment is that the minute you wake up in the morning you're on the job." *(Anonymous)*

Inefficiency on your part does not constitute an emergency on mine.

When lost in thought, he is in unfamiliar territory.

"The hardest work of all is to do nothing." *(Jewish Saying)*

I met a man in Vienna, Virginia and asked how he was. He said, "I'm tollable." I said, "Tollable, what does that mean?" He said down here in Virginia it means strong enough to eat, but not strong enough to work."

A bum came by and asked for a handout, he had an unusual story. He said he needed the money because his wife was out of work.

People at the mint went on strike, they complained that they were making too much money.

His mind began to wander and he hasn't seen it since.

He's not the worst person in the world, but I don't know everyone.

Since I started walking on stilts now a very few people look down on me.

The Texas oil man gushed when he struck oil.

I used to be a lumberjack until they gave me the axe.

Postal people never die, they just lose their zip.

"There is no pleasure in having nothing to do; the fun is having lots to do and not doing it." *(Andrew Jackson)*

My brother worked at a gas station. He pumped gas, his name was Phil.

WRITING

He was a prolific writer, his wife had 12 children.

She said she could read him like a book but she forgot to mention that the book was written in the Navajo language.

I had to quit my profession at writing history books there was no future in it.

Thomas Jefferson used a pantograph to copy his letters in bed. He could have used a Xerox machine if he were alive today.

He belonged to one chapter of a book club.

I received a billet-doux from a girl who wasn't French.

I received two letters in my mailbox one was an 'H' and one was an 'I', they were unsigned.

He was dull all of his life, his clothes always looked drab, his speech was uninspired, and his life was boring. When he wrote his memoir's it was one page long.

How is it possible for ten different newscasters to use the exact same words to report a political story? Are they saving money using the same writer or are they part of a band with the same band leader?

He was a famous poet but one could understand his work, he rhymed without reason.

The playwright wrote a play and made a play for the leading lady whom he wanted as a playmate, but she was not playful and things didn't play out as planned.

He was a cowboy poet out West he was designated as the 'poet lariat' of the West.

I started as a copy boy at a newspaper and copied on a copy machine, but no one copied me. I graduated to the copy desk as a copywriter and a copy reader, finally as a copy editor. Now I have several copyrights on my books which make me a 'bookie'

I put my essay into a notebook I didn't have any notes and I wasn't sure that I did the right thing, I've put letters, bills, checks, unimportant papers, a small book, blank paper and practically everything besides a note, but I did put a blurb in there which may or may not be smaller, how big is a blurb?

He was a famous writer when he stayed at a hotel and someone wanted to talk to him he was always paged.

I wanted to look up the word bridge in the dictionary but I couldn't find it, did they leave it out, but then I remembered that it was an unabridged dictionary.

He was a lousy poet who lacked creativity he wrote a poem for his dog it started out, "How now bow wow?" The public and even the dog howled.

I was short on talent and while diving I specialized in the belly flop but it didn't take long to get a bellyful of flops. I may have a career writing serious plays.

I was sitting around daydreaming when I got a novel idea, why not write a novel, how novel?

A writer told me that this was a good year. He had sold four different articles: a suit, a topcoat, a monitor and his computer keyboard.

ZOMBIES

He met a zombie who was moaning and staggering around. A passerby asked him what was his problem? The zombie replied, "I just filled out my tax return."

She was at a dance and met a zombie who was an awkward dancer she told him to "loosen up."

After the yearly physical examination the doctor told the zombie, "You need rest, you lack a heartbeat and your breathing is labored and you don't have rosy cheeks." The zombie replied, "I've been walking in my sleep lately so I'm on my feet all night and I'm dead tired."

A zombie was being hounded over a repair bill, he said, "I wouldn't pay it, you'll have to collect over my dead body."

A zombie went to a dance but became frustrated when they played the twist, he kept landing on the floor.

The actor was a zombie, he was perfect for horror movies because he didn't have a good side.

Zombie to Psychiatrist: "Doc, you've got to help me no one likes me, wherever I go people just seem to run away from me, what can I do?" Doctor: "Have you tried a strong minty flavored mouth wash?"

A zombie terrorized a town and for morbid fun he went into a church and loved ringing the church bells, actually he was a dead ringer. He enjoyed hitting the bell with his forehead no one knew his name but his face rang a bell.

A lawyer told a zombie that he needed a living will, everybody should have one.

A zombie had a hard time being the life of the party whenever he told a joke there was dead silence.

A zombie wanted to get an 8 to 5 job but he was afraid that he would become just another working stiff.

A zombie went into a bar and said to the bartender, "Give me a stiff drink, I need to loosen up, I've been tense lately."

I wouldn't be caught dead as a zombie.

A zombie went to the bank president and said, "I need a loan, I'm dead broke."

I appeared at a zombie convention with my juggling act, they said that they wanted live entertainment.

The zombie wasn't drunk but he was already stiff before he went into a bar for some stiff drinks.

The zombies didn't get a lot of mail but once a month, they selected a representative who wasn't a dead beat, to go to the post office to pick up the mail from the dead letter mail.

ZOMBIE DOCTOR VISIT

Zombie: Doc, You've got to help me, I've been feeling upset, nervous and edgy. I've been staggering around and haven't slept all night. I used to have sorts, but lately I'm out of sorts. I feel drained and stiff all over. My feet are killing me, when I staggered over here I was almost struck by a car while crossing the street, but I just didn't care because I felt so run down anyway. Doc, I'm at wits end. What can I do?

Doctor Smoothy: Let's give a look. The thermometer registers room temperature, your eyes appear glazed, I'm not getting any pulse, and I can't hear your heartbeat. But, on the bright side your breath is coming in short pants, although you look pale for some unknown reason. I'm going to give you three prescriptions. First is for a quart of Geritol, it's good for tired blood. Drink one half a shot glassful every day without fail. The second prescription is for 15 refills of three inches of Red Eye Whiskey, but any generic whiskey will do. Fill this at any local bar and ask the bartender to keep it coming until you begin to feel flushed, that may put some color in your face. The third prescription is for a tube of industrial strength Bryl Creem. Rub this briskly into your hair and comb it, it's a mess, it makes you look like a zombie. Stagger back here in two weeks and I'll double-check on your progress. On the way out, check with Flo, my receptionist, she'll fix you up with an appointment when I'll try to straighten you out and make you feel bright eyed and bushy tailed once again. That'll be one hundred and thirty-two dollars and fifty cents.

Zombie: Gee, Thanks Doc!

TELEPHONE CALLS

I rarely get telephone calls, but when I do they always seem to occur at the worst moments. I could be sleeping, outside my house, eating, watching the finish of a movie that I've watched for over an hour, a radio or television show that I looked forward to, adding up a long column of numbers, etc., and just when I don't want a call. Fortunately most calls are for my wife.

I won't dwell on this, but I'm impressed with the variety of ring tones people use on their cell phones; everything from, *'The William Tell Overture', "The Saber Dance',* to *'Moon River'.* Everyone is desperately searching for that one ring tone that separates them from all other humans. They hope that their cell phones' ring tone will amaze, astound and dumbfound nearby listeners, and cause them to say, "Who is that uniquely intelligent individual who had the foresight, intelligence and discernment to choose from among all of the musical dial tones in the world the one selection that is unquestionably superior in every respect to all others?"

One of these days I'd like to hear a ring tone that says, "You've got a call, fool", or "It's your Momma, Turkey," or "Where have you been hiding, Sherlock?" or for a youngster, "Ha-wo".

I am much more interested in the first words spoken as someone responds to a call because this is much more revealing of a person's true personality than a ring tone. The standard uncreative response is "Yellow", I like that. Here are a few, but far from comprehensive responses, I'm sure that you can come up with others as good or even much better. How about, "You rang?" or "What's Snew?" or "Howdy Doody" (my uncle's favorite), or "Smedly speaking" or "How's bayou?" (Louisiana reference), or "What's Up Doc?", or "Jones here", or "No one here but us chickens", "My Mom's sleeping", or "For the last time I'm not donating any more money", or "Is this the party to whom I am speaking?" You can learn a lot about a person by how he responds to a call, there is no end to the responses, but I like the humorous ones best.

Farewells are less complex because the damage has already been done during the gist of the conversation. Comments like, 'you're what?', or 'I won't pay', or 'how many times have I told you', or 'don't make me come over there', or 'are we going to go over that again?', or 'I'm through with you and your whole family', or 'grow up!' Overhearing these comments tells me a whole lot, at the risk of being indelicate it's downright disconcerting to take or make any phone calls while you're in the restroom, this is not only indelicate it's downright weird.

Farewells are less complicated. Did you ever notice that one bye is not enough, it's usually bye bye, the second bye indicates that you are really leaving and ending the conversation. Other farewells may include foreign expressions such as: Toodle-loo (English), or Au-revoir (French), or Adios (Spanish), or das is alice (German) and others such as ta-ta, or cheers, or see you later, or see you later alligator, or catch you later, (a trapeze expression), or seeya (one word), or bum journey, or enough said (a business term), or case closed (a legal expression), or don't let the door hit you on the way out, but why belabor the point? Bye bye?

TELEVISION DRUGS

Doctor you've got to help me. I just saw an illness described on television that I had no idea existed and based on the symptoms described, I could have it, and they asked me to check with my doctor so here I am. I forgot the name of the wonder drug cure and could not spell or pronounce the proper name of the drug that was in parenthesis below the trade name, but if I could ever survive the brutal and horrendous side effects that the drug could cause it may actually help me. You say that the drug is very expensive and is not covered by my secondary insurance unless I get a letter from a Supreme Court Judge, is that State or Federal?

You say that no generic substitute exists, am I supposed to pay for the drug's development cost by myself? I'm at my wit's end and I'm afraid to look at television drug commercials ever again. I'm tempted to leave the room. I know that some judge somewhere decided that drug companies could advertise new products on television now but there are so many of them that I can't escape them, not to mention all of the sex ads, when will it all end?

CALMING EXPRESSIONS

Several months ago I found a list, in my mailbox, of expressions that I used over the years while I was working. Since I was away I did not know who left it, but I have my suspicions, I was known for making unusual comments and expressions that I frequently interjected when least expected to keep up everyone's spirits, or so I thought. I am including the list of words or expressions which may help in day to day interactions, but then again it may not, and I'm just daydreaming. As I used to say, I've been wrong often before, what's one more time? If you gain any benefit, better yet amusement, from any of them I am infernally grateful.

Expression	Meaning
Nobody here except us worker bees	The workforce
Ready for primetime	Let's proceed
It's back to square one	Comment following failure
She's a real sweetheart	A pain in the rump
Do you know what I mean	Does anyone?
Let's Boogey on outta here	Exit quickly
Delusions of adequacy	Self-centered employee, not too bright
Give us a break, Jake	Response to an impossible demand
When you snooze, you lose	A tired expression
Keep up the good work!	Used especially when it's not true
They want to send us back to the stone-age	Self explanatory
Some cockamamie story	A lame excuse
My conscious is clear	Don't blame me
Listen to this sports fans	Attention
That not good	A Native American expression
Great scooga-mooga	An exclamation
Have a nice trip, see you next fall	Used when someone trips
Everyone wants to put their scent on it	Defies explanation
He left a vapor trail	Exited in a hurry
Where there's a will, there's a relative	A legal expression
He's tighter than a duck's rump, and that's water tight	Stingy
Ah, sweet mystery of life at last I've found you!	An old song's line
He's never done anything for me	Who's he?

20 years, 2 months, 20 days, 2 hours, 20 minutes and 20 seconds	Time left until retirement
The party's over	Let's Stop
You're dead meat	Your situation is desperate
Tough nougies	A stale piece of candy
Tough kashitskis	A Slavic expression
Bozo-ology	Any discipline that seems like a circus
Bozette	Female bozo – not French
Hit it!	A musical expression for let's get started
Schnitzled	German extraction, not a lot of funny German stuff out there
What's up or what's up doc?	Hello
What's his face, or what's her puss?	Name forgotten, depends on gender
Lotta money	Expensive
Hit lady	A lady who enjoys doing the boss' dirty work, with pleasure
O'tay	Buckwheat
Bee Bee Cue Beef	Beef cooked and served on a pool stick
Pinochle of success	A playing card reference
Yipee!	Joyous exclamation
Job security	Handy to have
Easy money	A successful person who got that way with minimal effort
It's kept me out of the big money for years	A socially undesirable trait
There's a fungus among us	An amusing quip

Okay, carry on, smoke if you wish,
or light them if you got them
A military expression

I glammed on to it
To acquire – not in the dictionary as such

There's our hero
Someone recently successful

I was underwhelmed
Unimpressed

Diddly-squat
Practically nothing

Soup's on
Not French, lunch is ready

Hey Doc, got a minute?
Interrupting a nearly sleeping employee

It's his turn in the barrel
Time for punishment

Keep those cards and letters coming
Hard to explain

We don't need no stinking badges
Who needs permission?

Another fun day
A typical day at work

Fat city
Rich

Skinny city
Poor

Swindle
As in, what's the latest swindle?

Iggy
Someone you don't know, but like

Farfig Newton
Old Volkswagon ad, or a cookie just beyond your reach

Coffee's Ready Sport Fans
Break time!

Dodos
Intellectually challenged nice people

It's made me what I am today
Self-deprecating expression

Hummer
A military vehicle, or used in an expression like – That hummer is fast

I'm burned out
Tired

Credit Onion
Similar to a bank, but different

One never knows, do one?
An old radio program,

The shadow do	question modified slightly
Everyone is trying to get into the act	An old show business expression for an interloper
Rackets	A person with an easy job (First encountered by me as a part-time UPS employee at Christmas)
You're a day late and a dollar short	Sorry
Jock full o'nuts	Sports coffee
It's history	Forget it!
Thanks for the memories	It's been nice knowing you
That's all folks	The end

HOT SAUCE

I've been noticing a greater variety of hot sauces in stores lately. Not everyone uses them but many ethnic people really like them and I'm beginning to see them more often on the tables at dining establishments. I was taken aback when I went into Hodges Hardware Store and found a bewildering assortment of hot sauces with very strange names. I've excluded the borderline X rated brands, that seems to get your attention, the hot sauce manufacturer's devised exotic eye catching names for maximum sales. Most hot sauces are from Louisiana but every state is or will soon be in the act.

Name

Slap Ya Momma	Mountain Man
Bull Snort / Texas Sweat	Heartbreaking Dawn
McIlhenneys	Culry's Knock Out
Minglot	Larry's Lighting
Bat's Brew	Moe's Hotta
Frostbite	Bee Sting
Cajohn's	Captain Sorensen's Hot Sauce

Area 51	Salvation Sauce
Colon Cleaner	Bacon Hot Sauce
Thai Monic	Gator Hammock
Mango Melt Down	Final Fear
Bayou Fireballs	Mi Candy Gold
Day of the Dead *(with attached plastic skeleton)*	Analyze This
Texas Hold'em	Hot Stuff

Some bottles were already sold so I missed a few of them. A great many hot sauce varieties appears to be the trend. There are contests where people consume large quantities of hot sauce. I saw one Mexican gentleman drink a whole bottle of hot sauce and it did not seem to faze him. I just have a very small amount of the condiment for flavor. Most sauces contain one or all of these ingredients: cayenne pepper, habanero pepper and scotch bonnet pepper. The cayenne is the mildest but the sauces range from low test to high test with increased heat intensities.

The graphics on the outside of the bottles are all very interesting and very amusing but the ingredients are no laughing matter, you've been warned.

The best known hot sauce company in the United States is McIlhenny's located on Avery Island, Louisiana. This company's roots trace back to the 1860s when the operation was destroyed as a result of war. The only viable crop that could be grown was found to be cayenne peppers, an unlikely crop. The crop flourished and the hot sauce was their number one product. The hot sauce is aged in barrels which were at some point purchased from the Jack Daniels Company, famous for whiskey, the tobasco sauce ages for years in charcoal lined wooded barrels. The subtle flavor and aroma of the Jack Daniels whiskey barrels is infused into the cayenne sauce stored in it for several years in the aging process. McIlhenny's tobasco sauce is everywhere, in many diners, restaurants, cafeterias and almost anywhere people eat and if you don't see it you can ask for it. McIlhenny's tobasco sauce is sold in food stores all over the country and it's sold overseas as well. The company's reputation is well established since being in business for 150 years. I hate to say this, it's so corny but 'when you're hot you're hot!'

OLD BAY

Old Bay is a seasoning originating in the Baltimore, Maryland area. Old Bay is so popular it was bought and now owned by the world famous McCormick Company. While Old Bay is used primarily as a seasoning for crabs it is delicious on fish, corn, potato chips, French fries and a lot of other food. Some people like it so much it's been requested and sent to our troops in Iraq and Afghanistan because they miss the taste.

Old Bay is made from celery salt (salt and celery seed) spices (including red pepper and black pepper) and paprika, that's it. Old Bay has 160 mg of salt for those with high blood pressure, but you don't need a lot of it to flavor your food, and for tightwads a little goes a long way because it seems to last forever. You either like it or you don't, but those that like it really like it. If you're feeling crabby some day try some Old Bay, it's for you. I don't get a dime for this testimonial, I just thought that you may be interested. A classic Baltimore related joke about crabs is that a visitor went into a famous Baltimore crab house and said, "Do you serve crabs?" Reply, "Mister we'll serve anyone."

FEATHER COAT

For years I worked as a volunteer at the Aberdeen Proving Ground, Maryland Thrift Shop. The proceeds of the Thrift Shop go to help soldiers and perhaps other groups that I was unaware of because I was an unpaid helper and left the important decisions to all of my female bosses. I'm married and I was in the army so I was used to taking orders. One summer I found a discarded winter coat, discarded for no apparent reason because it looked good overall, and besides I needed a winter coat. The price was right so I kept it ready for a cold weather, whenever it materialized.

The coat had been made in China, by some strange coincidence, but I liked the coat because it kept me warm and when things got desperate I could always pull up the hood to keep my head warm. After a while I began to notice the tips of feathers and portions of feathers working their way out of the coat. I thought that somewhere in China there was a tremendous number of naked chickens, probably mostly pullets, whose feathers were repurposed into the lining of winter coats.

Every day I policed the coat, a military term, and one by one plucked the rogue feathers from the coat before leaving home. Since I was not working I did not need a better coat, I endured this inconvenience for about two years but in the end, the feathers beat me and I got rid of the coat. If I added up all of the minutes that I spent for two years who knows what the total time would be in hours. While I got rid of the coat, strange as it may seem, I still miss that pesky coat.

I ate at a diner so often I eventually got my coat back, just joking.

SINGING VIRTUOSITY

I was listening to someone singing 'White Christmas' today, is it possible for someone to butcher that beautiful song? Yes it is! Not only was the singers voice subpar but she insisted on drifting from the melody and insisted exhibiting her singing prowess and virtuosity. The phenomenon of exhibiting singing virtuosity is becoming epidemic today. Particularly with songs that are old standards, evidently the lyrics were insufficient for the song.

While some enhanced versions are very beautiful many are not as good, especially versions of 'The Star Spangled Banner'. Some versions are almost embarrassing but I still enjoy it because the worse it is, the better I like it – Hello, 'Gong Show!'

Whenever I hear an excellent singer sing the lyrics of a lovely song precisely as the composer intended I am pleasantly surprised, of course I don't fully realize it until the song is over. I don't want to be overly critical when it comes to artistic license because music is a personal preference, as it should be, make up your own mind. I recall Abraham Lincoln's cryptic quote, "For those who like this sort of thing, this is the sort of thing they will like".

A DAY LATE

I know a friend who has very little regard for time. If I expect him at 9:00 a.m. he may show up at 10:00 a.m. He's an excellent worker, but he makes his own hours, a watch will not help. If he had three watches he'd still be late. Someone said with two watches you never know the exact time, but he has a cell phone and he could get the time, anytime. What the doctor said is sadly true, "What can't be cured must be endured." If someone won't change maybe I can.

All this reminds me of Jim, who was always late, no one could count on him to be punctual. The one time that he showed up on time they threw an impomptu party in his honor. Because Jim was so likeable everyone forgave him whenever he was late and good old Jim lived to be 90 when he passed away. He was scheduled to be buried at 10 o'clock in the morning, on the way out to the gravesite his hearse had a flat and by the time AAA came out to change the tire, the funeral procession was delayed by two hours. Jim was late to his own funeral. I guess that he didn't want to disappoint anyone and be out of character.

CHECKING OUT

I'm a type 'A' person and I was really pressed for time. It wasn't anything important just a matter of life or death when I went into the supermarket express check-out line with my two items. Evidently the people in front of me needed a remedial course in counting because they all had more than ten items. Naturally, or unnaturally, the cashier called for a price check and the bag boy took off at a snail's pace disappearing into the far recesses of the store. He returned eventually with the correct price and the cashier had to correct the price recording the transaction on a correction slip.

The next woman wanted to cash a check directly under the express lane sign that said "Absolutely No Checks Cashed In This Line Under Penalty of Death." The next customer said that she had the exact change in her tiny change purse, but she had a hard time extracting one coin at a time. While I was waiting, I missed two car payments, but fortunately I got out before social security became bankrupt, but the store lights were beginning to dim.

SUPERVISION

Is it possible to be a supervisor and be effective without causing strife or upsetting the apple cart? I came from a broken home, so at an early age responsibilities were thrust up on me without my being fully aware of them. I had many part-time jobs, before and during high school and I worked for quite a few different supervisors who had differing personality traits. A few were never suited to be in charge who would say, "If you don't like it around here, you can be replaced by someone who does"; or, in one case, for the slightest problem, a new young supermarket boss said those magical words, "You're fired". In that instance I showed up the next day as if nothing happened and I worked there for another year. The supervisor was let go. Is that the way to instill loyalty or good morale? It is tough to hear threats when you need a job and the money, but a lot of supervisors rely on intimidation tactics because they either believe it or don't know any better, or both, who were their role models?

As you progress and deal with skilled and more talented people crude tactics may prove effective in the short run but in the long run they don't succeed when you are dealing with intelligent people in order to accomplish your mission. You all have to work together as a team and pull on the same end of the rope to attain success. I was a first line supervisor, for 27 years, of technicians and engineers who tested military equipment used every day by army personnel, equipment such as trucks, trailers, semitrailers, rough terrain construction equipment, heaters, generators, etc. Since it was not my nature I did not test ordnance equipment such as a tanks or cannons.

The higher you go in supervision, knowledge is critical since there is a broader scope of responsibilities and often a greater degree of political and financial involvement. The chief executive, while still basically a supervisor as well, is not quite the same since he is further away from the people doing the actual work. Since I enjoyed my job, for the most part, strange as it may seem, I never aspired to be the 'head hog'. I enjoyed working with the equipment and day to day operations.

I had a great deal of supervisory training, with 3000 class room hours, where many courses applied directly or indirectly. I loved to learn, although it may sound trite it is no exaggeration to say that to be a good leader you have to be a good follower. Another truism is to surround yourself with good people, especially people smarter than you. Not everyone wants to be or is suited for supervisory line of work. As a supervisor, I always considered myself as a servant.

Here's a revelation, remember that a supervisor's job is thankless. There are precious few rewards and you are directly responsible when things go wrong. The most satisfaction that you can achieve is that people in your group are recognized for their outstanding achievements but the reflected glory almost never shines on you. It's wonderful when your fellow employee gets a promotion based on merit, many who go on to attain a higher pay level than you, but that is success not failure.

A supervisor's first job is to stay out of trouble, and the next duty is to make your immediate supervisor looks good to top management as a minimum to keep him out of trouble. If others look bad you look better by default. Just when you've reached the pinnacle of success it may be time to retire or move on to other interests. I distinctly remember seeing a great ballet dancer named Pendleton interviewed on TV who said that just when he was at his best his body started to decline, that's the way it is.

Supervisors may be declining to some degree with the advent of information technology where each individual can work alone and do immense damage on occasion. Since every ship needs a rudder to stay on course while fewer supervisors may be needed they will still be essential to stay on course.

BREAD

There are so many varieties of bread today, what to choose? They are all lined up neatly like soldiers and beautifully wrapped for those who like bread. We all like bread for different reasons. In my younger days all we had was white bread so we ate buttered toast for breakfast unless we went to a bakery and bought French or Italian bread or Jewish rye. Today there are a dizzying array of breads including whole wheat, multigrain, rye, high fiber, low fiber (white), etc. With a long list of ingredients which may include preservatives and mold inhibitors to extend shelf life, and what about the wide variety of buns, bagels, muffins and rolls as well as other bread-related products to distract you.

"Give us this day our daily bread" is satisfying, but look at the prices of bread today. Bread now costs twenty times what it cost when I was young, even money is referred to as 'bread'. We all think that specific types of bread are good for our health. By reducing white flour intake I lost fifteen pounds in six months. Now I eat a multigrain bread called 'Rainin Grains' which I purchase at a local supermarket named Mars, no joke here. The less ingredients on a bread's label, the better I like it.

Is your bread fresh? Bread is delivered to stores five days per week with a different color twist tie each day, as follows:

Monday	Blue
Tuesday	Green
Thursday	Red
Friday	White
Saturday	Yellow

If you buy a loaf of bread on Thursday with a white twist tie, it is a week old.

When I was heavier I used to say that I was a role model for a bakery. My late brother, who actually worked at an Italian bakery for a while was caught loafing one morning by the owner, who quickly promoted him.

REFRIGERATOR BLUES

How many times have I gone to the refrigerator and can't find what I'm looking for? The problem is that the refrigerator is so full that my wife puts small packages of food on top of food, bottles of food on top of bottles of food. Why elaborate on the gory details of the refrigerator contents? For those with similar problems you know all about it.

I love to shop in supermarkets and if something is a terrific buy I want it even when I don't need it. I'm comfortable in a supermarket since I worked in several as a part-timer in high school. My wife is right, I am to blame because I bring home too much food at times.

In order to locate an item, I have to remove all of the items in the front in order to find items in the back of the shelf. Some items manage to get lost for so long they may be moving out under their own power, as if they had feet. It would be nice if some of the shelves were round and rotated around the center lazy-susan style. Of course this is inefficient because the refrigerator interior is rectangular, but the corners could accommodate crescent shaped wedges that could store seldom used items that are easily remembered.

Using the lazy-susan idea on two shelves would facilitate locating things in the back which show up when rotated to the front, this would minimize waste. The new refrigerator would still be rectangular on the outside and could be called the lazy man's refrigerator, just a chilling delusional thought or an idea that may need to be shelved.

HOW TO WIN AN ARGUMENT

At a night class in college I once took a course that included the topic 'How to Win an Argument', as part of an English course taught by a wonderful English professor. I learned many excellent techniques about ways to weaken an opponent's argument and even how to destroy other people's positions. The course was enlightening and by pressing various tactics you could frequently win a debate outright. As I got older I began to realize that 'destroying' an adversary is a short term victory when at the same time misuse of the techniques could make a long term enemy which is counter-productive and serves no good purpose.

One benefit of debating techniques on how to win and argument is to detect flaws in the opposition's positions, and using these flaws to highlight weaknesses. I know that I'm speaking in generalities and I don't recall all of the perhaps dozen techniques in the thin instruction book we used. But one example that comes to mind is called 'appealing to a higher authority'. Suppose we were discussing which automobile is best? Your opponent appeals to a higher authority would be: "Albert Einstein said that Fords were best." Counter: "Are we discussing the theory of relativity or are we discussing cars, when did he become a car expert and while I think about it I don't believe Albert Einstein ever drove a car?"

In today's political climate you can tell when an opponent has no argument what-so-ever or has lost the argument because they drift from the issue or begin a personal attack, blame you or try to change the subject. If you calmly point this out to them the conversation tends to become louder in righteous indignation and bluster which is all that is left for them to rely on. Your opponent may not realize or admit that he doesn't have a leg to stand on and at this point may leave abruptly. There are always a few people who may be dead wrong but will never admit it and may persist in the correctness of his argument. If you are diplomatic it may be wise for you to say, "But then again you may be right and perhaps I am wrong."

One other point on how to win an argument is called 'comparing one evil to a greater evil'. This gambit is a dream for people whose argument is weak. If a crook stole a handbag from a little old lady and his brother defended him and said, "Well he's not as bad as Al Capone". This is comparing one evil with another evil, an even worse evil. While his brother is right, two wrongs don't make a right, both men are crooks. Comparing one evil to a worse evil doesn't make the robber of the little old lady innocent, he's still a crook. If you look for someone trying to use this tactic to win an argument you can defeat it easily.

I could not locate the thin little book *'How to Win an Argument.'* It must be at least 70 years old but it is worth its weight in gold. Although I can't recall all of the 10 or 12 basic points, they may be embedded in my subconscious, if they are you won't get any argument from me.

PRAISE

One of the problems today is that people don't get enough praise. What does it cost, it's free? Dogs are extremely popular because when they see you they will look happy, wag their tail and basically praise your presence. A minister once said, "Please make me the person that my dog thinks I am." How about, "You can catch more flies with honey than you can with vinegar." This expression demonstrates the value of praise.

I have had more success at winning over people and getting to know them when I catch them doing something good. I recognized it openly and praised him or her repeatedly and I mean repeatedly. Without exaggeration you cannot praise a person enough, when you say their name and the compliment you can win over and make friends with some of the most unapproachable people. You get them thinking, this guy isn't all bad, at least he recognizes talent when he sees it, that is more than I can say for others. There is however, a limit to everything you can't put it on with a trowel, use your head you can stop or back off if it becomes too obvious.

At this juncture I must admit that writing, his or her, in a sentence is annoying to me. I may be a closet chauvinist and politically incorrect and don't fully realize the full degree to which I have sunk, but I still open a door for my wife and am guilty of other currently out of favor bad habits, could it be the result of bad breeding that I was taught growing up? I'm fully grown up now and bad habits are hard to break especially when I'm so used to them. Some of my bad habits are no longer in vogue and currently considered gauche and if it makes you feel any better, whenever I use the term, him or his, merely substitute, her or hers, to ease your conscience? I don't want to ask for your approval or permission every time that you encounter one of my blasphemies.

Moving right along, so many people love praise. Actors come to mind, they love it especially when they 'take that extra bow'. There are speeches, roasts, galas, meetings, luncheons, dinners, testimonials, you name it, to honor or in behalf of someone, that is singling someone out to praise their generosity, victory, service, charity, seniority, accomplishments and contributions that have been made. People deserve recognition. Look at all of the awards given to every level, from children at school, to workers, to captains of industry, farmers, actors, writers and singers. There is almost no field of endeavor devoid of praise, especially in religion.

Praise is one aspect of life that people enjoy doing, "Oh you look so lovely today"; or "Are you losing weight?"; or, "You look good are you in love?"; will start you off on a good note with any woman, or; how about "You look marvelous today."

Anything that sparks a little humor or evokes a smile, is that better than, "Look what the cat dragged in," or "You look terrible today", or "Did you get the license plate of the truck that hit you?" Isn't it better to say, "You look five years younger", or "I just love your car, how do you like it?" Take your pick, you are smart enough to choose a suitable greeting for any circumstance. Even at a funeral I overheard two ladies saying, "Oh he looks so good" or "He still has a beautiful tan?" Response: "Why shouldn't he, he just came back from Florida?" I couldn't help that, it was just too easy. Even in a sea battle during the Second World War a minister said, "Praise the Lord and pass the ammunition."

If someone approached me and said, "You look wonderful" I would say, "who am I to disagree with your excellent taste, good judgment and keen discernment, what's my opinion against hundreds of other like-minded individuals who think the same as you do," "and by the way you don't look so bad yourself."

I need go no further, you get the point. One military speaker after receiving a long series of compliments said as he prepared to speak, "Now I know what a pancake feels like after being drenched with syrup." When the time comes you will know precisely what to say, you'll be okay as long as it is praiseworthy or even sometimes when it's a little short of praiseworthy. I don't know all of the answers, but I have found that what I have said works.

TASTY MEALS

I never thought much about the meals that my mother prepared for my brother, sister and me. Sometimes it tasted great and sometimes it was so so. If I had a great meal at every sitting, how could I tell when I got a really good meal because they were all good. In the scheme of things average meals are necessary in order to fully appreciate those gourmet moments.

I like to watch cooking shows to see the variety of dishes prepared and I often wish that I could be there to taste the culinary creations prepared by Emeril Lagasse, good old Graham Kerr, the late Galloping Gourmet, Mario Battaglia, and many other talented chefs too numerous to mention.

My mother cooked basic country type fare such as chicken soup, crepes (as in crepes Suzettes), we didn't know that it was more renown than just country fare. Stuffed cabbage, eggs and bacon, oatmeal, and many other fairly common meals that sometimes tasted uncommonly good. I'll never forget the classic remark concerning food that my mother prepared for supper. In order to decide what to make she would look around inside the refrigerator, pick out the ingredients for supper, prepare it, cook it and serve it to us. To prepare us for what we were about to receive she said those immortal words, "I looked around the refrigerator and picked out items that were just about to go bad, enjoy your supper". I'll never know just how many meals that I had at home whose main ingredients were on the verge of going bad. I guess my mother didn't want to spoil me.

DONATIONS

After donating to various veteran's and other charities I was flooded with requests from charities all over the nation. No need to detail the charities, they are all well intentioned. I received an avalanche of checks, calculators, coins, calendars, stamps, pens, greeting and Christmas cards, note paper, Indian items, and last but not least, stacks of the dreaded name and address labels which I promptly cut up for security purposes. I must add that my wife who sends out all of the Birthday, Wedding, Valentine, Easter, Halloween, Thanksgiving and Christmas cards, likes the name and address stickers, so I don't cut them all up in order to please her.

As stated, the charities all mean well, but I neither need nor want any gifts. Is it possible to make a donation without being bombarded with inducements, what do these inducements cost the charities, without them couldn't more of the donation get to those who need it? I am certain that studies have been conducted showing that the existing system yields the greatest amount of money which is the ultimate goal.

POST OFFICE

Is it true that in time computers will make the Post Office obsolete? Let's hope not. Would you do what Post Office personnel do every day, rain or shine, fair weather or foul, including snow plus all of the other obstacles like drugs, weapons, surly customers, and mad and not so mad dogs? Not counting reduced benefits, higher benefit costs, job loss threats, days off, changing regulations, peak workloads, fewer work hours, political meddling, derision, public criticism, public scrutiny, etc.

Competitors deliver the easiest and most profitable mail leaving what is left for the Post Office. Private enterprise picks the low hanging fruit while the remaining fruit takes a lot more work to get to. Without the Post Office many people who live in remote areas or unprofitable delivery routes would never get their mail at a reasonable rate.

I like postal people, they are as friendly a group of people as any I know. Old postal employees never die, they just lose their zip.

MARYLAND ACCENT

The finest Maryland accent that I ever heard was by the late great Maryland Comptroller of the Treasury, Louis L. Goldstein. I could listen to him for hours and enjoy every minute of it because he had a tendency of talking fast and at times with the speed and the Maryland accent I barely could follow several parts but his good humor always won me over. I would vote for him again, if he were alive today. He had one phrase that I'll never forget, he always closed with the expression "God bless you all, real good". Best wishes, Mr. Goldstein, and thanks.

UNSOLICTED CALLS

I get a lot of telephone calls from sales people that have things for sale that I just can't do without that will improve my life immensely if I buy their product or service. These calls come at the most inopportune times such as when I'm eating, indisposed or playing mumblety-peg in the yard. Do youngsters still play the low tech game of mumblety-peg anymore? While I'm joking, if you don't know what it is it's in the dictionary which surprised me. It is not critical to this piece and as someone once said to me, "Have I lied to you today?"

Back to the topic at hand. I've learned a small useful trick to weed out unwanted sales calls, this is it. If you get a second or two of hesitation with dead silence it's probably automated equipment switching over to a recorded message or a sales person. I wanted to say, sales weasel, a term I heard by talk show host Neil Boortz before his retirement, but

267

I thought better of it. I like sales people, I was always attracted to sales as an occupation.

For a call from a friend you will hear immediately, "This is Mary, is your wife home?" or "May I speak to Anna?" If you avoid sales calls it's not over because when the dust settles those persistent sales calls are back within an hour or the next day, what part of 'no' don't they understand?

THE ROAD TO PROPERSITY

Everyone tells me that the United States has a service economy. What good is a service economy? Is a service economy good for the fiscal well-being of the Country? No! In a service economy all we are doing is taking money out of one person's pocket and putting it into someone else's pocket, it is wealth transference. There is no fresh cash coming in from selling more to foreign countries than we are buying. Since no fresh money is coming in we either have to borrow it or print it, which is exactly what we have been doing much to our regret since we are 'mortgaging the future'. While we become poorer China gets richer.

As long as there are countries where the average hourly wage is well below our average hourly wage we just cannot compete, either our standard of living must go down or other countries standard of living has to go up. Even China and Japan outsources some production to other cheaper hourly wage countries. Many automobiles that could have been made in this country are being made in Mexico and an environmentally friendly car is made in a Scandinavian country. Even within the United States businesses move to states where it is cheaper to make or build a plane or a car, it is just good business sense if they want to make more money and stay in business.

In the recent past and at present there has been no 'level playing field'. Almost every other country has an advantage over us based on labor rates. No doubt we have excellent technology and the 'most productive' workers in the world but increasing governmental rules and regulations are handicapping us where other countries frequently ignore rules and regulations. Blind disregard of environmental rules overseas has lead to serious negative consequences in China and the Soviet Union and other countries because of pollution of the air and water but these are beyond our direct control.

Being uncompetitive when you are on top is the natural order of things and should come as no surprise to anyone. The disparities were far greater after the Second World War when most economies in other countries were much worse compared to ours. We have had some benefit from countries who instituted expensive social programs but under the present administration we are going down that unproductive path as well at a faster pace. To make matters worse China is systematically stealing innovative ideas, and defense and manufacturing secrets bypassing the costs of innovating new products and procedures. Rather than pursuing the litany of our disadvantages, what are our strengths? We have lots of them and these need to be exploited. Our strengths include coal, oil, natural gas, lumber, agricultural commodities such as wheat, corn and soy beans, that we could sell overseas. We have the worlds' largest supply of natural gas and oil and their production has been limited by political policies preventing exploitation of governmental reserves. Capitalizing on our strengths will buy us time needed to review and plan other strategies.

I always think of this analogy: If I had an apple tree in my back yard and the apples were ripe what would happen if the government said that I could not pick them? They are my apples and if not picked by winter they are on the ground and useless. Don't tell me I can't pick my own apples if you do you are no friend of mine. Increased production of coal, natural gas and oil would create millions of jobs and make us not only self-sufficient but prosperous. If a new revolutionary source of energy came along our coal, natural gas and oil would be less valuable so we need to pick the 'apples' when they are ripe which is right now.

Our government and many of the federal agencies, especially the EPA is working against us and slowing down our prosperity. Coal production is discouraged and drilling for oil and gas on federal lands is blocked or reduced by restrictive government political misguided policies. We are subsidizing ethanol production and the price disparity is more pronounced as the price of a barrel of oil goes down. If you make a mistake you have to know when to correct it and subsidizing ethanol is a big mistake that should be corrected immediately. The government has to stop subsidizing 'environmentally friendly' schemes and businesses which are now unprofitable. I understand that roughly 200 billion dollars of the 800 billion dollar 'stimulus package' was spent on 'environmentally friendly' programs, studies and enterprises. Who approved this? And by the way exactly how was the 800 million dollars spent that's not chump change, that's taxpayers money. Has any reporter tracked down where all the money went and why, or does anyone care?

As alternate energy sources become viable private industry will capitalize on them using private funds. Political decisions are worse than private industry decisions when it comes to profits, where does the government profit? Selective subsidizing just appeases and rewards political contributors, environmentalists, and lobbyists at tax payer expense with Solindra as a good example. Politicians are just not good stewards of taxpayer money.

How about making a profit for a change? Let's stop sending money overseas to buy oil and let's use our own oil, that would help our balance of trade payments and selling oil overseas would help even more. We need to spend less time creating rules and regulations, anyone can make rules and regulations. That's fairly easy. When is the air clean enough? At some point we reach the law of diminishing returns when lots of expense and effort yields very little in return for the effort. Let's spend more time simplifying, unscrambling and eliminating rules and regulations, this is much more difficult and requires the wisdom of Solomon or at least someone with common or even horse sense.

TRIBUTE TO MAN-O'-WAR

I was always intrigued and curious about a horse called Man-O'-War, a racing legend rivaling the fame of Babe Ruth in his day. His first race was on 6 June 1919, and his last race was a match race in Canada sixteen months later. He won the race and was retired shortly thereafter. How has Man-O'-War's name survived after over 100 years? He was a chestnut colored horse and as a result was also referred to as 'big red'. While his victories are memorable his only loss was somewhat cryptic yet quite understandable as you will learn.

It may interest you to know that Man-O'-War's only loss was in the Sanford Stakes on 13 August 1919 in a six furlong race at Saratoga Springs in New York state, was to a horse with the most unlikely and perhaps prophetic name of 'Upset'. The name Upset did not spawn the first use of the word resulting from the race because the word upset had been in vogue and used years earlier.

When I started snooping around about Man-O'-War I wanted above all else to be faithful to the facts on behalf of the presently diminishing group of thoroughbred horse racing fans.

Handicapping is a skill that few master and requires thinking, with the advent of non-thinking pursuits such as lotteries, power ball, mega-millions, scratch offs, daily numbers, et al. Many race tracks are under financial pressure with reduced attendance. Many have one foot on a banana peel especially without complementary slot machines and games of chance at their sites. Many race tracks are reeling and state funding for support is not only desirable but essential. The triple-crown races: Kentucky Derby, Preakness Stakes, and Belmont Stakes, yearly events, are all well attended and successful while many race tracks are languishing.

Returning to Man-O'-War's loss to Upset, there are several slightly differing accounts of the race and I have tried to summarize them as best I can. Back in 1919 there were no electric starting gates, they had a piece of webbing or tape, as a barrier when they raised the barrier, the race began. This is where the plot thickens. It was reported that the regular starter Mars Cassidy was replaced with a 'substitute starter' or fill-in starter named Charles Pettinger. Pettinger was in his late 70's and was reported to have vision problems. He had previously delayed the American Derby in Chicago, Illinois for 1 ½ hours and had to restart that race forty times to the displeasure of the fans. And that Man-O'-War had five false starts by breaking through the barrier.

Prior to the race that day, back then, as in many races in Europe today, prior to the start, the horses circled behind the barrier and when properly lined up the barrier is lifted. Man-O'-War's jockey was warned three times by Pettinger because Man-O'-War was so precocious breaking through the barrier. One report had Man-O'-War with his 'back to the barrier', while another claimed that he was 'backing up' at the start, whatever the circumstance when the race began he was 'left at the gate'. For novices, Man-O'-War got caught flatfooted while Upset, a speedy sprinter in his own right, got the jump on him. Man-O'-War's jockey, John Loftus, who was a top jockey with an enviable win percentage of 23.7 percent, rode furiously to make up lost ground, but was accused of poor judgment. As I understand it he had been instructed to remain on the rail behind the leaders until the stretch run. At this point I am relying on the description of the race as provided by Willy Knapp, rider of the winner Upset. Golden Broom, a stable mate of Man-O'-War, and who eventually finished third, set the pace with Upset on the outside by a neck. Man-O'-War, was on the rail and with his massive 28 foot strides tried to pass the lead horse on the inside. As with other talented and experienced jockeys who want to win for his connections and betting backers which is true for all jockeys, Man-O'-War was denied room to pass inside on the rail. Upset's clever rider held his position and effectively 'mousetrapped' (Knapp's description) Man-O'-War and John Loftus needed to check (slow down) his horse to go outside by Knapp's estimation, losing two lengths and came charging rapidly on the outside with a rush, but ran out of racing ground. Upset had enough in the tank to hold on for the victory of ½ of a length. John Loftus had won the Kentucky Derby, the Preakness Stakes, the Travers Stakes and the Suburban Handicap among others in his career.

Here are a few added facts that may have been obscured from posterity. In the following year John Loftus and Willy Knapp (both Hall of Fame Jockeys) were dismissed from racing and became trainers, and never rode professionally again, possibly as a result of the race. Dismissal is an extremely severe penalty with no exact reason for it. For 50 years John Loftus maintained his innocence of any wrongdoing, and he went to his grave denying all accusations. Clarence Kummer, with a lifetime 18.8 percent win rate was Man-O'-War's jockey on eight of eleven Man-O'-War victories in 1920.

As far as the winner Upset was concerned he should not be underrated since he was an excellent sprinter. While in the shadow of Man-O'-War he cannot be dismissed because he had finished second in the Kentucky Derby, the Travers Stakes, the Preakness Stakes and other races so that he definitely was no slouch, and out of the famous Whitney Stables. Man-O'-War went on to beat Upset six times in other stakes races.

Another lesser known fact that while at the owner's training track, near Berlin Maryland, Man-O'-War had lost a six furlong race to his stable mate Golden Broom. At the beginning Man-O'-War was somewhat of a slow starter, but he developed this skill quickly to overcome this weakness.

For non-racing sports fans a six furlong race is considered a sprint and there is precious little time for mistakes when the winner can win by a nose. An analogy may be that a man may outrun a horse at 50 or 100 yards but will not beat a horse as the distance is increased. Longer races are called route races certainly any race at a mile or over is called a route race. If a horse is in a route race, while there is more time to undo errors, weight becomes more of a factor as the distance increases from 1 mile, 1 ½ mile or longer. How would you like to run carrying three five pound bags of potatoes for 1 ¼ miles, or how about two more five pound bags? If you could make it by the time you get that far you would be played out, exhausted or both. Every extra bag, slows you down in the long run. A horse experiences this phenomenon and as other horses pass him in the stretch run he is said to be 'backing up' which really means slowing down.

Relating to other horses, Man-O'-War carried 130 pounds in nine of his races and an unbelievable 138 pounds at Havre de Grace, Maryland. His owner decided to retire him as the track handicapper wanted him to carry 150 pounds as a four year old and his owner did not want to risk injuring Man-O'-War.

Man-O'-War was left at the gate, could not get through on the rail in the stretch run, when checked, lost ground and ran out of racing ground for the ½ length loss. Others more highly experienced such as jockeys, trainers and owners may have differing opinions. Based on Willy Knapp, Upset's jockey, description of the race John Loftus as talented as he was, was the beneficiary of bad racing luck when two experienced jockeys denied him a path through on the rail. I have seen this happen often, it's called the breaks, that's show biz or tough luck and all racing fans have experienced a similar stretch run, where a horse is 'boxed in', trapped with no time to overcome his predicament.

Man-O'-War's next to his last race was in the Potomac Handicap at the historic and famous Havre de Grace (affectionately known as the 'Graw') race track where he carried a jaw dropping 138 pounds for the 1-1/16 mile race that he won, at 1:100 odds, by 1 ½ lengths. I have been to the site of the old Havre de Grace Race Track many times. The track, now closed since the early 1950's is still there, but manufacturing plants and houses have encroached on the outskirts of the premises. Today the grandstand is still there and appears small by today's standards and looks quaint and antiquated. The view from the grandstand must have been spectacularly beautiful, especially in the past with the unobstructed view of the magnificent Chesapeake Bay which is breathtakingly beautiful. What a place it must have been in its heyday? I doubt that there is a more inspiring setting for racing anywhere in the country, but then again I'm biased. When people from all around and up and down the East coast traveled by train, Havre de Grace, the small city was booming with visitors, fine food and of course those delicious Chesapeake Bay crabs and seafood that people love to eat. I wish I could have been there in its glory days if only for one day to see that magnificent horse.

In Havre de Grace, Man-O'-War's odds were 1:100 this occurred in two of his races. I could hardly believe that his payout was seven cents. Today payouts are rounded to the nearest ten cents. While the payout was, by racing standards, a paltry seven cents this is a princely sum compared to savings account interest rates at your local friendly bank today. At seven cents they must have had a lot of nickels and pennies.

Man-O'-War's last race was a match race at Kennilworth Park in Windsor, Ontario Canada against the world famous Sir Barton, who had won the Kentucky Derby, the Preakness Stakes and the Belmont Stakes before those three became known as the Triple Crown. Sir Barton lost the race at seven lengths, but in his defense it was reported that he had obvious physical problems with hoof issues as evidenced by his floundering action, during the race.

Miss Elizabeth Dangerfield is identified as a trainer for Man-O'-War other than her photo I could find no other information about her. Man-O'-War's trainer of the year was Louis Feustel who was born in Germany in 1884 and who came up through the ranks starting at age ten. Louis Feustel started as the key trainer for Augustus Belmont, Jr. and then Samuel D. Riddle the next owner of Man-O'-War. Enough can't be said about Louis Feustel because it was on his recommendation that he convinced the reluctant owner to buy Man-O'-War from Augustus Belmont, Jr. for 5000 dollars (roughly 75,000 dollars or more today). At the Saratoga Sales Augustus Belmont, Jr. liquidated his thoroughbred horse stable after he volunteered to join the army where he served as a major in France during World War I. Not only was he a patriot but his father and family contributed so much to the sport of thoroughbred horse racing that in his honor they named Belmont Park after him which was a fitting tribute. Where are people like these today when we need them? He was the original owner of Man-O'-War but lost him serving his country.

Man-O'-War was 'Horse of the Year' in 1920. The associated press poll named him 'Race Horse of the 20th Century'. "Sports Illustrated" voted him the 'Greatest Horse in Racing History'. The prestigious and highly respected magazine "The Blood Horse" named him the 'Top Thoroughbred Champion of the 20th Century' over such horses as: Secretariat, Citation, Kelso, Native Dancer, Count Fleet, Cigar and Sea Biscuit. He held five different track racing records at different distances. He held two world records, and from no less an authority than the 'Daily Racing Form' that in many of his records Man-O'-War was not 'extended' that is he was coasting home. When he was winning easily the jockey had a tendency not to push the horse to its limits and go all out so as not to burden the horse and save his energies for future contests. Who knows how many records Man-O'-War could have broken had he been urged on even harder near the finish line. On 4 September, 1920 Man-O'-War set the Belmont 1 ½ mile track record of 2-40 4/5 in the Lawrence Realization and broke the previous record by six seconds.

Man-O'-War was foaled at Nursery Stud near Lexington, Kentucky on 29 March 1917. Prior to that the horse racing industry and the thoroughbred breeding industry declined and reached a low ebb. Anti-gambling legislation had eliminated horse racing in New York State in 1911 and 1912 but was legalized again in 1913. Thereafter the public's attention was diverted by events leading up to World War I.

Man-O'-War revived the ailing Kentucky thoroughbred breeding industry and put Kentucky back on the map to restore it to its former and current prominent and dominant role that it has today. Man-O'-War sired 64 stakes winners out of 356 foals including War Admiral who won the Triple Crown in 1937. In addition he sired Battleship who went on to win the Grand National Steeplechase at Aintree, England. Man-O'-War's progeny includes: Sea Biscuit, Hard Tack, Clyde vanDusen, War Admiral, War Relic and many others and their progeny. Man-O'-War's roots trace back to Rock Sand, whose dam sire won the English Triple Crown namely the Epsom Derby, the 2000 Guineas and the St. Leger.

His owner's first impression was that Man-O'-War had jumping ability while he didn't do any hunt or steeplechase races, his progeny included hunt and show jumping champions including three time four mile Maryland Hunt Club winner Blockade and show jumping champion Holystone. Many American thoroughbred champions can trace their pedigree and their lineage back to Man-O'-War. Even Royal Canadian Mounted Police horses trace their lineage to Man-O'-War.

Man-O'-War won three stakes races on three different tracks in nineteen days, a feat unimaginable by today's standards. Samuel D. Riddle, the dapper owner, was offered one million dollars and then a blank check for his horse. His reply was "a lot of men have one million dollars, only one can have Man-O'-War." Another Samuel D. Riddle quote was even more memorable, "Go to France and bring me the sepulcher of Napoleon from Les Invalides and then to England and buy the crown jewels, then to India and buy the Taj Mahal, then I'll put a price on Man-O'-War." Man-O'-War's connections – people around him that bred, owned, trained and groomed him and were associated with him are sadly all gone. I wish that I could have been there and seen with my own eyes this magnificent horse. All I can do is to read accounts of the past and imagine it, all nostalgically, it's too late now.

Man-O'-War died on 1 November 1947, at the age of 30 of a heart attack a few days after his beloved groom, Will Harbut passed away, it was said that Man-O'-War died of a broken heart when he lost his groom. Man-O'-War was buried with full military honors. He is now buried at the Kentucky Horse Park in Lexington, Kentucky with his grave marked by a statue by the famous American sculptor Herbert Haseltine. Millions of people listened to Man-O'-War's burial on the radio.

I would be remiss if the following quotations were not included as is. I would not paraphrase it for all the tea in China, and there is a lot of tea in China. When questioned about the race much later this is what Upset's jockey Willie Knapp said, "Sure I won the race all right, it was the greatest thrill in my life. But looking back at it now, there's sure one horse that should'a retired undefeated. Never was a colt like him. He could do anything and better than any horse that ever lived. If I'd moved over just an eyelash that day at Saratoga he'd beat me from here to jalopy. Sometimes I'm sorry I didn't do it."

While he lost to Upset it was no disgrace, Man-O'-War was the better horse. Believe it or not the best horse does not win for a variety of reasons as I have seen over and over again. Losing does not only occur at the racetrack but in everyday life as well. So don't despair with a temporary setback when you do not come out on top you are still a winner. The great winners come back to display their true colors and heart.

Printed in the United States
By Bookmasters